"I've never wanted to be less sensible..."

Mavis gulped air into her lungs. "That's my point. This...all this... It's nice for now. But what happens in the end?"

The words shot Gavin's smile dead. "When I leave?"

Mavis lifted a shoulder. "Isn't that what you'll do eventually? You've been very clear. I've told you, I know you don't know your place in the world anymore and I'm aware of who you are—who you've always been. You'll go looking for it if you can't find it here. You—"

"I run," he concluded, gaze dull and far off.

She couldn't stop herself from reaching for his hand and gripping it tight. "I want you."

The truth snatched his head around, back to hers, brows hitched. He looked surprised. Then impressed.

Mavis nodded. "And that isn't something I'm capable of ignoring anymore."

"Anymore," he murmured. His jaw softened. "How long have you been ignoring it, exactly?"

Dear Reader,

Readers were introduced to Gavin as a boy in the first book in my Fairhope, Alabama series, *A Place with Briar*. Even then, he seemed caught between two worlds. Now in his thirties, Gavin has finally come home, though the wounds of war have sunk deep enough that any semblance of peace he hopes to find there seems to have dried up. He's caught between the need to flee and the desire to cling to the only home he's ever known.

It takes an outsider to know and understand one. This draws Mavis to Gavin and his journey back to himself. All too quickly, they forge an irrevocable bond that is tested time and again throughout the story.

The hardest part about writing *Navy SEAL's Match* was addressing how Gavin struggles and comes to grips with post-traumatic stress disorder. Alternately, the greatest discovery along the road with these characters was that although love goes a long way toward healing him, Gavin and Mavis embark on their journey knowing that it won't take the disorder away. Yet they still choose to pursue it. In a lot of ways, this book is for service members and those who love them, through the good times and the bad times. It is a great joy to give you my sixth Superromance novel and Gavin and Mavis's story.

Always,

Amber Leigh

PS: If you know a veteran in crisis, please contact the Veterans Crisis Line at 1-800-273-8255 or visit veteranscrisisline.net.

AMBER LEIGH WILLIAMS

Navy SEAL's Match

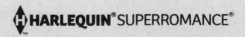
HARLEQUIN® SUPERROMANCE®

Recycling programs
for this product may
not exist in your area.

ISBN-13: 978-1-335-44922-1

Navy SEAL's Match

Copyright © 2018 by Amber Leigh Williams

For questions and comments about the quality of this book, please contact us at CustomerService@Harlequin.com.

www.Harlequin.com

Printed in U.S.A.

Amber Leigh Williams is a Harlequin romance writer who lives on the United States Gulf Coast. She lives for beach days, the smell of real books and spending time with her husband and their two young children. When she's not keeping up with rambunctious little ones (and two large dogs), she can usually be found reading a good book or indulging her inner foodie. Amber is represented by the D4EO Literary Agency. Learn more at amberleighwilliams.com.

Books by Amber Leigh Williams

HARLEQUIN SUPERROMANCE

Navy SEAL Promise
Wooing the Wedding Planner
His Rebel Heart
Married One Night
A Place with Briar

Visit the Author Profile page at Harlequin.com
for more titles

To those who serve.

And to Karen Reid—editor and friend.
May the Force be with you always.

CHAPTER ONE

MAN DOWN! ZACCOE'S DOWN!

The flashbacks had to stop. They came at him in the middle of the night when he was ready for them. They came at him in the middle of the day when he wasn't.

Fall back! Get him to the Bradley!

Gavin Savitt jerked from the clutches of sleep. Colors bled through his eyelids. He could hear civilian life. Better, he could hear the soft wash of waves against the shore and the chatter of wind chimes, the kind that hung from the eaves of his father and stepmother's bayside bed-and-breakfast. There was laughter, far off. Gulls crying overhead. He tasted sunshine on his lips.

The soothing sounds of the half of his childhood that had been good and whole and stable should've brought the unrest to a standstill. Should've obliterated it. It was fear that made the flashbacks hang around. The fear was all too real these days and had been his since his final deployment as a navy SEAL six months ago.

It was fear that he would open his eyes and the

civilian world would be less clear to him than the assault of vivid memories from another world.

Funny that he hadn't contemplated how stark and colorful those dreams were before his last mission, the one that had robbed him of half the visibility in his right eye and all of his left.

Gavin took a moment to quell the anxiety, to manage the fear, even if he couldn't kill it any more than the flashbacks.

He braced himself, stomach tightening. Then he opened his eyes and confronted the odd blur of light and shade, the merging of shapes. He picked a fixed point out of his right eye to study...

The white house was like a beacon on a hill. Hanna's Inn spread prettily, overlooking Mobile Bay. Even Gavin could see the proud and regal way it held itself up—columns, balconies, long narrow panes that glistened as the sun shrank from its high post. The winding paths through the gardens... he knew them by heart. Just as he knew the sand skirting the kempt lawn curved in a crescent shape to follow the slope of the Eastern Shore. Beneath its peaks and tumble-down kudzu-lined valleys, the beach formed the watery border of Fairhope, Alabama, the small town that had called to Gavin for most of his life.

He'd ignored that call, returning to Fairhope only out of necessity. However, nothing could compete with the inn that his father saw to alongside his stepmother, whose family it had belonged to for generations.

A smudge detracted from Gavin's focal point. It was black and willow-slim. As he fixed on it instead of the inn, he frowned. It was getting closer, if not bigger, and he was definitely in its line of fire.

He knew only one person in the world who wore neck-to-toe black in July in the south.

Gavin sat up in the hammock and placed his bare feet in the thick grass his father tended well. There was a catch in his neck and his muscles were taut as wires. He had learned how to snatch his mind out of the dreams, but his muscles rarely followed suit.

He'd sought the hammock and the company of waves for relaxation to break the vicious cycle of PTSD, even if only for a short while.

He might've been able to do it if he hadn't given in to fatigue and dropped off.

Smoothing his hand over the outer edge of his thigh, he wiped the damp from his palm. *Oh, great.* Night sweats were turning into day sweats, and the first person to find that out was potentially the last person he *wanted* to know.

"Have you seen a dog?" Mavis Bracken asked as she bore down on him in her combat boots.

He offered her a lazy salute. "Freckles."

In spite of his limited field of vision, he knew she scowled. She'd hated the nickname he'd given her as a youngster. The dark speckles on pale cheeks made her stand out in a sea of faces. While his father, Cole, and stepmother, Briar, ran the inn, Gavin's half sister, Harmony, had become bosom pals with Mavis, the daughter of the florist next door. Mavis was always younger—always aloof.

Some would say she was odd—those same people called him a loner.

With their close ties to Hanna's, the flower shop, Flora, and the two families that had grown tight between the establishments, Gavin had always felt that he and Mavis shared similar experiences; they were both outsiders.

"You don't look too good," she observed.

He tried to release the tension ball inside him. It didn't work. Gavin passed a hand over the back of his shorn head. "Hard to shave when you can hardly see a mirror."

"That's not what I meant." Mavis paused and he felt her. His toes rolled in on themselves and a shimmy went through the fine hairs on the back of his neck. Mavis had a way, an eerie way that spoke of something otherworldly. She saw people in ways others didn't understand.

She was downright spooky, and he felt far too raw to be the center of her attention. "You're looking for a dog," he repeated.

"Yes."

"What kind?"

"He's big," she provided. "Black. Goes by the name Prometheus."

"You're kidding." When she didn't answer, his lips parted. "Right?"

Familiar sarcasm flooded Mavis's voice. "Well, I thought *Killer* was overdone."

"Prometheus." Gavin shook his head. "Because that's not over the top."

"Have you seen him?" Mavis asked pointedly.

"Was he carrying a torch and running really fast?"

"Gavin."

"No," he answered. "I haven't seen a dog or a Titan."

Her arm rose to her head as if to shield her eyes from the sun. "Damn it," she muttered. "It must've been herons. He always chases the herons."

Gavin scratched his unshaven chin. "Is, uh, this by chance *your* dog?"

"Yeah. What about it?"

"How'd you lose him?"

"He wanders," she said by way of excuse.

"You've heard of leash laws," he guessed.

"He's called Prometheus and he weighs nearly as much as I do. You think a leash is going to make a difference?"

"He sounds like a legitimate beast," Gavin mused. "At least you got the name right."

Her arms crossed and her weight shifted. "You used to have a dog. Boots. Wasn't that his name?"

Gavin's hands folded. He clenched them against his thighs. "He wasn't my dog."

"What do you mean? During your visit two years ago, Harmony said you couldn't shut up about him."

"Boots belonged to the US government," Gavin said. "Not me."

"Oh." She said nothing more. Because, again, Mavis sensed things. Like the fact that Boots had been shot outside a checkpoint in Kabul. Almost exactly like Benji had years before.

Don't go to that place again, Gavin told himself. Once more, he focused on what was present. He picked Mavis as his focal point. A dark beacon. The kick-ass combat boots were followed up her slender ranks by black pants, or leggings. The heat index today was 102, which meant she either hadn't checked today's highs before leaving her bat cave or she was crazy.

Crazy, he thought. *Let's go with crazy.*

There were white slashes in the fabric for venting at least. They went well with the punk look she'd owned since the tender age of sixteen. Or was it fourteen? By that point, he'd been in BUD/S, fighting to fulfill his dream of joining the SEAL teams.

"What are you doing out here?" she wondered out loud.

He spread his empty hands. "Reading the newspaper?"

She answered with knowing silence, making

him more aware of the tremor in his knees. Mavis probably also knew by now about that vase he'd broken in the hall upstairs at Hanna's and the semi-argument he'd had with his father as a result.

This isn't working, he had told Cole as he stood by like a chump listening to the man and his wife clean up his mess. His third, in as many weeks.

We'll move things around, Cole had replied.

Briar was quick to jump on the bandwagon. *Sure,* she'd said in her feather-soft voice. *It's my fault, really, for leaving the vase in your way.*

The fact that they'd worked their butts off to accommodate him did little to temper the hot-burning coals inside him. The coals had been there since the surgeons informed him that he would be legally blind for the rest of his life, effectively shutting down his military career the only calling he'd ever known.

It wasn't fair to resent Cole or Briar. Yet with every valuable Briar had to sweep broken off the floor, those coals smoldered.

"When was the last time you slept more than an hour at a time?"

Gavin frowned at Mavis's inquiry. *Yeah, no. Not going down that road.*

"There are people," she suggested.

"People?" he chimed.

"That you can talk to."

"I don't want to talk to them," he said quickly. He'd seen enough doctors. They were all in agreement that he was a head case who needed to be on the antianxiety meds that made him spin out of turn.

He'd take his chances with the flashbacks.

Gavin pushed himself up from the hammock, finally feeling steady enough. He crossed his arms and lowered his head, hiding the pink scars raked across his face by the winter's RPG blast. He'd forgotten to use sunblock again, as instructed. What did it matter? The scars wouldn't fade any more than the blindness. He started to walk away, then heard her drawn-out breath and stopped. "What would you know about it?" he ventured. "Ever had a flashback, Freckles? Night sweats? Hypertension brought on by stress?"

"No," she answered plainly.

He gave a nod and began to walk toward the inn again.

"But I know someone who has," she said at his back.

"I'm sure," he replied, and kept walking.

"Which is your good side?" she asked, following. "Your right or your left?"

Why was she following? He'd never been one for glossing things over. Would he have to bite her head off to get her to stop chasing him with the same good intentions as everyone else? "I don't have a good side," he replied. When she only continued to follow, he elaborated, "The left's worse. Why?"

She didn't answer, but he found her in his right periphery. A shadow. With a quick glance semi-close, he was better able to pick up on her dark hair, cut raggedly, longer in the front where it tickled her fine-arrowed chin and shorter in the back where it rode just above her hairline. He could see she was wearing a flowy sleeveless top, feminine even if it was black as brimstone. A hint of skin underneath turned him on to the dark cut of her bra.

When in God's name had Mavis started wearing flowy, see-through blouses? She was in her late twenties, but when Gavin *could* see twenty-twenty, he'd never known her hips to swing quite like they seemed to now.

Gavin studiously turned his attention to other features, ones he knew. The freckles. They marked her for the distinct thing she was. They reminded him of the quiet girl he'd known—the freckled Wednesday Addams. The sarcastic teenager he'd never thought of as womanly.

Her sharp-cut jaw still looked too much like her older brother's.

Kyle. Like Harmony, Gavin had found a Bracken bosom buddy in the early years in Fairhope. Kyle had joined him at BUD/S after a year of college. They'd earned their Tridents together.

Kyle could boast just as many battle scars as Gavin. Most of his had come from walking into a frag grenade during his second deployment.

Seeing Mavis's big brother hung up in traction five years ago hadn't settled well. Gavin hadn't stayed long at his buddy's bedside as a result. No, he'd pushed himself back into the fight with grim determination that smacked of vengeance.

He should've slowed down, taken some time to decompress before going on the op months later that had ended abruptly with him carrying Zaccoe's limp body from conflict.

Benji's blood. Gavin would never forget how it seeped warm through the back of his digi-camo. He'd never stop cursing how his hands had shaken in the armored vehicle on the way back to base, making his job as medic impossible.

He'd lost that battle. He'd lost it hard, and, with it, a friend. Benji was gone, and he'd left Gavin's sister a widow.

Everything started to blur once more. The ringing in Gavin's ears warned him of return flashbacks. He tried blinking to snap himself back to present, then remembered. *You're blind, asshole.*

He took a detour, hoping to lose Mavis so he could orient himself.

"Where are you going?" she asked. The question floated to him. It got chopped by the blender in his brain. When he veered into the floral undercroft of a lengthy bougainvillea-wrapped awning, she tailed him. "Gavin?"

He held up a hand. In the shade, things were

cooler. The humidity clung to his skin, a wet blanket he couldn't dislodge any more than the fresh scent of blood in his nostrils or the feeling that brought the tremor to his fingers. His heart beat heavy, the ache behind it keen. His lungs pushed the air in and out, rapid-fire. The overdose of oxygen made him dizzier. Groping, he found one of the awning supports beneath the vines and tried not to stumble into it. Pressing his brow into his forearm, he worked to bring himself out of it.

"You're having a panic attack."

No shit. It was what he wanted to say. Along with a whole lot of, *You're* still *here?* What came was more along the lines of, "Mmmph." And even that caught in his throat.

Mavis's expressionless words came to him, closer. "Is it okay if I touch you?"

She still sounded muddled. Everything did when the anxiety peaked. Still, he frowned when he grouped the words together. *Is it okay... if I touch you?*

Had Mavis ever touched him?

He wasn't coming down—his pulse, the Tilt-A-Whirl in his head, his breathing. He was being swept up by the sights, sounds, smells from another time and place. The sights, sounds and smells of death. He'd lost track of the self-assertions and tactics that sometimes simulated a sense of control.

Mavis didn't take his hand. Her cool fingers

wrapped loosely around his wrist. Her thumb found the flexed tendon in the center and applied pressure.

The fighter in him punched through. His muscles twitched. Damn it, he was jumpy enough to take her above the elbow and apply pressure of his own. The urge was knee-jerk and wrong. A remnant of his training.

"Do you feel that?"

The question bobbed to the surface. *Mavis*, he told himself. The brief image of her racing a horse against his at breakneck speed through a crowded wood stopped the training from taking effect. It stopped the urge altogether. He still didn't know what the hell she was doing, but he nodded in answer.

The pressure of her thumb increased, enough for the blood flow inside the pulse point to slow.

She didn't hurt him. If anything, the slight discomfort and the odd awareness of her skin against his tuned him in to her further.

While his pulse careered and the battle raged inside his head, she held him. Then, over the same spot, she began to knead.

It was several minutes before he realized that his focus had shifted. The pressure lifted off his chest enough to breathe. The words he usually told himself came to him. He chained them to the flight rhythm of his heart, slowing them by minor increments until the chant became a mantra and his heart rate leveled.

It wasn't until he opened his eyes that he realized he'd relaxed enough for her to grasp his other arm. She kneaded his opposite wrist.

When he was able to bring his voice to the surface, he swallowed, fighting against a dry throat. "What're you doing?"

"Acupressure," she said. After more kneading, she added, "How does it feel?"

He raised his brows in answer. He lifted his lids again. Her dark head was beneath his. She was looking down between them. She smelled nothing like brimstone. He caught a surprising waft of fresh, cool mango. Her jet hair looked soft, so much so that he considered resting his cheek against it.

But that would've been weird.

Gavin bit off a curse. "Don't you know better than to approach somebody like me with his guard down?"

She shrugged, letting her touch slide across his palms, down his fingertips and away. "You held yourself together."

"I wanted to snap your arm." He grated the words through his teeth. "Like a ruler."

"You didn't."

He tilted his head at her. Who was this creature? With him so determined to stay away from life stateside, he and Mavis had rarely crossed paths after adulthood. As a boy, he'd been too distracted to take more than a second or two to fan the mystery of her. As a man, he'd been too busy elbowing his way back into the fight to really notice her. Cut to his return to Fairhope three weeks ago; she'd been the one who'd seemed busy, rushing in and out of the inn to drop off Harmony and Benji's daughter, Bea, or grabbing a quick bite from Briar's kitchen on her lunch break.

She had no reason to trust him—who he was then, who he was now. What the hell had he ever done for Mavis Bracken? "Your brother's a SEAL," he reminded her. "You know what goes through an operative's mind."

"What's your point?"

"Keep your distance from me, Mavis. I'm a house on fire."

"When a house is on fire, you throw water on it," she told him. "You don't stand back and let it burn."

"You do if it's too far gone."

"Not everybody does."

This wasn't working. "Would you approach a wounded predator in the wild?"

Mavis took a step back, perhaps out of respect. "That depends. How well do I know this predator?"

"Huh?" he asked, dumbfounded.

"If this were any normal predator in the wild, I'd walk away. But if I knew, for example, that he liked blondes not brunettes, mustard not ketchup, and salty foods in lieu of sweets…more than likely, I'd use that to my advantage."

He stared through the damaged veil of his eyes. "You remember all that about me."

"Gavin, you hung out at my house with my brother every day you were in town as a kid. That's ten years you and I ate at the same table. I can't tell you how many times I saw the two of you turn out your billfolds for the customary condom count when Mom wasn't looking."

Gavin gave a startled laugh.

She narrowed her eyes. "You're still proud of that, are you?"

He coughed slightly, bringing his fist to his mouth. "Uh, no. Of course not, no. You remember?" He wasn't able to get over it.

"Don't you remember anything about me?"

"Yeah," he said with a nod. "When you were little, you had these big screech-owl eyes that seemed to know everything. You were spooky. You still are."

She studied him again. He picked up on the slight sound of her sigh. "You're still white as a sheet," she observed. "But your eyes are clear."

"They are." The careful non-question rang with surprise.

"The pressure point helps alleviate anxiety," she explained. "It can also work for nausea and motion sickness."

He was close enough. He might be able to count the freckles. Because it helped him hug the present closer, he started. *One, two, three…four…*

Forked pain struck his temples. He closed his eyes to shut out the light. The migraines nearly always followed the hard forays into insanity.

"Stress headache?" she ventured.

He laughed cheerlessly, webbing his fingers over his face. "Did you train to be a medical professional while I was away or are you psychic?"

"I get them, too," she explained. When he only scrubbed his hand from his face to the top of his head and lowered his chin into his chest, her hands lifted between them and spread. "Look, if I touch you again, are you going to freak out?"

I might. She had a way, too—this new Mavis. "I'd prefer a sledgehammer to knock myself out with."

"This is healthier."

He raised his chin and tensed to stop her from edging in closer. "Since when are you the touchy-feely type?"

She paused, fingers curled toward him. "I'm not. But do you know why I'm a vegetarian?"

"No."

"I can't stand to see an animal in pain. Teeth or no teeth." When he wouldn't relax, she sighed at him again. "Stand still."

Personal space be damned, she stepped right up into his. He wasn't overly tall like her six-foot-four brother, but she was small even in combat boots. He remained rigid as her front buffered his, as she touched him, his face. More pressure points, he assumed. A snide remark formed on his lips when her thumbs came to the base of his cheekbones. It fell flat when she began to massage again.

"This is yingxiang," she said in a low voice he found strangely hypnotic. "It targets the pressure points in the wrinkles of the nose. It works for stress headaches, but it can open up the sinuses and relieve hypertension, too."

"Mm," he said, trying not to drag the syllable out like he wanted to.

She massaged his cheeks for a minute or two more before her thumbs lifted. His face felt loose. Most of his tension he held in his neck and jaw. It had lessened to the point that he could feel the soreness around the joints and the relief that sang behind it.

Under his stare, she seemed to hesitate. This close, he could definitely count those freckles. He could also trace the shape of her big screech-owl eyes. Dark and uncharted. Like the far side of the moon.

Her lips parted and her tongue passed briefly between them before she moved her hands slowly to the place where his neck met his shoulders. "Or…if that doesn't do it for you…"

The tendons beneath her kneading fingertips all but cried out at the attention. He gave up deciding whether it was from pleasure or pain. The muscles moaned under the ministrations. It was the exact spot the stress of the last six months had taken up residence. The stress of the last decade, now that he thought about it. He hoped she didn't notice his eyes rolling into the back of his head.

No. Yes. Yes, no.

For the love of God, touch me. Touch me tender. Touch me hard. Freckles, just...

...touch me...

Gavin expelled a breath. It gave him away, he feared. It gave him away hard.

"You're brick."

"Hmph?" he responded, at a loss for better.

"Your muscles," she muttered, exerting more pressure. "They're like mortar."

No, her hands were mortar. Crashing into his brick walls. Exploding them into dust.

"You'd really benefit from yoga."

His snort was a half sound. "Who does that new age shit?"

"Friend of mine owns a school. Yoga helps you stretch the right way, loosen joints... It helps you learn to breathe..."

"Breathing's involuntary," Gavin said. "You're either breathin' or you're..."

Dead.

Her low voice smoothed through the juncture. "Most people never give themselves over to all the multifaceted ways breathing can act as a tool for everyday life. Or they're never taught to begin with."

"Stick with the massage."

She did, utilizing her fingertips until he'd lost his breath completely. "Only if it's working for you."

"Hmm," he replied, at a loss again.

"These are simple techniques you can practice on yourself," she murmured, quieter, "anytime you need them."

He couldn't bring himself to open his eyes so he raised a brow. "Is this what they teach you in ghost-hunting school, Buffy?"

"Buffy hunted vampires," she told him levelly. "Not ghosts."

"I think it's all relative," he drawled.

"Oh, you do?"

He opened his eyes to search for her. Up close, the familiarity struck him. High, leopard-spotted cheeks. Pert nose. Insouciant mouth. Eyes like the frigging Mariana Trench. There was something silver shining from each of her ears, a very small diamond in the crease of her nose. Her dark makeup was pronounced.

He was shocked when the ghost of a smile touched the corners of his mouth. "You are a little spooky still."

She loosened her grip, falling back. "Well. At least you're not still tense."

He wasn't. *Wooow.* When her hands lowered

from him, he very nearly grabbed hold to bring them back.

Placing a palm to his sternum, she backed herself off so the length of her arm stretched in the marked space between them. "You'll get better," she told him. "It'll get better."

The certainty caught him. Not only because it went up against his own, but also because she believed it. "How do you know?" he found himself asking.

"You're a survivor."

"I used to be," he replied. He no longer felt like one. More like something tattered and unrecognizable that washed ashore after being picked over by birds and fish.

"It's not just the SEAL in you. It's who you were before all that, too. A survivor." When he said nothing to that, she went on. "Despite all you've been through…your heart's still beating."

If only she knew. Sometimes, he wondered if this was it—that, after everything, he'd be defeated by the mind-fuck he couldn't seem to get a handle on. Mavis's hand was still on his sternum, and he tuned his awareness to it. "It doesn't beat evenly," he admitted. He wet his throat. "What about the dog?"

She looked around at the reminder. Her hand moved off so that she could shield her eyes from the glare off the distant bay. "He's somewhere around."

"Will he come back on his own?" he asked,

falling into step with her as her slow gait brought them back into the sunshine.

"Yes, always," she said. "Growing boys never miss a meal. Not to mention, not all who wander…"

Are lost, he finished silently. Not all, Gavin agreed.

Maybe just him.

He let her walk ahead and her pace quickened. He wrapped the fingers of one hand around the other fist, coming to a halt. "You wear black, but you like red."

She stopped. Doubling back, she faced him fully.

He went on. "You have a tattoo…somewhere. I don't remember. But you got in trouble for it when your mom found out. You rode a horse named Neptune. You liked to ride English because, even though you were weird, you were a cut and a half above the rest of us."

Still, she was silent. She was too far away for him to read. He was beginning to sweat nonetheless. "And when your family would have their Saturday music round, you wouldn't play. You'd sing. You could turn an acoustic version of 'Come Together' or 'Don't Come Home A-Drinkin'' into something classy and unexpected."

"Oh, God…" she said.

"Don't laugh, Freckles. You killed the Loretta."

She did laugh. It was a low noise, like the drone of a hummingbird's wings. It didn't last long enough. "I hated when you called me that."

"I knew it," he returned. "Anyway, you were... different. I thought it was kind of badass that you didn't care."

"Just like you didn't?"

Gavin lifted a shoulder in answer. Yes—they had more in common than it seemed either of them had anticipated.

Quiet fell. The gulls droned from the shore. Tires moved over gravel in the parking lot beyond Briar's garden. The world moved, lively and fierce. But there was a measure of quiet in Gavin's head. He'd forgotten what quiet, in its purest form, was. Damned if he wasn't grateful—and a little spellbound.

Mavis spoke again in a sober light. "Look. I might've overheard what went on upstairs with the vase."

Gavin's frown returned. He sought the inn, the place he'd known he shouldn't come back to. He hadn't fit in before the RPG. What had made him think he could fade into the wallpaper now with his face a veritable grid of violence?

"Before you think about disappearing again," Mavis continued, "you don't have to leave Fairhope entirely."

He moved his shoulders in a brusque motion, the tension climbing up the back of his neck again. "You know a good bait bucket I can crawl into?"

"You'll break their hearts if you skip town like all the times before," she said.

"Yeah, but think of the antiques," Gavin said, gesturing to the pristine white building and the treasures it held. "At least they'll live long and happy lives."

"If you knew your parents at all, you'd know that when it comes to your well-being, they'd burn every single one of their antiques if it meant having you here."

Judgment had a bite to it, he found. He didn't much like it. Remembering the tone he'd struck with his father and Briar upstairs, he scowled. Okay, maybe he deserved it. But in spite of the steadier ground he found himself walking on after the detour with Mavis under the bougainvillea, the coals still burned, low and blue.

"I might know a place you can stay," she continued. "While you take the time you need to decide what the future holds. It's close enough to town to keep your parents happy, but far enough and quiet enough to give you the freedom to piece your thoughts together."

"Where is this place?" he wondered.

"On the river," she told him. "Fish River."

"You live on Fish River," he remembered.

"Along with a slew of other folks," she pointed out. "The place is at the end of my road. There's a catch, though. You'll have to put up with a roommate."

"I think we all know I'm no good at sharing," he pointed out.

"Yes, but this is just temporary," she said. "And your potential roomie is very into feng shui. No antiques, few breakables. Plus, she's likely to stay out of your personal space."

She rounded out the last words nicely. "Huh." Gavin considered. "Is she hot?"

Mavis's laugh was full-throated. When it didn't end quickly this time, Gavin asked, "What's funny?"

"You like a good joke, right?" she asked, wrapping her arms around herself and backtracking to the inn.

"Normally," he replied. "Don't leave me hanging on the punch line."

"Her name is Zelda Townes."

"And?"

"And you can find the rest out for yourself," she tossed back, intriguing in all her unsolved mystery.

Gavin frowned at her back. "Is this because I can't stop calling you Freckles?"

"No," she said. "It's because you won't."

CHAPTER TWO

PEOPLE NORMALLY PERFORMED hot yoga in a studio. Thanks to the heat and humidity July had to offer the Gulf Coast, Zelda Townes's Bikram classes were held on the wide veranda of her old river house. The sun fell through the square slats of the pergola, fighting through a canopy of hanging ferns and fuchsia. If the screens didn't keep the wolfish mosquitoes at bay, the plantings of lavender, mint and thyme would have made the pests turn tail.

Not only did Miss Zelda's porch offer the perfect environment for hot yoga. It smelled like the inside of an apothecary. With the backdrop of the river and the grand weeping willow in the yard that spilled down to its fishy shores, achieving peace of mind wasn't difficult here. The happy burble of shallow fountains, the hollow knock of bamboo chimes, and the light refrain of kirtan devotional music brought the morning class to its culmination.

Despite this and the stalwart nature of each of Miss Zelda's advanced students, nearly all of them shrieked and fell out of their standing bow when a loud bang rent the quiet river air.

"What in the holy name of Babylon…?" Zelda scowled, her svelte spandex-clad form straightening from her mat. "That sounded like a Desert Eagle .50."

Mavis felt the frisson of alarm go through her fellow classmates and injected a note of sardonic cool into the scene. "Yes, because Desert Eagles are a dime a dozen." A chorus of barks reached her ears. "Damn it," she said, already up. "That's my dog."

"Water's still as molasses," Zelda said, peering down the lawn to the river's surface. "Go 'round back and see what's doing. The rest of you, a few sips of water before we pick up on the last vinyāsa."

Mavis wove her way through the sweaty bodies to the barn doors that led into Zelda's sparse domain. The house had been built before hurricanes were named and outhouses had died. Zelda had done well to update the place. The water ran fine, just like the electric. Two large bathrooms had been added to the floor plan, with an additional powder room near the patio and sunrooms where Zelda held her classes, depending on the season.

The house had once been crammed wall-to-wall with furniture. Zelda's parents and grandparents had been notorious hoarders. They'd run a down-home antiques business from there. Long before the business passed to her, Zelda announced she had no intention in furthering the enterprise. She'd cleaned house, burning most possessions before cheerfully planting the willow amid the ashes.

Longtime river residents still spoke about the great bonfire of '76 and how it had lit up the night sky like the Second Coming. Of course, all this was decades before Mavis joined the river community. She'd grown to know the strange woman living in the old house at the end of the road, so much so that she and Zelda had started their own enterprise—Greater Baldwin Paranormal Research & Investigation. More commonly, they were known to locals by the tongue-in-cheek nickname the Paranormas.

The office to the right of the house's entry point housed most of the ghost-hunting gear that Zelda and Mavis had carefully invested in. When Zelda wasn't a yoga guru and Mavis wasn't filling time cards at any of her parents' small-town industries, they could both be found screening calls, dissecting claims of activity or out doing fieldwork in Zelda's vintage red Alfa Romeo.

Mavis peered through the window to the right of the door. The pane of glass was old and waxy, but the distortion of smoke over the cracked drive and the fits of excited barking made her snatch the door wide. She looked right, then heard the cursing to her left and crossed the porch to get a better look.

"No, Prometheus!" someone said. "Back away! Down!"

Mavis broke into a run upon hearing her dog's

yelp. She opened her mouth to yell for him before she rounded the last car.

The smoke wafted from the hood of a familiar orange eighties-model Ford truck. The person shouting was Mavis's friend and Gavin's sister, Harmony Savitt. Which made the person on the ground underneath Mavis's gigantic canine...

"Prometheus!" Mavis shouted, stumbling forward. "Get off of him! Get..." Her steps faltered at the sound of more yelps. They weren't distressed. They were yipping. Happy. Walking sideways, tilting her head, she reevaluated the scene.

Gavin's arms were up, the cords of his neck drawn into sharp contrast as he torqued his face away from the dog's mouth. It was the dog's tongue that was attacking him without mercy. The strained sound of high-pitched laughter fought through Gavin's teeth.

Harmony had one leg over Prometheus's back and was jerking on his silver-studded collar with all her might. "Oh my God! It's like moving a *planet*!"

Prometheus got lucky with a tongue-lap across Gavin's mouth. "Ah!" he grimaced. "Come on!"

"Prometheus," Mavis said again, finding her feet. She joined the fray, grabbing the dog's collar, too. She grunted, yanked. "Would you move your butt?"

Together, she and Harmony managed to tug Prometheus off the soldier. "Sit!" Mavis instructed, keeping hold of her dog as Harmony doubled over. Mavis crouched to Prometheus's level, drawing his attention to her. "What were you thinking? You can't just go knocking people over." Shifting to her heels, she reached out to offer Gavin a hand, but he was already on his knees. She frowned at the Oakley sunglasses in his hand. "He broke them."

"They fell off my head," Gavin insisted. "I should've grabbed hold of 'em when I heard him coming."

Harmony nodded agreement. "Those paws. They sound like a mammoth stampede."

"I'm sorry," Mavis said. "He usually doesn't jump people like that."

"You're right," Gavin said simply in return. "He definitely is a Prometheus."

At his name, Prometheus strained forward, sniffing for Gavin's hand. To Mavis's surprise, Gavin obliged him, pressing his palm warmly against his flat-topped cranium and feeling his way to the dog's ear. Prometheus's lapping jowls closed quickly as he leaned into the caress and groaned, loudly, bending his head low. Mavis's lips pressed together. She stared at Gavin over the length of Prometheus's back.

Was that a smile? The scars stamped across his face didn't interfere with the lines of his mouth, but it was a mouth that had grown far too accustomed to not smiling. Vague and hesitant, his eyes were more than just the epic clash of bottle green and unfinished copper. Tapered at the corners, they held the same sad glint as an abandoned pet.

Her heart misfired. She frowned at him. The wounded Gavin. He held himself together, as always. However, the bruising was on the surface. She could see the stitching. She could see the steel cables and the double coat of duct tape holding him together. Yet still the damage was close.

She hated that she could read him. It was easy for her to read people. Exceptions were rare. With his cool exterior and easy charm, Gavin Savitt had nearly always been the exception. He'd split his time annoying her and—unintentionally perhaps—compelling her. However, for all his past, there weren't too many people who had ever found Gavin uninteresting.

He'd always been far too good-looking and she knew he'd used it to his advantage. Not with her. Others. His fighting edge had started young. He'd been in enough scrapes in high school to get him kicked out for a time. People vouched that he never started the fights, but he did finish them, and not always with an assist from Kyle.

The fighting edge was still there, but it had turned inward. As a result, his guardedness was down, the coolness had dropped, and Mavis could read him like a book she shouldn't want to finish. She tried to look away in front of Harmony, at least. Things were strange enough since

Harmony and Kyle had happily announced their march into coupledom.

Gavin couldn't see her clearly. She knew that. So why did it feel so intimate to hold his steady gaze? Maybe because even after they couldn't see, the eyes were still the door to the soul?

Mavis locked herself down. Whatever it was that she was feeling, she felt it too much in too many places and she had to lock it down because, per her directions, Gavin had come here to live with Miss Zelda at the end of the road.

Prometheus showed his appreciation by pressing his head against Gavin's thigh. "Hey, hey," Gavin said, easing back. "Easy there, Cujo." He *was* wearing a smile. It might no longer look natural, but it wove into his hard-angled features until Mavis *had* to look away.

Prometheus nuzzled against Gavin's shoulder, earning more ear-scratching. Mavis's spine snapped straight at the touch of envy. "Okay, enough," she said, wrapping her arms around Prometheus's middle.

"He's fine," Gavin said. "He seems like a good egg. He's Lab, right?"

Harmony belted a laugh. "Try rottweiler."

"Nah," Gavin said doubtfully. He hooked his arm around Prometheus's neck and glanced at Mavis.

"One hundred percent," she confirmed. "Dad picked him up at the shelter for me when he was twelve weeks old. He said if I was going to live alone, I had to have a guard dog."

Harmony shook her head, watching the display between man and dog. "If that's a guard dog, I'm a canary."

"Breeds like rottweiler can be seriously misunderstood in terms of behavior." Mavis gestured to the lovey canine licking the seam of Gavin's jeans near the knee in a slow savory manner. "Exhibit A."

"So you're a righteous beast, eh?" Gavin lowered his crown to Prometheus's bowed one. "That makes two of us."

The gesture from man to dog did something. Mavis's palms dampened. Her lips parted as a rush of warmth flooded her. It started in her belly and curled like a wave before she sucked it back. *Feelings,* she reminded herself. *No.*

She studiously rolled her eyes as Prometheus continued to vie for Gavin's affections. Trying not to follow the path of Gavin's stroking hands on Prometheus's ruff, she looked to the smoking truck. "What happened?"

Harmony groaned. "Overheated. Liv's going to kill me." She shivered as though contemplating the response of her cousin, Olivia Leighton, to having her beloved Ford maligned in such a way. Squinting from beneath the brim of the baseball cap that advertised the cropdusting and flight instruction business she shared with Mavis's father,

Harmony frowned at the steam. "We'll have to call James for a tow."

Gavin gained his feet. "It wouldn't have blown its top if you didn't drive like a heretic."

"I drive just fine," Harmony said dismissively.

"You drive like somebody trained in low-level aerobatics," Gavin argued. "Which you are."

"You like my driving," she pointed out. "It puts you back in action, which you miss."

Mavis watched his mouth fold and she quickly changed the subject. "At least you made it to Miss Zelda's."

"Everybody calls this woman *Miss Zelda*," Gavin pointed out.

"So?" Mavis asked.

"So, normally that would mean she's a person of importance or she's older than…you know… Betty White."

"Betty rocks," Harmony declared.

"Actually, nobody knows how old Zelda is," Mavis informed them. "I'm pretty sure anybody who does is dead."

"So, great. She's like biblical," he muttered. His arms crossed over his big chest. "You set me up with an old lady?"

His smile was on the verge of creeping back into play. She sighed a little. *A little*, she told herself when the noise made her cringe. "You know what they say," she said with a shrug. "Age is only a state of mind."

"Uh-huh."

He kept looking at her, stance stern, eyes amused and…unseeing. So why, again, did she feel like…

Like he was touching her?

Harmony's voice broke into the interlude. "Wait a second. You two aren't…"

Gavin slowly turned his head to her. "Aren't what?" he asked when she only gawked at them.

"You guys aren't *into* each other, are you?" Harmony asked. She held up her hands and took a step back. "Because *blech!*"

"Seriously?" Mavis responded. "When my brother's not in training, aren't you two normally camped out in bed together when your daughter's not looking?"

"Good point," Gavin said with a nod.

"Still, this better be some sort of revenge joke," Harmony told them. "A new tactic to show me how awkward it's been for the two of you since Kyle and I got together."

"Of course it's a joke," Mavis said. Because how could Harmony's brother be flirting with her? He was dealing with God only knew how many issues. For example, she was pretty sure he hadn't yet come to terms with his disability. And she definitely, *definitely* was not his type.

She backtracked, jerking a thumb over her shoulder. "Grab your stuff. I'll go tell Miss Zelda you're here. Harmony, you can call for a tow inside. Come on, Prometheus."

The dog reluctantly fell into step. She reached down and laid her hand against his snout when he sought her. It was still warm from Gavin's touch.

If she wasn't Gavin's type, why did she feel his eyes on her as she walked away?

CHAPTER THREE

"SOMETHIN' WAYLAID ME in the shower," Gavin announced to Mavis as he wandered into the kitchen, closely following the mental blueprint he'd drawn of Zelda's house during the introductory tour. It wasn't the simplest layout, but he wasn't blind enough that he couldn't trust his keen inner compass. It only made most tasks he'd once thought simple now frustrating and a few everyday skills, like driving, impossible.

He found a halo of hair underneath one of the florescent lights on the other side of the high countertop. "Some kind of tree," he elaborated.

Mavis answered, "Eucalyptus."

Gavin frowned. The light had gone from the windows. There were a lot of windows in Miss Zelda's house. The harshness of electric lighting burned the working parts of his right retina. "So the old lady's aware she's got plants growing in places they shouldn't?"

"If you call her 'old lady,' she's likely to strike you dead at some point. And, yes." He heard a rustle. Pages turning. She was reading a book. Here

at Zelda's, half past dark? "The plants are refreshing. For most people."

He wrapped his fingers around the edge of granite and jerked his chin at her. "What're you doing?"

"Studying," she said plainly.

Feeling around the prep space, he found a large
wooden bowl. Recognizing the cool touch of a
smooth apple's surface, he palmed it and brought it
to his nose to sniff. "Algebra test in the morning?"

"In your mind, am I still a fresh-faced fourteen-
year-old? Pre-tats? Pre-piercings? Prepubescent?"

Not at all, he mused, remembering what had
transpired at the inn under the bougainvillea. Ah,
that bougainvillea.

Passing the apple from one hand to the other,
he countered, "Studying what?"

"Genealogical records." More rustling. Gavin
saw the white face of a page flash as she flipped
to the next.

"Mmm." He took a crunchy, satisfying bite from
the apple.

Her head was low over the book. Her hair fell
forward at a slicing angle. "It comes with the territory."

"Territory?"

"The paranormal investigation and research territory," she explained. She lifted her face. It shone
under the bright light, freckles pronounced. He
could see the red bow of her mouth. It'd always
been lush, like that of her mother, Adrian. The dark

slant of her eyes was masked by a large set of reading glasses. Old-fashioned, from what he could tell, and cat-eye. "Didn't Miss Zelda tell you? This is where our spooky little business comes together."

Gavin stopped chewing. "Here?"

"Yes. Here."

He worked his jaw, deciding to study the red coating of the apple instead.

After several seconds, Mavis said, "Is that a problem?"

"No." He shook his head. "No. Just…on the tour earlier, nobody mentioned athames or cauldrons."

"Why would it matter if there were athames and cauldrons?" Mavis wondered. "I thought you didn't believe in that stuff."

"When I trip over a chair and fall on or in either, that'd be a big problem. Unless you witches have broken into the field of advanced healing."

"You do realize neither Zelda nor I practice Wicca, witchcraft, or anything of the spiritual or magic variety?"

"Communing with the dead?" he said pointedly.

"We listen," she corrected. "It's more science than anything."

Gavin lowered his voice. "And what do people who do actual science have to say about that?"

Mavis's sigh floated to him. She flipped more pages, with more force. "Some pay attention. Some don't."

"Most don't," he wagered.

"Haven't you had anything happen to you that you can't explain?" she asked.

Rotating the apple as if he could study every facet, he said, "If I can't explain it, and nobody else can explain it, why would I want to know more about it?"

"I'm trying to decide if that makes you ignorant or irrationally skeptical," Mavis said thoughtfully.

"From your side of the field, I imagine everyone's a skeptic. Except the freaks who pay you."

The book slammed shut. "Nobody pays us. Only scammers and con artists demand payment for the type of work we do."

"You work for free?"

"Second," she said, "while the people who call on our services do sometimes turn out to be a little nutty, it's unfair to lump them all as freaks. Especially since a percentage suffer from any number of psychological disorders such as depression, paranoia, schizophrenia...even PTSD. EMF sensitivity alone can lead to extreme bouts of paranoia. You know as well as I do that mental illness is no joke. Am I right?"

Gavin raised his brows but said nothing. *Low blow, Freckles.*

"Miss Zelda and I take what we do very seriously," she added. "As seriously as you did playing modern-day advanced warrior with Kyle and Benji."

Did she have to bring up Benji? "You argue like your brother."

"How's that?"

"Heavy on the guilt."

"Really? I thought I was talking truth."

"Sucker punching me with it." Gavin rolled the apple onto the counter.

"Aren't you going to finish that?" she asked when he turned to walk out.

"Nah. I've lost my appetite."

"May I ask why?" she said to his back.

He stopped at the door and turned halfway back. "I don't know. Maybe it's poisoned?"

It took her a second to answer. "Athames are on the left when you walk up the stairs. Good luck not tripping."

He chuckled, then wondered over the sound. Okay, that was twice now she'd made him laugh. Tapping his fingers against the jamb, he said, "Tell me something, Freckles. Why *did* you get into the paranormal racket?"

"When you stop thinking of it as a racket," she replied, "I'll tell you. Maybe. Anything else?"

"When's the naked séance? I might need to see that."

"You won't."

He cursed. "Are you really here working or are you keeping tabs on me for the folks?"

"Well, now's a good a time as any to make an entrance," Zelda said as she breezed past him. She patted him on the biceps. Her sleeve brushed his arm. It was long and silky. She raised herself to her toes so he could hear her mutter, "For God's sake, handsome, stop while you're ahead."

"When was I ahead?" he wondered out loud.

"Mavis thinks well of you," she pointed out. "She rarely thinks highly of anyone. Be a good soldier. Keep to her good side." She spoke briskly. The arm pat became a squeeze before she moved on, and Gavin found himself murmuring a quick, "Yes ma'am."

He'd already decided that he liked the mistress…er, matron of the manor. Meeting her in person, he'd had difficulty assimilating the keen woman with old age despite her pixie mop of silver-tinged hair. She was tall—like Harmony, nearly as tall as him—narrow as an arrow, and shrewd. Like Mavis, she smelled great. Herbal, refreshing. He saw the bright streak of her head scarf as she moved to the counter. She made him think of jewel-colored birds in the tropics.

The river house was everything Mavis had promised. Clean lines. Open space. In the daytime, there was the added benefit of a flood of natural light with the outside literally coming in, as he'd discovered in the shower. The furniture was sparse and, oddly, close to ground. The low-level effect from the dining room to the bedroom brought to mind an Oriental theme. Judging by some Mandarin words he'd traced on the wall of his bathroom, he didn't think he was far off there.

Zelda lived in the bedroom downstairs facing

the river. *My wing*, as she called it in her deep silky voice. *Rules are, I don't enter your space, you don't enter mine.*

That's fair, he'd said.

He was told to expect an odd assortment of visitors on weekdays and weekends and phones ringing late into the night. He'd thought that was due to Zelda's so-called yoga school, which also operated out of the river-facing first floor. Now he knew to attribute it more to her and Mavis's side business. Thankfully he'd found the soundproofing in his wing of the house to be impressive, despite the warning.

"Stunning rhododendrons!" Zelda said, approaching a tall spray of bright flowers in the corner. "Carlton Nurseries. Must be. The Bracken family trade always comes up with the best."

Mavis made an assenting noise. "Dad picked it out. The Leightons sent it, as a thank-you for Saturday."

"I'll have Errol plant it in the front bed, in front of the office window," Zelda announced. "That is, if he doesn't mind working in the rain. We're going to have a wet week. How's the research coming for the Muculney case? Find anything?"

"It's more in what I'm not finding," Mavis said, her head low over her book again. "I can trace the girl's Acadian line to Canada, but it stops expanding after the Civil War. No records that I can find of a child born of the Isnard estate after fighting broke out. Nothing at all under her name anywhere in Louisiana."

"Did you try the internet?" Zelda asked as she fussed over the stovetop. Pots rang with the sound of silver as she removed a lid. The scent of soup filled the air. "Censuses? Area cemetery records?"

"I spent most of the afternoon at the computer."

"Omissions can be telling. How hungry are you, Gavin?" Zelda asked him. "Soup's been simmering since the a.m. and there's more than Mavis and I can eat."

Gavin lifted a hand. "I don't expect you to cook for me. I can find my way around the kitchen."

"Yes, I see you've been at the apples. Errol brought these from his backyard."

"Who's Errol again?" Gavin wondered aloud.

Zelda's tone warmed over a purr. "*Mon choupinou.*"

Gavin frowned. "Is that code for boyfriend?"

"I'm pretty sure it's French for 'cabbage,'" Mavis said.

Gavin leaned into Zelda. "You sayin' there's another man around here?"

"Don't you worry, toots." She dug her elbow into his side. "There's plenty of Miss Zelda to go around."

Gavin felt a grin cracking across his face. "I like her," he said, pinpointing Mavis over Zelda's bright head scarf.

"Peas in a pod," Mavis decided for herself.

Zelda used the ladle in her hand to tap him on the rear. "Have a seat at the counter, sugar loaf. There's nothing heartier than minestrone soup at the day's end. And you look like you could use some soul food."

Gavin thought about going up to the solitude of his room. They were talking business and he couldn't pretend not to be weirded out by the ghost-hunting side of it. However, the fragrance of minestrone hit him in the gut.

He crossed the room and rounded the counter, following the edge of it with his hand around the elevated bar. He tripped over something and looked down to see the prone dark lump on the floor. There were sounds coming out of it. Gavin realized it was Prometheus. "Is he okay?"

"Just sleeping," Mavis informed him. "Why?"

Gavin waited for the noise to rise from the beast again. "When a helo makes that noise, it's time to bail."

"You know this from experience?" she inquired.

"Among other things." From his previous, adrenaline-loaded life.

"The only thing he's suffering from is exhaustion," Mavis said. "I don't know if you noticed, but he's shadowed your every move since you got here."

"I noticed," Gavin said. He skimmed the side of his foot along what felt to be the dog's ruff in a quick rub before grabbling for the back edge of the stool next to Mavis's and pulling it out from under the ledge.

"If he bothers you, all you have to do is say so," she said while he took his seat.

"He doesn't." Gavin had forgotten how companionable the silent presence of a canine could be, though he'd felt a clench when the shaded form of Prometheus had blurred into another dog's as the late-afternoon light failed.

Gavin turned his attention to the stacks of books on the countertop. The rubbed scent of lignin stirred memories of libraries and secondhand bookshops. They were old books, he assumed. Big, from the sound of her closing and stacking them. He squinted at the spine of one. When the letters blurred, he scowled. He'd never been a big reader, but there had been freedom in knowing, should he choose, it could serve as a distraction.

A bowl clacked onto the granite in front of him. The steam wafted up his nose and his stomach grappled for the contents. *Sustenance.* "Mmm," he said, unable to help it. "Thank you, ma'am."

"No *ma'am*," Zelda insisted, waving a napkin in front of her face before she set it down next to his bowl with a spoon on top. "It makes me feel retro."

"Are you?" he asked experimentally, picking up the utensil.

"You're a rascal," Zelda realized. "I like that in a man."

"Is Errol a rascal?" Gavin muttered in an aside to Mavis.

"He's been known to listen to metal on occasion…"

"All men are rascals in some vein," Zelda chimed in. "Even the deeply repressed type." Zelda stopped in front of Gavin. "I doubt you're the repressed type."

The corner of his mouth curved upward and kept tugging. "What makes you think that?"

"Well, for starters, look at our girl. Does she look like she'd go for that?"

Mavis looked up as she became the center of attention.

"I don't know," Gavin said. "I always thought deep down Mavis was kind of a tight-ass." The snug grin dug in further when her oval face slowly revolved his way under the light. His smile pulled at the scars on his face.

"Pat my head and call me Freckles," she said. "I dare you."

Zelda chuckled. "Here's your soup, dear. Stop and eat."

"Thank you," Mavis said, taking the bowl in both hands. She took the spoon and napkin, then began to stir. Her elbow nudged his. Then again. "This isn't going to work, lefty," she told him. "You should sit on my other side."

He nudged her elbow again. "You're wearing wool," he said as her sweater grazed his arm.

"Yeah, why not?" she asked.

"It's ninety degrees out," he pointed out.

"I'm cold," she said, her shoulder lifting close to his. Muttering, she went back to her reading. "I'm always cold."

"What would you like to wet your whistle, Gavin?" Zelda asked him. "There's water. We have herbal tea. There should be some organic orange juice. No liquor. Neither Mavis nor I drink much, particularly during working hours."

"Water for me, thanks. And some working hours, by the way. You don't drink?" he asked, turning to Mavis.

"Only once in a blue moon," she admitted. "Dad's a recovering alcoholic. Mom never kept liquor in the house. Some of us had better things to do in high school and college than binge drink."

"Not me," he remembered fondly.

"No, I never said anything about you, did I?" she said drolly.

"So you don't drink when you go out?" he asked.

"Out where?" she asked, mouth full of soup.

"Out," he said. "That place people tend to go when they leave the house. Particularly single people on Friday and Saturday nights." He peered at her when she turned her face to his without answering. "You do know what I'm talking about, don't you, Freckles?"

"Do I look like an idiot?"

"You look like a blur," he said. "A sweet, spotted blur."

He could tell she was frowning. "I work three jobs. One fielding customers at Flora for Mom. Another doing bookkeeping for Dad at the garage. And another on nights and weekends here with Miss Zelda. My social agenda is pretty limited. Not that I mind. And not that it's relevant."

"I think it's relevant," he claimed.

"Why?"

He shrugged, scarfing another bite. He stopped for a second to enjoy its impact before spooning another. "Because you are a tight-ass." She scoffed at him and he added, "And in another life, you might've been a cheap date."

Mavis made a choking noise, then coughed. Gavin dropped his spoon into his bowl, lifted his arm over the back of her chair. He gave her several raps on the back.

"Another life?" Zelda spoke with all the nonchalance of an innocent bystander. "Why not this one? Gavin, I assume *you're* single. That Leighton boy was the last one to tickle Mavis's fancy. And that was back when he was still a man-baby."

Gavin demanded, "Which Leighton?"

Mavis choked again.

Zelda called his bluff. "So you *are* interested. Hot dog!"

When Mavis reached desperately for his glass of water, he asked, "Are you okay?"

"Mmph."

He heard the water going down her throat. He thought about it—her throat.

Stop being weird, Savitt, he chided himself.

She was talking again, to Miss Zelda. She sounded husky. Vital. He felt an odd stir, the same one she'd cranked to life in the bougainvillea. Something told him to reel it in, but he kept his arm across her back, cupping her slender shoulder blade through the thin wool of her sweater. He'd never been good at listening to sense, especially when it came to warm, smart women of the unconventional variety.

This one happened to be his best buddy's sister. But Kyle was training hard somewhere out in California. Helicopter rappelling. The bastard. And Mavis. She was in arm's reach. The threat of Kyle was lessened by the miles between them and conversation with Mavis… Her proximity had kept the lingering threat of that afternoon's headache at bay.

"The meal's put color in your face," Zelda observed as she ate from the other side of the counter. Her tone slid homily into something sly. "Or is it the company?"

Gavin felt Mavis go rigid and circled the spot of her shoulder blade beneath his hand before removing it, going back to his meal. "Both are unrivaled," he granted. Zelda's low laugh was one of approval. The knuckles of his drinking hand knocked into something hard. Another book, he surmised. Cautiously, he asked, "What about this genealogy thing? How does that factor into…whatever it is you do?"

"Cases are confidential," Mavis informed him shrewdly.

"He's living here," Zelda reminded her. "There're things he's bound to overhear. Such as, Vincent and Phyllis Muculney out of southern Louisiana are investigating the family lore of an alleged presence in her family's planation homeplace. Vincent and Phyllis are friends of mine from the eighties so I knew a drive there wouldn't be a waste. They've drawn attention to the property over the last year because of its rich landscape. Phyllis is very into conservation; Vincent is very into history. Local media have drawn widespread interest in the family lore and reports of paranormal activity. We got some interesting EMF readings off what's left of the Isnard Plantation, didn't we, Mavis?"

"Sure," Mavis said mildly. Pages flipped. She was back to her research, multitasking as she spooned more minestrone into her mouth.

"Excuse me," Gavin said, holding up a hand. "EMF?"

It was Mavis who answered. "Electromagnet fields. The theory is that ghosts are able to manipulate them. Our EMF meters can detect this."

"And this is how you find Casper? Beetlejuice? Bruce Willis?"

She stared at him a second or two before answering with amusement. "If you will."

"The audio was most revealing," Zelda said, excitement growing. "Tell him about the audio."

Mavis spared a weary glance for Miss Zelda before continuing. "We often take voice recordings, particularly in areas of EMF anomalies," Mavis told him, adjusting her glasses. "While playing back the Isnard tapes, we found something."

"You heard voices?" he asked, back to skeptic.

"Just one," she said, nonchalant. As if they were discussing the ingredients of minestrone soup.

"What did it tell you?" he asked. "Have you unlocked the mysteries of the universe? Should we call Stephen Hawking or—"

"No," she replied. "After passing what we heard on to Vincent and Phyllis, they told us about twin brothers who owned the planation jointly before being called off to service in 1862."

"Here's where it gets intriguing," Zelda said conversationally.

Mavis paused. "Neither Josiah nor Daniel returned from battle," she said finally. "Those who remained were convinced that the family line ended there. Until, of course, a kitchen girl revealed that she was pregnant with an Isnard heir."

"So?" Gavin said.

Zelda smiled. "She didn't know which twin was the father."

"Which means either one of them cornered her

in one of the secret passages under the cover of night," Mavis said admonishingly.

"Or she was having an affair with both," Zelda finished.

"The first theory's more likely," Mavis murmured. "I don't see a ménage à trois happening in the grand master suite."

"People back then were no different from people today," Zelda informed her. "There was scandal. And secrets aplenty. Besides, I like the idea of the servant girl getting her own."

"Was this voice you heard on the tapes by chance female?" Gavin asked.

"Why, yes," Zelda said, glad he was catching on.

"So you think it was the kitchen girl," he surmised.

"It's a sound theory," Zelda said. "One Mavis, Phyllis and I are in agreeance on. But what's most interesting is that she spoke two names. The first in what remained of the living quarters above stairs. Josiah."

"And the second in the chamber Phyllis told us about behind the servants' stairwell. Daniel," Mavis added. "That's where the family claims most activity has occurred throughout the years."

Gavin scraped what remained of his soup from the sides of his bowl, mulling the information. "Did this baby and its mother wind up reaping the estate benefits and carrying on the line?"

Zelda laughed. For once, it didn't ring true.

"Hell, no, she didn't. Cousins came in, Phyllis's ancestors, and turned the place over. The servants were dismissed and nothing was heard of the girl or her baby. The place wasn't fit for living for another whole generation. The cousins eventually gave it up cold turkey."

"Phyllis's grandfather eventually inherited the mess and decided to rebuild most everything from the ground up," Mavis told him. "It took years because workmen kept walking off, claiming they felt a tap on the shoulder or they could hear whispering when they were alone."

"Phyllis's first encounter herself was in the chamber behind the servants' stairs," Zelda divulged. "She was playing hide-and-seek with friends from grammar school. She was alone in the dark, but someone brushed the hair from her face. She lit outta there like someone had planted live firecrackers in her saddle shoes."

Gavin sniffed. "And which of you ladies volunteered to take your recorder into the servants' stairwell?"

"Oh, that was Mavis," Zelda replied. "She usually volunteers for the tight spots. Attics. Basements. Crawl spaces. You name it, our Mavis is there."

"That's great," Gavin said. He downed half his water before letting the glass clack against the counter next to his empty bowl. "Does your family know about this?"

"Did yours know anything about your combat injury for six months after it happened?" she responded in kind. "I didn't think you were judgmental, Gavin. And I didn't think you believed in this stuff anyway, much less cared."

"I'm having trouble with the belief thing," he admitted. "But I never said anything about not caring."

"If you don't believe, why's it necessary to care?" Mavis asked. "It's all just a racket. Right?"

"It's big creepy houses that belong to strange people," he told her. "Sure, Zelda's friend Phyllis might be all right, but her family home sounds like it's been a meal for more generations of termite colonies than you can trace. How carefully do you screen callers before showing up? It's just the two of you? No muscle?"

"Well, Errol," Zelda said. "He likes the country drives."

"How old is this Errol?" Gavin wanted to know. When neither of them answered, he scowled. "Uh-huh."

"Our screening process is thorough enough," Mavis explained. Her tone had grown taut from irritation. "You can't tell us that the process we've operated under for the last five years isn't up to standard. Who do you think you are?"

"I'm a goddamn navy SEAL," Gavin told her. "I think I know a sight more about the ugly parts of humanity than you do."

"Try me," she invited.

"Don't tell him about that meth lab two weeks ago," Zelda suggested. "He'll blow a gasket."

"You've got to be kidding me." He groaned. The slow-roasting coals were growing in temperature. "Did you know they were cooking meth?"

"They didn't announce it," Mavis responded.

"They weren't hiding it, either," Zelda noted. "They were nice boys. If you like mullets and missing teeth."

"These are drug dealers we're talking about," Gavin said. "Drug dealers."

Mavis rolled her eyes when he slowed the words down to mocking speed the second time. "Yeah, we got that."

"But we scored," Zelda said. "EMF and confirmed audio."

"Wait," Gavin said. "You walked in, saw what they were doing and you went ahead and did the job anyway?"

"Well, sure," Zelda answered readily. When he cursed a stream and mashed two fingers against his temple, muttering disbelief, Zelda added, "You think we're simpletons? You think we don't know to arm ourselves with more than curiosity and flashlights? You've known her a long time, handsome. You really think Mavis is crazy?"

"I'm starting to," he said. At the sound of books closing again, he reached out for Mavis. He closed his fingers around the back of her hand to stop her from scooting off. "Drug dealers, Freckles," he re-iterated. "*Drug. Dealers.*"

"One of them hit on her," Zelda revealed, uncovering the mischievous streak Gavin thought he'd gleaned earlier.

Exasperated, Mavis slid from his grip and off her stool with books under her arm. "I'm so glad you two are living together, because you deserve each other. Night-night."

"I have an idea," Zelda announced, stopping Gavin from reaching for Mavis again and preventing Mavis from retreating. "You're going to like this, the both of you."

"Aren't we optimistic?" Gavin said.

Zelda went on. "Why doesn't Gavin accompany us this Saturday…?"

"What's this Saturday?" he wondered.

"Fieldwork," Mavis muttered. "For our next case."

Gavin felt a stone drop in his stomach. It sank to the bottom and spread cold everywhere. "I don't think so."

"Oh, why not?" Zelda asked hopefully. "You'd get an idea of what we do. He'd enjoy our approach at least, I think, Mavis. Tell him!"

"Every job we take," Mavis said dutifully, "we approach as skeptics. Our main focus is debunking claims of paranormal activity. It takes up the bulk of what we do."

"I still don't think it's a good idea," he said dully.

"Come on, handsome," Zelda said. "There's nothing worse for the mind than confining oneself to the indoors. It'll make you crazier than a holy roller on Sunday. The cure is fresh air and the outdoors."

"With all due respect, ma'am," Gavin said coldly, "I'm not going anywhere." He lifted his hands from the counter. "Excuse me."

He sidestepped Prometheus, nearly overcompensated and leaned unintentionally into Mavis. When he felt her hand on his arm for balance, he straightened, veered around her and made a quick exit.

Not quick enough to miss Zelda utter, confounded, "He called me *ma'am* again. I'm not sure I deserved it."

CHAPTER FOUR

"I KNOW HE'S not eating like he used to," Briar Savitt said as she walked alongside Mavis through the pecan grove. The salty breeze adhered the clothes to their backs. The swelling heat index hadn't stopped Briar from taking Mavis aside just as soon as she'd arrived at the Leighton orchard. "He's so much thinner than he was when we saw him last. But do you think he's sleeping better now that he's at Miss Zelda's where it's quiet?"

"I couldn't tell you." Since the brush-off from him several days ago, Mavis had steered clear of Gavin, opting to stay home for dinner as opposed to lingering at Zelda's in the late afternoons.

"You and Miss Zelda talk every day," Briar said. "She must tell you…how things are going."

Briar was the kindest person Mavis had ever known. Her reasons for the inquest were genuine. Regardless, Mavis wasn't comfortable. Especially since Gavin had already accused her of keeping tabs on him for his parents. She cleared her throat. "I think Prometheus sees Gavin more than Zelda does. I understand he comes down for meals and weight lifting. Zelda gave him one side of her private meditation room for his bench. She says he isn't conversational." Mavis shrugged. "That's really all I know, Briar. Sorry."

"I don't mean to put you on the spot." She rubbed Mavis's arm in a motherly fashion, then seemed to remember that Mavis wasn't the affectionate sort and eased back. "But Cole's eaten up over the whole situation."

"Because Gavin's living at Miss Zelda's?" Mavis asked.

"No. Well, yes. He wishes he was within arm's length again. We all do. But the injury. The trauma. I wish we could do something to help Gavin be free of it."

"He'll probably never be free of it," Mavis reminded her. Briar's mouth folded into a line and worry knit her forehead. Mavis hated to see her this way. "He came back. And he tried to make it work at the inn. He's never done that before. Not since he was a kid."

"We think it's only because it wasn't working elsewhere," Briar said, "on his own. He tried that first."

"In my experience, admitting you need help is the first step to recovery."

"Yes, but how long before he convinces himself again that he doesn't need us?" Briar asked. "That he's better off alone? We'll do anything to make him stay."

"You're doing the right thing," Mavis assured

her. "Letting him be on his own—or with Miss Zelda… Letting him have his own space…it'll all work out. Especially if he gives in to her. Miss Zelda wants him to try meditation. Maybe some yoga. It won't help if he's skeptical. And if Gavin is anything, it's skeptical." *Of everything—of everybody,* Mavis thought. There had been that moment under the bougainvillea where she'd seemed to get through that coarse web of suspicion. It had vanished at Zelda's.

"It wasn't just his experience on the far side of the world that made him that way," Briar said. "You do know about his mother."

"Yes." Mavis frowned. Gavin's mother, Tiffany Howard, had made large upsetting waves whenever she visited Gavin as a child.

"Thank goodness he cut off communication with her," Briar stated. "I'll never forget him as a boy, caught between two worlds. I know she tried for the longest time to poison his opinion of us and Fairhope."

"He was smarter than that," Mavis said.

"Yes," Briar said, a small smile making the lines in her brow retreat briefly. "Though I'm afraid when that didn't work, she tried another tack. She made him think *he* was different—that he'd never have a place here. That try as he might, he'd never belong."

"That's horrible," Mavis muttered.

"The strongest minds can yield to the basest

ideas if they hear them enough. So we understand why he feels he's never been able to stay, and all we can do is reinforce that he does belong. To all of us."

All of us.

"If you think he's in trouble," Briar said, "or you see he's about to run, will you..."

"I'll call," Mavis assured her. "But I think you're right. He is strong. He doesn't think he is." She thought of the weakness peeking through the bandage he'd placed around his open wounds. She'd seen the strength behind it, flagging but real. "I don't think he wants to be alone. Not completely."

"Thank goodness for you, Mavis," Briar said, ignoring boundaries and squeezing Mavis's hand as they approached the deck of the Leightons' brick house. "I feel better knowing you're close to him."

"Why exactly?" Mavis asked.

"Because he's always respected you," Briar revealed. "A friend can save a life."

Mavis felt a frisson of awareness scaling her spine. She crossed her arms. Did Gavin need saving? Would he want her to be the one to save him?

Doubtful. Regardless, she couldn't let Briar down. And just like at the inn, she wouldn't let him drown on his own. Not without him taking her down with him, if necessary.

The door to the Leightons' rear deck swung ajar wide enough to bash the handle against the wall behind it. A short blond head streaked through, bounding down the steps to the ground. "Mammy! Mavis!"

"Here comes trouble," Mavis said, a fond smile tugging at her lips as Briar waved a cheerful greeting.

Briar crouched to wrap her granddaughter up like a present. "The world is right again," she murmured. She chuckled low in her throat, hugged Bea tighter, then sat back on her heels to skim curls from the girl's brow. She pressed a kiss to the center of her forehead. "Your grandfather showed up early with you, as promised. Good man. But did he bring watermelon?"

Bea nodded eagerly. "They were selling them on the side of the road. There were *hundreds* of them, big and dirty—like they'd just popped out of the ground. He let me pick two, but I wasn't big enough to carry them..."

"Give it time," Mavis said, amused. The precocious four-year-old was growing like a weed.

"...so Uncle Gavin carried them for me," Bea concluded.

"What?" Mavis said, slack-jawed, while a surprised Briar said, "Gavin? He came?"

"Uh-huh," Bea replied. "He might not see so good anymore, but he sure can carry a watermelon!"

The happy report of barking brought Mavis's head up. Prometheus, who'd been gleefully chasing squirrels since arriving in the back of her Subaru, trampled a shrub of Indian hawthorn as he made a break for the raised deck.

Gavin was ready for him this time, folding to one knee and hooking one muscled arm over Prometheus's collar. He rocked back from the torrent of kisses Prometheus rained over the surface of his face. "Back," Gavin said, gentle. "Back." Prometheus's wriggling body went still as Gavin found the place behind his ear that made the canine groan. "Good boy," Mavis heard him murmur. He ran a hand along Prometheus's spine before glancing up.

The frown was never far from his face. It returned in force. Replacing the Oakley sunglasses he had wisely removed before receiving Prometheus's attentions, he straightened, his feet braced apart on the decking. He didn't say a word when Prometheus began to wind circles around them, bumping his head and body against the man's knees in a motion that would've looked feline had it not been for the speedy whip motion of the dog's tail.

Briar didn't hesitate to approach Gavin. "You made it," she greeted, taking his rigid form into her arms.

"I'm sweating." Gavin's hands lifted, lowered, then rose the rest of the way to hug Briar back. After a second, his head dipped so that his cheek touched her temple. He let her go, but not without a small rub over the slender line of her back.

"I heard rumors about your potato salad and Gerald's rum ribs."

Briar patted his flat tummy. "You could use some of both, I think."

"Thanks," he said without seeming to take offense. He reached down and ran his fingers down Bea's upturned face, pinching her nose lightly between his knuckles. "This one charmed me out of wrestling Harmony for shotgun."

"He taught me how to make a spitball," Bea revealed.

"Lord help us, Gavin," Briar said, and sighed.

"Yeah," he said. "Sorry about that." His gaze relocated—to Mavis. "How's it hangin', Frexy?"

Mavis narrowed her eyes. "Frexy?"

He lifted a shoulder. "Since you hate Freckles so much. Thought I'd change it up."

"Frexy?" she said again.

When he said nothing further, Briar pointed out, "We were just talking, Mavis and I, about Miss Zelda."

Lines barred the sides of his mouth, his attention all over Mavis again and displeased. "And me."

Rigid as he was, he still emitted a waver of suspicion around his full lips. "Well, yeah," Mavis answered. She crossed her arms. "Your stepmother wanted to know if you can do a Fallen Angel yet."

He hesitated, measuring her. "What'd you tell her?"

"That I can't wait to see you try."

His features didn't ease much. Mavis knew him well enough, however, to see them smooth, even if the frown persisted. He shifted his feet beneath him. "Can *you*?"

"What?" she asked. *Jesus*. It'd been nearly a week. She'd forgotten how little effort it took for the center line of his focus to knock her off-kilter.

"Do a Fallen Angel," he said.

She spread her hands. "Come to class and find out."

A hint of a grin flirted with the edges of his mouth.

Her heart reeled. *Son of a bitch*, she thought. Uncomfortable, she snapped her spine straight. There was a crepe myrtle encroaching on the deck. The white blossom heads were heavy enough to bow to the ensuing heat. One tickled her elbow. Irritably, she pinched the crown of blossoms until she rent flowers loose between her fingers. She stared at them for a moment before handing them absently to Bea.

She and Briar made a motion to escape into the air-conditioned house. Mavis's feet shuffled in an awkward ball change to follow. "I taught a beginner class a few months ago. I could teach you a few poses or help you build your own flow to manage tension, stress…even head and neck aches."

"I don't think stretching's going to solve all my problems," he said.

"Probably not," she agreed. She let the door

close after Bea and Briar, lingering with her hand on the knob. He pivoted slowly to face her, giving her a second to measure the solid slope of his shoulders and his T-shirt-clad back. Briar was right. He had lost weight. "But if you can't punch your way through the bigger problems, you might as well start chiseling away at the small stuff. Otherwise, you're just…standing still."

He stared. It wasn't like being bathed in sunlight. More, moonlight. Lots and lots of super moon–light. It was mystical in its intensity—as was Gavin's effect on her.

When she realized neither of them had spoken in nearly two minutes, she opened the door. The sounds of family conversation lured her in. The door was solid paneling, heavy. She hid a grunt behind her teeth.

A large fist clamped over the top of hers, spreading the door wider from the jamb. He was there, close.

They'd been close before, but she couldn't remember ever being this aware of him, his large, roughened hands, or his arms roped with muscle and dark hair. Under his white T-shirt she could see the outline of black tattoo work. Body ink was her weakness—the darker, more pronounced and exquisite, the better.

Dark, pronounced, exquisite—like him.

What are you doing? she wondered. She stopped

from shaking her head. *He didn't move the frigging earth; he opened a door.*

She wasn't into chivalry. She quelled the urge to trace what she could see of the tattoo's design through the thin cotton. When her fingertips—and other areas—grew hot at the idea of tugging down the collar of his shirt altogether, she moved over the threshold out of his way.

Harmony seized the moment by shouting across the room, "You two! We've got frozen lemonade over here. Stop letting the heat in!"

Mavis rolled her eyes at her friend for calling them out. "I'm surprised you came," she muttered at Gavin.

"I haven't had Gerald's cooking in years," he pointed out. "When he and Briar get going in the kitchen…it's like religion. Also, I heard there'd be a show."

"Oh." He meant her and Zelda. Olivia and Gerald had called them to their orchard in hopes that their EMF meters might be able to help find a lost time capsule of Olivia's grandparents. Decades ago, the orchard had belonged to them—Ward and the first Olivia. Rumors of activity at the grove had been rife among their circle for decades. Olivia claimed she could still hear her grandmother's laughter tinkling on the wind in autumn months. Gerald told intriguing anecdotes about the scent of pipe smoke heavy in the evenings near Olivia's grandfather's old woodshop. Their second son,

Finnian, could jaw for hours about supposed conversations he'd had with Ward. His brother, William, was more close-mouthed, falling quieter whenever the topic was broached.

Today Mavis and Zelda weren't here to debunk the Leightons' claims. They were on hand to aid in what was sure to be an exhaustive search. Mavis had come dressed for dirty work in a gray cropped T-shirt and a thin plaid work shirt unbuttoned over fitted workout capris and black-and-white hightops. She came prepared with EMF readers and a shovel of her own. Olivia had called on Briar, her first cousin, and Cole. It was Gerald's idea to prepare the family-style fiesta.

"I thought you weren't interested in what Zelda and I do," Mavis said as they joined the queue for plates.

"I'm not interested in joining the revelry," Gavin claimed. "But I bet from a distance it's fair entertainment."

"That proves you've never seen EMFs operate," she said. "Ever worked with a metal detector?"

"At least they find treasure," he said, handing her a plate off the stack and motioning her ahead in line. "Or tinfoil."

"Depending on the contents of Olivia and Ward's time capsule," Mavis replied, "we might be finding more than that today."

"I'll believe it when I see it, Frexy."

THE BLADE CUT deep into the dirt. The smells of earth, clay and rain enriched the air as Gavin worked under the baking sun.

"Mind you don't come up against any bones," Olivia stated. "'Round here's 'bout where we buried Rex."

Gavin's shovel paused. Visions of a clumsy Irish wolfhound he'd chased through the inn gardens alongside Kyle hit him full force. Next to him, William Leighton's shovel stilled, too. "Now you tell us?" he demanded of his mother.

"No worries, gents," Gerald said, and grunted. He'd joined the digging. The polished vowels of his British upbringing rang clear. "Rex is entombed under that iris bed over there. Remember, love?" He addressed his wife. "To keep a fair distance from the roots."

The roots. *Right*, Gavin thought. They'd come up against a rough dozen as they dug around the tree closest to the brick house. It was an ancient specter. On the few occasions he'd visited Olivia and Gerald and their boys at the pecan orchard in the past, it had been an impressive sight. He recalled thick gnarled limbs weighted by healthy green foliage, perfect for climbing. It had had a rope swing tied in its boughs and the initials of Olivia's grandparents carved into the trunk.

It was difficult to reconcile memories with what remained. According to Gerald, the tree had taken a direct hit from a lightning strike. Now it was as black as night. Not a speck of green decked its stark skeleton. Most of the branches had fallen or been removed for safety. From the house, its bare silhouette looked like a dancer stuck in a painful arabesque.

But the damned roots remained. Gavin's arms sang as the shovel blade sliced into another thick offender. He lifted the shovel with both hands, bringing it down in decisive strokes to break it up. The tree was dead. How was it that so many of its roots remained lodged in the earth—as if time or disaster had never taken place?

He stopped to sweep his forearm across his brow. Sweat had built there. It soaked through his clothes. He thought of removing his shirt.

"They should take a break," he heard Briar say. "The heat. It's getting worse."

"They can hear you," William called to her. Humor lilted from his voice.

"Yeah," Cole piped up from Gerald's other side. "They'd like a beer, maybe."

William and Gerald made affirmative noises. Gavin kept slicing the blade through unbroken ground, tuning in to the song of metal and clay. His blood, too, was singing. He ached with effort. The release was sweet.

His head had screamed all morning, since 3:30 a.m. when dreams had tripped him awake. With a meal in his belly, however, and the lull of early

afternoon on the orchard, plus the added work…
the feeling of industry…he could almost convince
himself he was enjoying all of it.

And there was Mavis. It had all started with
her, the shovel in her hands. The EMF meters had
found anomalies, suggesting activity of some kind.
Gavin had heard her struggling with the blade near
the woodshed, then the front porch of the house,
and finally closer to the irises. When she'd stopped
to drink the glass of lemonade Briar brought her,
Gavin had yanked the shovel and picked up where
she left off. William and Cole had followed his
lead. Soon there was a trench around the dead tree
beside the irises.

"We close, Frexy?" he called out to her without
looking. He felt her watchful eyes.

"It doesn't work like sonar. There could be
something here. There could be nothing."

"It's a hotbed, for sure," Zelda said.

"If it's buried here, it shouldn't be but a few feet
down," Mavis said.

"They wouldn't have buried it deeper," Olivia
said.

A hand found Gavin's shoulder. He looked
around to find his father as flushed as a red pepper. "Dad," Gavin said, alarmed. "You okay?"

"Yeah," Cole grunted. He leaned into Gavin.

Gavin cupped an arm around his shoulders. Like
the others, Cole had sweated through his T-shirt.

His breathing was a touch more labored. "Sure?" Gavin asked.

Head low, Cole nodded. "The heat. Can't take it like I used to, I guess."

Gavin had already lifted a hand to his step-mother.

Briar linked an arm around Cole's waist. With the other, she took a firm grip on Cole's shovel. "Let's go back to the house for a breather." Steering her reluctant husband in that direction, she reached back to pass the shovel off to Gavin. "Don't any of the rest of you let it get to be too much."

Gavin watched the line of his father's back retreat until it wavered and became shaded. *Damn.*

The weight of the second shovel lifted. Mavis tugged at the handle. "Go with them. I'll pick it up."

"I can't let you dig," Gavin said. "Not after that."

She tugged again until his hold loosened. "Move aside."

He watched as she shed her overshirt, the plaid number. She tied it around her waist, then hoisted the shovel. He moved to the right until her blade split fresh topsoil he already knew to be soft. And he watched her, her hair slicing backward just like the dull edge of the long-handled tool. The pale curve of her cheek. The lines of her. She was small with, he suspected, curves that she drowned subtly with her wardrobe of ceaseless black.

There was muscle there, too, he found. Will

and might. He considered changing her nickname
again, this time to Mighty Mouse. She dug without slowing or even a grunt of effort. She culled
clay from its earth bed. He nodded approval, then
began working beside her, letting their actions fall
into rhythm.

He'd knowingly overlooked her for most of her
life. Who knew Kyle's sister would wind up an
endless source of fascination?

The end of his blade met something solid as he
sank it decisively into the loose ground. The impact sang up his arms and filled the air with a satisfying *thunk*. "Aha," he heard Zelda utter.

Mavis dropped her shovel and knelt as he raised
his blade. She didn't hesitate to sink her hands
into the red-tinged dirt, combing it up the sides
of the hole.

Gavin took a knee beside her. He took over,
leaving her to tug aside loose black roots moist
from internment. The smell of earth was darker,
richer. Gavin could practically taste it. It coated
them both to the elbows as inches gave way to the
flat face of a handmade box.

They worked together to loosen the ground hug-
ging it close on either side. Finally, with one hand
over and another under, Mavis hefted the box from
its resting place. Gingerly, she placed it on the
ground as Olivia and Gerald flanked her.

The flat of Olivia's palm dusted the lid. Gavin
leaned in until he could make out the carving of

a rose. Until he could inhale Mavis's mango scent
and realized how close he was to brushing his lips
across the point of her shoulder.

Gerald found a screwdriver to loosen the lid.
As he pried the old screws from their corners, nobody moved.

"It should be you," Gerald said as he looked to
his wife. "Go on, love. Let's see what Ward and
his Olivia found worth saving."

"Not me," Olivia said. She beckoned William
closer. "Come 'ere, Shooks."

William obeyed, hesitant. "Mom. You've
waited…"

"You never knew them," she told him, scooting so that William could wedge his way between
her and Gerald and take a knee. "I should wait for
Finny, but God knows he didn't give me a single
patient bone in my body." Placing a hand on William's arm, she lowered her voice and said, "Go
ahead."

William paused only briefly before appeasing
his parents' ill-contained curiosity. He pried the
lid free. Mavis, who had shifted over with the
others, was practically beneath Gavin. He felt
the excitement all but zipping from the top of her
head even if it wasn't her gasp that rent the air.
"Letters," she said.

"What's the date on the postmark?" Olivia asked
as Gerald lifted a ragged envelope to the light. "Is
the stamp still legible?"

"It is." A wondering laugh shook Gerald's shoulders. "July 18, 1953."

"Six months before they were married," Olivia calculated. She handled the envelope with care. "From her to him."

"It's not the only one," William said as he riffled through the collection. "The bundles tied with the ribbons are the ones she wrote, from the looks of it."

"You can tell by the writing," Olivia noted. "I'd forgotten how precise her penmanship was…"

"And the ones tied with the leather straps are his," William finished. "Look, Dad. We found someone wordier than you. But I don't get it."

"What don't you get?" Olivia asked absently as she thumbed through a stack.

"They both grew up here, or close by," William said. "Didn't they?"

"He was from Fairhope," Olivia said. "She lived more toward Malbis."

"They had cars in the fifties," William expounded. "Why so many letters? It's not like they lived on opposite corners of the globe. Even if they did, there were phone lines, telegraphs…"

"People used to communicate differently," Zelda explained.

Olivia carefully unfolded a page of a letter. She sounded far off, near dreamy, when she added, "And when you love someone that much, there's nothing like writing it down on paper."

"It's recorded," Mavis concluded. "This way they could relive the feeling and pass it on."

Gavin frowned at the side of her head. "Since when're you a romantic?"

She glanced up. Her eyes went round when her nose nearly touched his. The gap widened as she edged back, but he saw her dark gaze race across his face in quick perusal. His mouth went dry. "I'm not," she claimed and looked away.

"Mmm-hmm," he said, unconvinced.

Underneath the point of his chin, Mavis's shoulder hiked in a shrug. "It's history, right? I like history. Especially the kind I can hold in my hands."

Like those giant genealogical tomes back at Zelda's.

A smile crammed, foreign, in the ball of his jaw joint. It felt out of place, but it hung there, like a lazy, back-sliding moon in its crescent. He was aware of it, just as he was aware of Mavis and aware of all the places inside him that didn't feel dark when she coaxed it out of him.

He should move away. It was too hot to be this close. The contents of the box were too intimate. Ward and the first Olivia's messages weren't for him.

But Mavis smelled like earth and life and threw all the shady parts of him into stark contrast when he breathed in and filled up with her scent.

The heel of his shoe caught the lip of a hole and he nearly tripped into it. Stumbling only slightly as he straightened, he looked down to keep from twisting his ankle in any of the rest of them.

They were spread out under the dead eaves of the tree, the grass-covered glade broken up by ruts and dirt tossed haphazardly. A minefield.

No. He blinked. The battlefield couldn't intrude here.

But he had intruded, and the battlefield was always with him. Damned if he'd ever be rid of it, anymore than the stench of the loner—the outsider.

His mind began to grind into the sick death spiral of anxiety. He braced his palm against his brow. It was covered in clay. Red clay. Even the cloying scent couldn't stop the visceral flash-bang of memory.

"He's down! Benji's down!" he all but wailed into his comms over the sound of cover fire. "Bring the Bradley! Bring that bitch around!"

"It's four minutes out," Pettelier said.

Benji was bleeding out against the underside of Gavin's palm. "Get inside my pack. Get me the gauze."

Benji struggled to talk through a taut grimace. Gavin couldn't hear him over the sound of M60s going haywire. He leaned down.

"...in the gut."

Gavin shook his head automatically. "Nah. The ribs. We'll stop the bleed. You'll be a'right."

"No bullshit," Benji muttered. "Don't... b-bullshit me."

Gavin knew where the bullet had gone through. He knew what gutshot meant as much as the next soldier in line out here in no-man's-land. And he denied it. "Bradley's comin'. Gonna be fine."

Benji coughed.

Don't do that, *Gavin shouted from the walls of his head.* "Pete! Where's the fucking gauze, man?"

"Got it right here," *Pettelier grunted.*

Another team guy shouted from behind, "We're covered up!"

From comms, he heard, "Bradley, five minutes out!"

"Slow son of a..." *Gavin pressed his teeth together. They stayed clenched. If they weren't clenched, damn it, they'd be chattering. He moved his hand to plug the wound.*

Blood rushed at him. Benji shuddered. Spasmed.

Gavin pressed his hand against the flow. He wasn't a goddamn surgeon. He needed a surgeon!

"Harm."

The name had Gavin riveted to Benji's pained expression. The light hung there, but it was hard and forced and it caught Gavin like the last blind scream of sunlight off the bay at the end of a winter's day.

Gavin shook his head. "Shut up, you're fine."

"I got somethin' to say."

I'm not a surgeon! *"We're not doin' this!" Gavin said out loud.*

The ground shook, the world coming apart with

noise. Gavin threw himself on Benji as dust and mortar fell.

"The hell...we're not," Benji said. And he coughed again.

"I'm gonna save you," Gavin persisted. He ground it from the marrow. "I'll get you to a surgeon. This ain't but a flea bite on a dog's ass and you're going home, you son of a bitch."

The faint flicker of humor eclipsed pain momentarily. Benji's mouth fumbled. "A s-s-sheepdog's ass."

"Right." And thinking of his sister, Benji's wife, thinking of Kyle and his father, Cole, the inn and the bay and everything about life there that was growing harder and harder to retrace in his mind, Gavin placed his hand over Benji's brow and stroked. "You're damn right, brother."

The rest came at him in a rush. The squad hadn't been able to hold their ground. The Bradley was eight blocks away. Running retreat was all they had. Benji had gone out on Gavin's shoulder.

He died in the stupid Bradley, less than half-way back to base where even the surgeons couldn't do a damn thing for him. He'd wanted Gavin to tell her—Harmony. Benji had wanted it to be him.

Gavin had failed there just the same. He hadn't made it back stateside before Kyle had raced off to Wisconsin where Harmony was flying aerobatics to deliver the news.

She and Benji had been married less than a year. She had only just found out she was pregnant with Bea.

And Gavin hadn't been there. Because even if he had made it back to the States before Kyle had gotten to her…he wasn't sure he could've told her he was the one who couldn't save Benji.

It was the anger that came swinging through the flashback, crashing through it like a ram. Gavin grabbed it by the horns, rode it bucking and thrashing—

A hand closed around his elbow. He threw it off to dislodge the hold, poised for attack.

Mavis's features struck him, freckles dark, eyes round.

He let the fight go out of him when the shock painted her. He stepped away, seeing the others casting looks in their direction.

She shook her head and spoke first. "I'm sorry."

"What for?" He shot it off like a curse. He forced his feet into backward motion, winding away from her and the rest.

"Are you okay?" She reached out.

"Fine," he said, still verbally swinging. She needed to go. He needed to get away from her before she found out how cold and vast the dark side of the moon really was. He moved in the direction of the house…or what he hoped was the right direction.

She came after him. "Gavin…"

He pointed at her. "Stay. I mean it," he added in resignation before lengthening his stride.

CHAPTER FIVE

"WHERE IS HE?" Mavis asked. She'd changed from the work wardrobe she'd dirtied up into black jeggings and a tank. After checking on Cole and Briar to see that Gavin's father had recovered from the heat, she'd hunted Gavin through Olivia and Gerald's homey abode.

Harmony came down the stairs. "He's taking a shower."

Mavis could tell by her expression that she'd seen him. "How is he?"

"I don't know." Harmony shrugged. "He won't talk. Not that he ever has about how he's feeling."

Because it's weakness, Mavis knew. Gavin didn't accept weakness. Most men like him, soldiers, didn't. "Where is he, exactly?"

"Liv told him to use William's room," Harmony said. She grabbed the stair rail to stop Mavis from climbing up. "Whoa. Where're you going?"

She'd promised not to let him drown alone. "I'm going up."

"Mavis." Harmony grabbed her hand to stop her from passing. "I'm not sure you should. Not right now."

"Look," Mavis said shortly, "you're trying. Cole's trying, Briar's trying. No approach seems to be working. The other day at the inn, he was having flashbacks and…and I helped him."

Harmony's wide-arched brows lifted. "How?"

Mavis forced an exhale. She couldn't tell her friend everything that had happened with her brother in the bougainvillea. And not because she didn't know *why*, precisely, Gavin had responded to her touch. She couldn't tell Harmony because of what Mavis had felt the moment she'd sensed Gavin's walls trembling…when she'd thought maybe she had done the impossible. "All I really know is that for a few moments he felt safe enough with me—he *trusted* me—to help him out of it, and it worked, if only temporarily."

Harmony searched Mavis's face. She stepped aside. "I can't stand to see him like this. I'm scared of what's on this path if he keeps going down it alone. Do what you can for him."

"Okay." Mavis climbed the rest of the stairs. Glancing back briefly, she said, "Thank you." *For trusting me, too*, she added, silently.

When Harmony nodded in answer, Mavis moved from the landing. The Leighton house was laid out with rooms tightly knit. An ideal nest that kept its inhabitants close. The master suite was on one side of the hall and William's and Finnian's rooms were on the other, connected by a Jack-and-Jill bathroom. Mavis had been there once. She'd gone from one boy's room through the bathroom to the other so she could climb out the back window and escape without Olivia and Gerald's notice.

It felt odd choosing the first door on the left. She'd dated William in secret so their families wouldn't find out and make noise about the two making things more permanent. It was strange seeking another man through the same door, intruding on the space of her ex.

Gavin's shirt she found hung at the foot of the full bed, and his shoes near the bathroom door. She heard the shower running.

She bypassed the shirt, stepped over the shoes and came to the door. Raising her fist, she quelled hesitation and rapped her knuckles against it.

She heard a curse. The door was snatched from the jamb. Gavin filled the space of the frame.

Mavis blinked. He was a mountain. Like Prometheus, he was a fricking beast. Toned. Muscled out—definition on top of definition.

There were ribs, however. Enough of a hint that on anyone else might've looked ordinary. On him, they smacked of self-neglect. His rib cage as a whole should've been lost to the ripple of abs and the scintillating muscles that honed his waistline to perfection. Behind the eyes, she saw truth. There, he looked gaunt. As if the sharp bones of his honest self peered through the coat of naked flesh.

She caught the moment…the very brief moment

that his honest self reached for her. She nearly reached back.

Then he blinked. Resignation resumed. Annoyance followed. "What do you want?" he asked.

"No questions." Placing her hand on the deep-inked, red-eyed wolf as black and forbidding as the storm he held inside him, she moved him back into the bathroom, stepping in, too, until she could shut them both in.

His expression turned puzzled as she shut off the tap in the shower stall. "What're you up to now?"

"This is me pouring water over the fire," she told him.

He stared. Shook his head. "No. No, this is you dressing up as a can of lighter fluid and throwing yourself at it."

"Give me your thumb," she said, extending her hand.

He held it back. "I'm fine."

"You let me in the other day," she reminded him. "Why?"

"I thought we weren't asking questions."

"Gavin. Why?"

"Maybe I was desperate."

"Maybe you do need someone."

"This is hell. I'm not dragging you into it."

"I do what I want. And what *I want* is to help you. So stop being a man—a big *stubborn* man— and let me help you!"

The staring didn't cease. She wondered how

much he could see in the closeness of the white-washed room, under the single bright vanity bulb. Not her pulse tripping against her throat. Not the frisson of nerves in her wrists and knees. Hopefully not the desperation pressed between her lips.

He brought his hand up to meet hers.

She fought a tumultuous sigh. There was dirt on his fingertips still. There was dirt on hers, too, despite several scrubbings in the powder room downstairs. It was caked red under both their nails. The scent of it, of their work together, came between them. She hoped he found it as grounding as she did. Gripping him lightly, she extended his thumb toward her. She moved her shoulders back, trying to grind the edginess out of her joints. She started to press her thumb and forefinger against the web between his. Then she stopped and bent her head, releasing a long breath that streamed cool over his thumb.

The shower steam, fine and damp, was suspended around them. Silence closed them in. She saw his lungs expand against his ribs and noticed his pulse trip against the base of his throat. His breath moved over the center part of her hair, at the apex of her brow.

She blew until she had to take several deep breaths of her own to catch up. Then she blew some more, until the silence was less entombing than it was enveloping. She blew until he relaxed by gradual inches. "When I was little…whenever I got anxious in the doctor's office or something… my mom would do this. It helped me come back to myself. Just enough, anyway, to focus on my own coping mechanisms."

"You could be speaking Latin right now…" he murmured.

She glanced up. His eyes were closed. *Good.* Letting her gaze rest on the ink of his chest, she licked her lips. It was beautiful. The wolf's snout closed over the sinewed bridge where his arm met his shoulder. Teeth extended, it lunged from his right pectoral, fur matted. It was every bit a tribute to all the dark places she knew existed inside Gavin.

The sword was more telling. It scaled his left ribs and was sheathed beneath his beltline. The banner wrapped from hilt to point had writing on it. *NOTHING LASTS FOREVER*, she read. She didn't have to ask to know that the roman numerals inscribed in the sword's cross guard were Benji's DOD.

It was skillfully rendered, just like the wolf. Beautifully done. *He* was beautifully done, ribs and all. She went back to applying pressure to the web between his thumb and forefinger and worked to bring her voice to the surface. "Wanna hear a joke?"

He gave a slight shake of his head. "You don't have to do this."

"How do two admirals greet each other?" she persisted.

"I don't know, Mavis," he said. "How do two admirals greet each other?"

"With a navel salute."

He closed his eyes and winced. "No…"

"So I took a tour of a submarine once."

Gavin rolled his eyes, rubbed his fingers against the underside of his chin. She heard the rasp of new stubble and was pleased when he played along. "Yeah? How was it?"

"Riveting."

The stern line of his mouth wavered. "That's… terrible."

"A marine and a SEAL walk into a bathroom…"

Gavin's mouth split wide in a grin. "That one's better. *Much* better."

Mavis struggled to inhale as her heart ratcheted against her throat. "You're still here," she told him plainly.

"Am I?" The mirth drained quickly, washing through like water in a sieve. "How do you know it's me when I can hardly recognize myself in the mirror?"

She wanted to touch the laugh lines dying on his face. Except for when her father had been released from jail, Mavis couldn't remember ever wanting to hold someone as much as she wanted to hold Gavin.

If he could just see himself the way his family saw him. The way *she* saw him…

She licked her lips, steadied herself. "What scares you most?"

The question caught him off guard. Still, a contemplative silence took hold.

"Say it," she encouraged, bringing gentleness to her tone. "Out loud."

Gavin rubbed his lips together. Then he said, "Using you." He blinked, checked himself. "Using anybody."

"Becoming a burden?" she asked.

After a beat, he said in a low, dark voice, "I am a burden."

"That's not what they say," she said. "That's not what anyone says." He began to shake his head and she held up a hand. "When you love someone…*really* love someone, that's not what it's about. Ever."

"Your rose-colored glasses are disappointing, Frex. I thought you knew reality better than that."

She doubled back and tried another route, crossing her arms over her chest. "You used to run, long distance. You were the high school cross-country star. I don't see you run anymore."

He lifted a shoulder. "Don't have a lead rope."

"You're the last person I expected to box himself in with his own weaknesses."

Frustration struck his face. "What're you talking about?"

"Miss Zelda's house is at the end of the street. Mine is at the beginning. It's a straight shot, uphill one way, downhill the other. Perfect for running. My house is stacked on stilts, round, and is the only one with climbing roses on the mailbox. It's hard to miss."

"So?"

"So, run," she told him. "Zelda's right about at least one thing. Locking yourself indoors will get you a free neurosis spin. You won't try yoga or meditation, but something familiar might give you a leg up. A conduit for all the adrenaline I know goes into the flashbacks—"

"Mavis."

"I'll lend you Prometheus. He knows the way like the back of his paw."

"Look—"

"Try it," she urged. "You're an adventurer at heart. You must be craving a natural high like your next breath."

"The way you talk, you know me better than I know myself."

"Tell me you think about the future even if you can't see one for yourself. Tell me you feel like you have a place in this world. Tell me you've lost your dream job but it's okay because the civilian world holds so much promise." When he only scowled at her, she turned her attention to his hand, took it back into hers. She massaged. "Tell me you refused Zelda's job offer because you don't think she extended it out of pity."

He waited to answer, looking over her head. "What good am I to you? If it's added protection you want, how're you going to get it from Mary Ingalls?"

"Mary Ingalls is a badass and you know it."

"I'm not. Not anymore."

She visually stroked his features. It would have been wrong to trace them physically. The line of his lashes looked denser when he was fatigued, hooding eyes that appeared more copper than green under all this light. He was raw in every aspect and the metallic edges of him were pricking like briars through the iridescent undergrowth. "You *are* a badass. You've just lost your mojo."

He shook his head. "I was trained to think differently. I was trained to channel fear into action. I shouldn't have to deal with psychological BS."

"But...?" she nudged when he stopped.

He shrugged a weathered breath from his chest. "But then Benji. And Boots. Then waking up one day without my sight... I can't drive. I can't read. At the inn, I've broken nearly everything in reach because I have no visibility on my left side—my *dominant* side. It's the same reason I can't cross traffic anymore, by foot *or* by car. It takes me a quarter of an hour to send a text message. You're damn right I lost my mojo. I used to wander off, get lost just to see if I could make it back whole. The itch is still there, but now I get lost in supermarkets.

"It's not just my sight, Mavis. Dad and Briar had a barbecue on the inn lawn to benefit the American Legion a week after I got back. The smell off the grill triggered me. They did all that for me and I couldn't stay because I kept seeing burning bodies in my head, clearer than I could see the faces around me. I shouted at Briar because she came after me like you, trying to fix it…"

He stopped. His ribs pressed against his skin as he took a breath, to stop himself. To steady himself. Mavis watched him swallow and blink several times. The effort not to embrace him, cling to him, nearly overpowered her, but she kept herself back because he was holding it in. He'd been holding so much in.

He swallowed once more, shifting his weight from one foot to the other and back. "I've spent my whole life punching my problems. Now I can hardly see to hit them."

"The SEALs didn't teach you?" Mavis asked, quiet. "To fight in the dark?"

His gaze settled on her once more, seeking for the first time.

"You were trained and conditioned for the fear that comes with war and combat," she went on. "Not the kind of life you'd have to learn to live in the aftermath here, where there's none of that."

A vertical bar grew between his eyes. "Why are you doing this?" he wanted to know. "Why does every word out of your mouth sound right?"

She didn't answer. The web between his thumb and forefinger became her primary focus as she deepened the massage.

He gave in to another sigh. "And why is it when you touch me—" his voice became gravelly "—I feel like you're the only person who does so without a heavy dose of pity?"

She should let him go. Not that she could, any more than she could meet his eye.

His head dipped close over hers. "Explain that to me, Frexy."

It was her turn to shake her head. Her heart was a drum. A big, loud drum in a silent room. Could they hear it downstairs? She knew Gavin could, with his adept, heightened senses.

He exhaled on a tattered laugh. "Kyle needs to come back and give me a good ass-whooping."

"If he does..." she began. She stopped to wet her mouth. "I'll give him one."

"Because I'm at a disadvantage?"

"No," she stated. She let go of his hand and found it best to say nothing more. She stood for a minute, staring mutely at his chest, unsure how to get around him to the door. When she spoke again, she was down to a murmur. "I'll let you shower." She moved in, intending for him to step back. He didn't.

"You don't feel safe anymore?" he whispered. "With me?"

She felt too much and that was a big, unprecedented problem. "You've never given me a reason not to feel safe with you," she replied.

He cursed. Hanging his head, he stepped aside. "Go," he gestured. "Go on."

She went to the door, trying not to lunge for escape.

How did one escape oneself?

When she was on the other side of the jamb, she glanced back. His hands were braced on his hips and his head was still low. His right ribs faced her. She wanted to climb them with her fingers as if up a ladder. Her fingertips burned, guilty with possibility. "Let Miss Zelda, Prometheus and me take you home." When he raised his head, she added, "We're headed in the same direction."

"Are we?" he questioned.

"Yes," she answered, trying to avoid any subtext. His shorts were unbuttoned and loose around his navel when he moved. Her fingers weren't the only parts of her that burned anymore, and she wondered how she'd gotten this deep when she didn't remember diving.

He walked to the jamb. He reached for the door to close it, stroking her with metallic eyes. Reaching up, he grazed his knuckles across her cheek. "You've got dirt on your face, Freckles."

She backed up quickly. "You said you were done. With Freckles."

His lowered his hand and anchored it with the other by pressing his thumb into the center of the offending palm. "Sorry. I'm no good at promises."

"You realize that's a choice, right?" she said. "You *choose* to keep a promise or run from it."

Gavin frowned. "Guru Bracken. That's what I'm calling you from now on."

"I'm not sure that's any better," she said as he shut the door. She heard the water running on the other side and showed herself out.

THE DOG BARKED at everything, even leaves skittering across pavement. He ran hell for leather after squirrels and other vermin. Gavin had even woken one morning at the sound of snuffing and howling from down below where Prometheus had wedged his large backside beneath the subfloor after he trapped the neighbor's cat there.

It was too much to hope that the beast knew how to handle a leash. As Gavin tied his running shoes on the front step, he heard the dog panting lightly at his shoulder.

Gavin had stopped wondering if Mavis missed the brute. He'd stopped waiting for the dog to give up on him and go back to her. Prometheus had loped after him for ten days, straying outdoors only to do his business and flush trespassing critters and one skittish deliveryman off the property.

Gavin made sure both shoes were good and knotted before sitting upright. He eyed the road ahead. He eyed the dog who stared back at him companionably. Reaching out, he spread his fingers over his snout and rubbed. The connection had become unspoken, ironclad, the kind Gavin had only ever felt with another four-legged friend. A part of him had held back because of his experience with Boots. However, where he'd been avoiding Miss Zelda and Mavis, he hadn't been able to reject the dog's company.

"No leash," Gavin decided. "You're in charge. You with me?"

Prometheus pounced to all fours.

Gavin had snagged a ball cap from his duffel. He pulled it down over his head. Prometheus went down the porch steps and Gavin followed. "It's been a while," Gavin warned. "Go easy on me."

Once they reached the street, Prometheus trotted across the asphalt. Gavin stopped as he sniffed a gray minivan parked on the tree-lined shoulder. Waiting for the dog to lift his leg on one of the tires and be done with it, he dug deep into a lunge. Muscles protested. He stretched them a mite farther before trying the other leg. He stretched his quads, holding each foot behind him.

He'd warmed up his calves and hamstrings when he realized Prometheus had drawn a full pacing circle around the van. Standing straight out of a groin stretch, Gavin left his hands on his hips and moved closer. "What's up, boy?"

Prometheus lifted a paw to the van door. Gavin took a few steps down the road to view the van from the front. A shining silver sunshade veiled the windshield. He frowned as the dog continued to sniff at the seam of the closed passenger door. Then he whistled. "Come on. We can check it out later."

Prometheus answered the summons, falling into a light trot. He looked back only once before closing the gap between him and Gavin, staying close to the narrow lane's outer band. He stayed to Gavin's right. Intuitive—just like his owner, who also never strayed to Gavin's blind side.

The breeze picked up, peeling back the tight shrink-wrap cloak of humidity. The trees veiled most of the sun from street level, dappling asphalt that was cracked with age but not broken under Gavin's feet.

He picked up the pace. He was sweating already. He was out of shape. But he wanted to push. To prove Mavis right, or to prove Mavis wrong? He wasn't sure which.

The road inclined. Prometheus ran in time with the slap of Gavin's shoes. Gavin's ribs protested, but he fought it out.

Prometheus bounded ahead, giving a joyful bark that knocked Gavin off course. He saw the rose-covered mailbox out of his periphery. He gleaned the round house stacked on pilings beyond it. Slowing, he ground to a halt just before the road's rocky edge.

Prometheus yapped up the walk to Mavis's empty drive, all but skipping home. Gavin planted his hands on his hips as his lungs took gulps from the tepid, merciless air. Pivoting, he looked long in the direction he'd come.

Zelda had mentioned that the road from her house to Mavis's was three and a half miles. The distance was nothing to what Gavin had run regularly while in the SEAL teams or even high school. But still…

When he had his breath back, he whistled through his teeth to catch Prometheus's attention before tearing off down the lane back to Zelda's.

They lapped it once, and then again the following day. On the third day, Prometheus chased something off into a neighbor's yard. Gavin let the dog catch up, keeping the pace.

He drank fresh air, as thick as it was. He sipped it deep. He reacquainted himself with the zap of blood that moved like magic through every inch of him, the music of it swimming against his inner ear.

He forgot about the gray van. So eager was he to get it on again with his Nikes, he hadn't thought to check or help Prometheus investigate, as he'd promised previously. He was halfway to Mavis's when he noticed it again.

His pace slowed. This time, Prometheus gave the van a wide berth. Gavin, however, stared, trying to identify it as the same one from three days ago. As he and Prometheus ran on, he saw that the sunshade was gone. He thought he could make out a round face behind the wheel.

Something rumbled in the distance, bringing Gavin's attention skyward. Also something he'd forgotten? To check the forecast. The overcast glint hadn't seemed threatening when they struck out from Zelda's. But he could smell rain as the wind dredged off the river, bringing its fishy perfume to crescendo. Prometheus pulled ahead. Gavin hurried to catch up as thunder knelled.

Prometheus bolted, his sleek back curving as he lunged up the incline.

Gavin waved when the dog tossed a look back over his shoulder. "You're all right. Keep going." Feeling like an old man, he lengthened his strides.

It wasn't until Prometheus let out a frantic set of barks that Gavin thought to look around again. He nearly tripped over his feet when he saw what was creeping some fifteen yards behind him.

The van. Gavin stopped. The tires grabbed pavement and the vehicle came to a standstill.

Followed.

The skin on the back of Gavin's neck tautened. Wariness sank in. The anger, too, and frustration. *Goddamn. Not this again.*

It'd been years since he'd been tailed. As long

as a decade. But he knew what happened when he strayed to Fairhope and stayed there long enough for the news of his return to travel upriver.

Still? he wondered wildly. He was in his midthirties and she was *still having him followed*?

Anger quickly morphed into rage. Gavin couldn't see the driver, no matter how hard he squinted. That didn't stop him from following the towering impulse to approach the bastard in gaping steps. He raised his arms and his voice. "You and me. We got business, asswipe?"

The engine revved. Gavin kept approaching. The driver swung wide, but Gavin managed to grab hold of the passenger mirror anyway. He held on for two seconds, feet tapping fast on the asphalt to keep up. Six seconds. The van clipped a mailbox. Prometheus shrieked. The van was level with him now. The dog lunged for Gavin's feet.

Gavin could see him going under the back tire. Boots entered his mind and he let go, instantly. He twisted to catch Prometheus's black blur, going down on his arm and latching onto the dog's studded collar with the other.

The van's tires screeched to a halt, sideways across the road. Gavin glowered at the back window. His pulse came down as he waited for the driver to get out or drive off. The reverse lights on the van made Gavin come to his feet quickly. "Off the road," he ordered Prometheus, watching the vehicle carefully.

The van crept back. It reversed slowly until Gavin could see through the driver's window, whirring mechanically so he was face-to-face with the driver.

The man had donned a pair of sunglasses and a hat, pulled low over his forehead. "You all right, buddy?"

Gavin stared for a moment as Prometheus whined behind him, pacing a restless circle on the sandy shoulder. "Yeah." He spat onto the asphalt. There was blood in his mouth. Hostile, he added, "You could've hit my dog."

"Sorry," the man said. He was younger than Gavin expected. Younger than Gavin, and by a stretch. "I got jumpy when you came at me like that. Didn't know what to do."

This guy knew who Gavin was and knew what he'd done overseas. He knew because *she'd* told him. "New on the job, are you?"

"Job?" the man said, feigning ignorance.

Gavin shook his hand. He looked around. The street was still. The rain was coming, the breath of it blowing sand across his legs. Prometheus's whining heightened at the signs of the encroaching storm. His loyalty to Gavin kept him posted at his side. "You're a PI. Right? Private investigator?"

"How do you figure that?"

"Because you aren't the first," Gavin volunteered. "Or the brightest. You boys are usually either a PI, a lover or both."

The kid had the decency to bluster. "I—I don't know what you're talking abo—"

"I'm talking about Tiffany Howard," Gavin snapped, "and how she hired you to shadow me. Don't play dumb, Junior. You know what I am."

The kid licked his lips, looking around once. Checking for witnesses. "She said you were a SEAL, but not to worry about it because you're retired. You can't see."

"I can see plain enough!" Gavin lobbed the words in the kid's face. When he twitched, Gavin fought the urge to draw circles with his feet, like Prometheus. Lightning tossed white light from a distance, setting Prometheus off with a fit of barking. Gavin tried to calm his anger.

It didn't help that she'd thrown this greenhorn at him. She'd sent a sacrificial lamb on the hunt for an operative. Gavin could all but hear her...

He's wounded. Just don't make any loud noises. He won't see you...

The hell with her, Gavin fumed silently. The storm clouds were closing in, making the world dark. "Where is she?"

The kid didn't think to challenge the graveled question. "Panama City Beach."

Gavin waited a beat. Prometheus's head bumped against the back of his thigh, almost a shove. Gavin nodded. "Don't let me catch you here again," he told the man behind the wheel.

The guy didn't hesitate to put the van in gear.

He mumbled something about "thank you" and "goodbye" and was gone.

Gavin ground his teeth when he failed to read the license plate. He watched until the taillights disappeared around the corner. "Damn," he said, scowling.

Did she think *he* was still a kid? Did she think there was anything left that she could say anymore to hurt him? Threaten him? Scare him off?

Tiffany Howard—the woman Gavin had once thought of as *Mom*—had left him well enough alone after Gavin had told her to stop talking to him, stop interfering. As a teenager, he'd learned to see the behavior for what it was, something he hadn't been able to see as a child—psychological abuse. When he was a child, it'd been easy for her to love him. Tiffany only loved those she could manipulate.

That child had disappointed her, however. Because he'd grown into a man. Gavin was the picture of his father, Cole—Tiffany's ex-husband. Bitterness had forested over the fertile ground of disappointment when he made it clear he knew his father was the better parent and that he wanted to live with him and Briar on a permanent basis.

There were times, like now, when he could remember how his face had stung. Being slapped was something he'd earned on and off as a mouthy boy.

Mommy won't do it again. Promise.

He'd believed. Until she'd taught him something different about promises.

Tiffany had never been happy and she punished those around her who thought they could be. Even when that person was her own flesh and blood. Her offspring.

Prometheus brought Gavin back to the present, lapping his fingertips with his tongue. "All right, all right," Gavin said, brushing him off. "It's all right."

Thunder rattled. Prometheus's whine reached fever pitch. He hopped back and forth, then took off. Gavin joined him. His elbow burned. He'd jarred his right knee. More bleeding, he saw as he twisted his arm around to view the damage. Cursing raggedly, he picked up the pace. Zelda's was farther behind than Mavis's was ahead.

At Mavis's drive, Prometheus made a quick turn off the road. The hiss of rain, a wall of it, chased him from the street and under the eaves of the odd round house.

Gavin came to stand in the mist blowing sideways under the covering. Soaking it in, he closed his eyes and listened. The patter of rain on water was near and seductive. God but he'd always loved the water, whatever body of it he could find.

Prometheus whined some more. Gavin touched the dog's head, inviting him against the side of his leg. A summer storm had been the only thing to stir Prometheus before sunrise, cracking enough lightning for a club strobe and shaking the walls of the old house with the din of the righteous. Gavin had found a hundred-pound animal planted firmly in his lap, squealing like a lost piglet. He'd responded as any man should, by wrapping his arms around the beast, laying his head down close on the pillow next to his and rubbing his ear until the chaos ended.

It had been two nights since Gavin had dreamed of Benji—storm or no storm.

Maybe Mavis was right.

He knew she was right. Therapy dogs weren't a joke. Trained or adopted from shelters, they comforted veterans with PTSD. Gavin had never thought of getting one of his own, but the potential had planted itself as much as Prometheus had on his right side.

The dog fit.

Unless Gavin left. The PI had been here for days. The news that Gavin was back in Fairhope, trying to make a stab at civilian life for the first time as an adult, had reached Tiffany, clearly. He'd see her at some point or another, he was sure. And he had little doubt she'd try to tell him what his itchy feet had told him at the inn...

Run. This is no place for you.

To *hell* with her, he thought again, with such vehemence his temples rang with it. He didn't want to think about the headache that was Tiffany. He didn't want to contemplate the mess that was his future with or without her telling him all the things he'd heard before. Not when, for a second, he'd learned to stretch inside the bounds of his own mind again—stretch and, just maybe, breathe.

"Stay," he told Prometheus before ducking under the spray of the rain. Prometheus gave a protesting yap and the sky remonstrated. Nonetheless, Gavin went toward the promise of the river.

The grassy yard started to yield, softening to the water's edge. He found the shape of a dock. The planks were stable, he noted as he walked to the end until the sound of water spread around him in a triumphant 360. Lightning flickered, not far off judging by the deafening boom that flattened over the top of him. Gavin didn't move. He closed his eyes against the gray cast of the sky and the fast fall of fat raindrops and let his other senses open to the deluge.

"What are you doing, muttonhead?"

From overhead, the voice sounded teeny. Gavin followed it around and up in the direction of the first floor of the house. He shook water from his face, peering blindly. "Frexy?" he called.

"Get up here!" she called to him.

It wasn't a question.

Through the rain, Gavin couldn't see much except the dark flash of Prometheus as he scrammed to a set of stairs. Gavin found them, too. They led him to an open balcony. Gavin nearly grinned when he saw Mavis's form leaning out of the open glass door to the interior.

"Wait," she said, holding up a hand at his approach. "Jesus. Let me get a mop."

Gavin glanced down. Rain sluiced off him, as freely as it peeled off the heavy bottom of the clouds. He ran his hand over his face, then over the top of his head. His hair was starting to grow, thick and black. It was about time for another fade. "I'm all right," he called after her.

"You're going to get struck by lightning," she admonished from within. "I'm bringing you a towel!"

He waited several seconds before she came back. "Inside," she instructed, handing him the towel as he crossed the threshold. "Prometheus, sit on the rug. You're both drenched."

Gavin dried his chest, then his neck, before rubbing the terry cloth over his face and head. It smelled like her. As he moved the towel down the length of his arm, he peered at the dim surroundings. "Athames?" he wondered, only half teasing.

"I'd be more worried about the poison broth," she informed him. "Full moon brings it to totality."

He cracked a smile and finished drying off. Still he dripped on her rug. Terry cloth was no match for sopping running shorts. "I forgot how quick these things pop up in the summertime," he admitted, squinting through the glass of the door.

"You're running," she said in surprise.

"As if the info chain that runs hot between here and Zelda's hasn't already brought you in on that fact." When she only stared at him, he forced the truth out. "You were right."

"It feels good," she surmised.

"Feels great," he said. He sensed her silent mental probe. "Slept okay the last few nights. Don't know if it's something Miss Zelda slipped in the vegan entrées or…"

"At least you're eating," she said. "That helps, too. How're the headaches?"

He lifted a restless shoulder. His good eye was slowly adjusting to the darkness. "Your power's out."

"Just," she answered. "It'll come back. The power company's usually quick on the jump out here."

He roved around the short space of the rug. He was still running high on adrenaline. It didn't do well to keep him in place.

"You're bleeding," she realized.

"Huh?" he said. He extended his elbow. "Oh. Yeah."

Her fingers were light on his skin as she went up on her toes to get a better look. "It looks like… road rash. Did you fall?"

He grunted.

She sighed at him. "I'll get the kit."

"Ice will be fine," he told her instead.

"I can fix you up."

"Just bring the ice, Frexy," he told her. "I'll do the rest." Once she'd disappeared in what appeared to be the kitchen, he sniffed. He could tell her the truth. He could tell her about the van. Something stopped him. He didn't want her to fuss, and he wasn't going to stop running. And he wasn't threatened. He wouldn't cave to anyone who tried telling him he should feel that way, either.

He might be partially blind, but underneath, he was still a SEAL. SEALs took care of themselves—and of their own.

She came back with an ice pack. "This won't do much."

"It'll do fine. At least 'til I get back to Zelda's," he reasoned. He made a grab for the pack. She kept it back, rotating around him to press it to the abraded skin herself. It was cold. His skin burned beneath it.

She paused a moment, waiting for him to flinch. When he didn't, she said quietly, "You should be more careful."

"It won't happen again," he informed her.

"Good," she said, patting the point of his elbow over and over with the ice. "You're lucky it wasn't your face."

"Ah, better the face than anything else," he noted. "It's already FUBARed."

"I wouldn't say that."

He glanced in her direction. "You like my face?"

She kept her attention on the rash. Her voice

was a murmur. "I have trouble imagining anyone complaining about it."

He felt a grin warming the rim of his lips. He laid his hand over hers. "It's all right now." When she took the pack away, he said, "Thanks. I haven't seen you much lately." Was it just him or was she wearing something strappy? He tried not to peer too closely. He saw legs, her legs. Pale, just like the rest of her. He wondered if they could boast a few leopard spots, too. Her feet were bare, he couldn't help noticing. He cleared his throat and went back to being restless. "Avoiding me much?"

"You flatter yourself."

"Maybe," he mused.

"You look…better," she observed. "Much better than the last time I saw you close-up. That makes me happy."

He liked that she was looking at him. "You miss him? The beastie?" he said, pointing in the direction of hardwood flooring where he could hear Prometheus's nails clipping in listless circles.

"He's helping you. Far be it from me to pull rank."

"Canine mommy trumps first-class petty officer?"

"Always," she said. "But he likes being with you. Otherwise, he'd come back for more than just a rainy-day visit."

"But I've robbed you of your guard dog." He thought of the van. "You got a gun?"

She pulled a face. "Yes. A gift from my brother."

"Do you know how to use it?"

"I don't want to use it."

"Do you *know* how to use it?" he asked again, planting his foot on the subject.

"Kyle taught me how to rack and fire," she finally admitted. "I haven't exactly been practicing. But I can handle a weapon even if the need for it won't arise."

"It could," he warned. "If I doubted for a second you'd use whatever munitions you've got, I'd hand the dog back to you in a second."

"I'll use it," she said, exasperated.

Thank God. "Thank you," he replied. Again, he looked at her, good and long. He lifted a hand. "What are you wearing now?"

"What does it matter?"

"Well, it appears that your gams are showing."

"Yes. We call these shorts," she said, grabbing the high hem of the article of clothing that revealed so much.

"So you finally got the memo," he said.

"What memo?"

"That it's hot enough for the river to boil crawfish on its own."

Mavis shifted toward the glass door. The light from outside undulated over her torso in a watery wave. "I guess with this water rising we might finally find out if there's really an alligator living under my dock. And you'll have a little trout to break your vegan fast at Miss Zelda's."

"You have a gator?" he asked, impressed.

"Possibly. Why do you think I told you to scoot from the river's edge?" she asked, sounding amused at least.

He tried to see through the runny lines on the other side of the pane. It was no use. "I hear you and Zelda are driving to Mobile tomorrow to do your ghost thing."

"Are you interested?"

With his forearm propped high on the door, he muttered, "You might want to start with a less loaded question."

She didn't touch him. Still, he felt her like a cattle brand. His neck heated.

She was the only one who, he thought, might still see him as a whole man, rather than half. Still, the skin at the base of his spine prickled, setting off a chain reaction until he felt the effect across the width of his shoulders. His toes curled.

Damn but Guru Bracken had a way.

They stood facing the wall of water for a long minute. Her Zen tone filled the vacuum. "I meant, 'Would you like to tag along?'" He rolled his shoulder in a doubting shrug. She skipped ahead of his denial. "The job isn't in the city. It's rural. The bank foreclosed on a large property. The area is ripe for resale, but the family who lost the land hyped rumors that it was haunted. They ran a hay-ride attraction every year around Halloween."

"The bank doesn't think anyone will buy it with Overlook Hotel vibes?" he asked.

"You'd be surprised how fast a real estate prospect can dry up once neighbors start talking anomalies."

"How often do banks call Scooby and the gang?"

She snorted softly at the reference. "The man handling the deed to the property is an old friend of Zelda's."

"She seems to have a lot of those."

"Jealous?" she teased.

"I met Errol."

"What'd you think of him?"

"Not what I expected," he said. "He never says a word, just comes over to fish. I've never seen him exchange anything with her other than fruit and fishing tackle. He's a lot like you."

"How?"

"He stares holes into me," Gavin said. He traced the shape of her nose in the runny light. "Great big holes."

Her gaze turned from the window again to swallow him up.

He gnawed on his lip, then winced when the abrasion on the inside tore open again. He sucked on it for a moment until the blood flow slowed. He sealed it with a flick of his tongue.

If he could see anything clearly again, he thought…he'd want it to be her. He didn't know exactly what is was about Mavis. "I don't think I've made much of an impression on him. At least with you…well, you seem to like what you see."

The sharp cut of her hair came down to veil the unshaded portion of her face, leaving him groping for an impression. "Errol is a man of few words. I think I've only ever heard him whistle on drives."

"He doesn't like drifters living with his girl," Gavin wagered.

"You two have a lot in common," Mavis said cryptically. "I'm sure you'd get along, if you took the trouble to get to know each other."

"Blind and mute make a winning combo," Gavin said sourly.

"You're not totally blind; he's not entirely mute, from what Zelda tells me. And there are thousands of different forms of communication. Pick one. Start from there."

He gave a miniature salute. "Yes, ma'am."

"Come with us." The light hit her face again. "The weather's supposed to be sunny. There's no digging involved. As I understand, the land's something to see." When he rolled his eyes, she added, "You used to love coming to the farm and running like a fiend through the woods and fields."

"I was twelve," he reminded her. "Adolescence. Adulthood. War. You tend to lose the urge to run like something imaginary's chasing ya."

"I don't think so," she said, incisive. Her voice dropped as she tapped his sternum. "Weren't you still trying to run two weeks ago?"

His mouth quickly settled into a frown.

"I'll buy you a burger," she offered. "A thick juicy one slathered in gooey white cheese."

"Careful, Frexy," he advised. "You're talking food porn."

"There could be mustard involved," she went on. There was mischief in her voice. "Maybe onion rings…"

"Mmm." His mouth watered. He shook his head, closed his eyes, to fight the temptation. "You know how to make a man *hungry*."

"What do you say, frogman?"

He stopped fighting the need to smile at her. "You play dirty, Bracken. I like that."

He was halfway sure she was smiling back.

The dog ruined the moment with a loud, solitary *woof.*

Mavis jerked. "Storm's breaking."

Gavin had to sidestep quickly as Prometheus bounded at the door. Mavis opened it just in time for his paws to scramble across the doorstep. They heard him darting quickly across the deck and down the steps. "He has a nervous bladder," Mavis explained. She braced her hands against the small of her back. "So…we'll see you tomorrow?"

"You win," he stated with some surprise. He took a step back and told himself to keep going.

"See you tomorrow, Velma. And the rest of Mystery Inc."

"You're not funny," she remarked.

"I'm a little funny," he said in parting before descending the stairs to the yard.

CHAPTER SIX

"YOU'RE MANSPREADING."

Mavis tried not to watch how Gavin's brow creased down the same center line she'd seen before, from his hairline to the bridge of his Oakley sunglasses. Arms crossed, knees spread, he took up half the back seat of Errol's Cadillac. "I'm what?"

"Manspreading," she said again. She planted her hand on the denim-clad knee that had crossed over the middle, moving it back. "You see this line?"

He only scowled at her.

She grabbed him. "It's here," she indicated, planting his big palm across the center of the roomy bench seat.

"So?"

"*So*...this is your dance space," she said, pointing to his side. She fanned her hands toward her side. "This is my dance space. Capisce?"

He flipped the notebook nearest to his thigh closed. "Look, if you're crowded, it's because you brought half the damn library."

"Ah, no," she said sharply, palming his knee

again when he encroached once more. "It's simple. Stay on your side. And don't touch my books."

He grabbed a loose sheet of paper from her side of car anyway. He brought it up close in front of the black screen of his sunglasses. "You've been reading since we left. This isn't more about that plantation girl in Louisiana, is it?"

"That plantation girl has a name," she said, extracting the page from his hand so she could file it numerically back in with the rest. "America."

"God bless," he murmured.

"That was her name," Mavis elaborated.

"You're making that up."

"Am not," she retorted. "Her given name was America. We know that. The surname's a mystery for now, but I'll find it."

"America." He shook his head. "There's some political or poetic irony in that. Especially if you tell me one of the siblings fought opposite the other."

"They were both Confederate officers," Mavis admitted. "Josiah died at Antietam. Daniel followed at Gettysburg. However, those papers you were looking at don't have anything to do with the Isnard case. As another thank-you for finding the time capsule, Olivia and Gerald gave Zelda and me photocopies of her grandparents' letters."

"All of them?" he said, lifting the binder he'd closed to test the weight of its contents.

"All of them," she confirmed.

"Have you read all of them?" he asked, passing it back to her. When she hesitated, he tipped it out of her reach. "You have."

"I might've." She shrugged at him when he tilted his head. "What?"

"You are a romantic sort, aren't you?" he said.

"No," she protested. "I told you. It's history. And... I *guess* it interests me how two people can commit their entire lives to each other. What it takes. How they choose who that person is."

"It's not that much of a mystery," Gavin said, stretching his legs out as far as the confines of the floorboard would let him.

"No?" she asked, surprised.

"All you have to do is ask your parents. Or your grandmother, for that matter. Edith and Van were married forever before he passed on."

"My grandparents couldn't stand each other. And what about your parents, Gavin?"

"My father's on his second marriage," he said.

"He and Briar have been married thirty years. That's some longevity."

Gavin folded one arm behind his head. "I don't know. I always figured they were crazy."

"Happy crazy." When he lifted his shoulder, she asked, "You've never felt that crazy about somebody?"

"No."

She demurred. It wasn't like her to probe. But she liked figuring him out. She liked the idea of swimming in the mystery of him. Even if she knew better.

"How about you?"

"What about me?" she asked.

"You've never found anybody you wanted to exchange lofty promises with?"

"Obviously," she answered truthfully.

"Not even, say, one of the Leightons?"

She frowned at him. "No."

"Which one was it? Zelda won't tell."

"Why do you want to know so badly?" she asked, turning the ready irritation away.

"Did you love him?"

"What's that got to do with anything?" *Okay*, she thought at the snappishness of the reply. *That's a negative on quelling the irritation.*

"I might need to kick his ass," Gavin told her.

"You're assuming he deserves it," she said. "What if *I* broke things off?"

Gavin thought, then asked, "Did he get to second base?"

"Um, none of your business."

"Hmm," Gavin said, gleaning the answer for himself. "I'd still kick his ass."

He couldn't know that she'd ended things with William because she'd wanted something more. That they'd seen each other long enough for their feelings to get mixed up in all the secrecy. That at first, it had been exciting—the sneaking around, the near misses with her family and his. But she'd grown weary of the concealment after a while. Weary enough to realize she wanted something more.

It was funny how feelings worked. At first, she'd wanted to keep them to herself—keep William to herself. Somewhere along the way, she'd done a 180 and the desire to be open, to go so far as sharing what she felt for him with her friends and family, had taken on a life of its own.

But a relationship born from secrecy and evasion had made it difficult to express ambitions to the contrary. Not to mention, past experience. The only boy she'd seen before William, Aaron Quarters from high school, had gone so far as introducing her to his parents and grandparents. It had helped that his grandparents had been friends of Mavis's grandmother Edith. Or so she'd thought...

The grandparents were taken aback by her. Maybe it was the nose ring she'd worn at the time. Perhaps it was her penchant for sarcasm, which she hadn't thought to check at the door. They'd made a snap judgment, the grandmother going so far as to tell Mavis baldly at the end of the night that she thought Aaron deserved better.

What had stayed with Mavis most was Edith. Her grandmother had driven her to the evening's introductions. She'd been there when Aaron's grandmother had told Mavis that she wasn't the right type of girl. Edith declined to say a word in Mavis's defense. She'd hardly spoken at all until they were halfway home. *She's right, you know,* she'd said quietly. Almost smug. *If someone like you came sniffing after your brother, I'd have something to say about it.*

Mavis loved the Leightons—William, his brother Finnian, Olivia and Gerald. And the idea of them rejecting her as any sort of prospect for their son had kept her awake at night. Not to mention William's silence on the matter. If he'd wanted something more, like her, if he'd thought her worth the risk, wouldn't he have eventually wanted to break the chain of clandestine behavior and spoken up about it? She'd waited for him to do so until those feelings had verged on that perilous four-letter L-word. They'd been friends for a lifetime, so she put a decisive end to the whole affair to make sure their friendship could remain.

Her feelings for William were so far in the past and they'd withdrawn so far into their old friendship that she'd all but forgotten the sting of not being good enough—for him or Aaron What's-His-Name.

Now in the back seat with Gavin, she did her best to shrug off the uncomfortable memories. She riffled through the binder to the last xeroxed letter she'd read and thought of something that might knock Gavin off course. "You wouldn't happen to know how a yucca branch wound up on my balcony, would you?"

He didn't twitch, but there was a pause. "What kind of branch?"

"Yucca," she repeated. "They have large white flowers that bloom in spires and grow on the river's edge. Particularly near Zelda's place."

"Mmm, no," he replied, a shade too quickly.

"Right," she drawled.

"I don't bring people flowers," he pointed out.

"Ever?" she asked.

"Ever."

"As a florist's daughter, I'm inclined to ask why."

"I don't know," he said with an insouciant shrug. "Too predictable. Too traditional."

He was neither of those things, she agreed. She couldn't help but admire that. "What *do* you bring people?" she asked.

He raised an indicative hand. "Charisma."

She barked a laugh. "Cute."

"Thank you."

She told herself that he was being arrogant and to stop smiling. Her mouth didn't get the transmission.

"Why're you wearing red again?"

Her attention strayed from the page once more. "I always wear red."

"Since you were, I don't know, fourteen or something you've dressed like you're going to Slash's funeral. But you've been splashing red in since I moved to Zelda's. Red sweater at her place that night at dinner. Red plaid at the orchard. I happened to see you wearing those candy-striped Jane Fonda tights to yoga earlier this week."

"You saw those just before you decided to turn tail and run, did you?"

"How else do you evade someone?" he asked.

"You knocked over a lamp."

"It was in the way."

"I won't ask how you managed to pass BUD/S."

"Wasn't blind then. Anyway, don't change the subject. While you weren't wearing much when I walked in on you yesterday in the storm…"

"I was wearing plenty. It wasn't my fault you showed up uninvited."

"True," he granted, lifting the water bottle from the cup holder near his elbow. Methodically, he unscrewed the cap. "But you did paint your front door red."

"It was always red."

"Nope. It was black, too." He took a long pull from the bottle, draining it most of the way. Pointing to her shorts, which were studded and frayed nearly to the point of disuse and red as a decadent pinot, he added, "So I have a theory. You want to snag my attention—"

"Toro toro," she cheered falsely.

"—by making it easier for me to know where I'm going."

"And I'm so haughty as to think the place you want to go is toward me?" she finished doubtfully.

He stared at her for a second too long. "Maybe it *was* me who left the yucca."

Her heart picked up pace as he let the admission hang between them.

"Maybe I found it along the riverbank near Zelda's, like you said. Maybe I thought it looked nice…what I could see of it. Maybe I thought, 'It doesn't smell flowery and it's kind of prickly' and I'm pretty sure I heard a ma gator growling at me while I was trying to saw one of those goddamn spires off with a pocketknife but I thought of you when I saw it so Prometheus and I dropped it off at your place on our morning jog."

Mavis swallowed. In the confines of the back seat, practically shoulder to shoulder with him, looking, she saw the strain beyond the indifference that he'd been throwing off for most of the journey. She saw the infinitesimal beads of sweat starting to gather on his brow. She saw the tight muscles rimming his jaw. She could feel him searching.

"What would you say to that?" he asked, tripping through words packed with potential.

Fumbling, she took several breaths to cool the endorphins already going for a happy joyride in her brain. *He brought me flowers. The man who doesn't give flowers brought flowers.*

There was some sort of inevitable and ill-advised countdown going on in her glands. He wanted to know if he was cleared to race and her body was waving the green flag. *Boogity boogity…*

Because it was Gavin, though...because of what she knew of his struggles and how well they knew each other—how well their families knew each other—she took another breath. *He doesn't need this now,* she reminded herself. *He's raw. He might even be confused...*

Why else would he want her?

She wet her throat again. Her lips were dry, so she wet them, too. Even wanting as she did to stroke the smooth side of his nose and the other side where scars had tried to write their name, she said, "Gavin—"

Errol slammed on the brakes.

Despite her seat belt restraint, her head took a fast dive into the cushioned back of the driver's headrest.

Gavin cursed in a loud, long torrent.

Zelda twisted, half of her profile sheathed in white Hollywood shades and an O'Hara-worthy wide-brimmed hat she held in place. "It's all right! It's all right, kids! Just some bastard in an eighteen-wheeler trying to turn us into sardines."

Mavis groaned, blinked. "Wow." She lifted her hand to cradle the side of her head.

Something wide and warm beat her to it. It spanned her ear, covered her cheek and chin.

"*Shit*, Frexy," Gavin spat. "Are you all right?"

His tone in no way mirrored the ginger care of his hand. She blinked several more times, not because he was fuzzy. On the contrary—he seemed too far in focus. Almost as if she needed to tamp down on a zoom function she hadn't known she possessed. "I'm okay."

He scanned her. His glasses were down. His eyes were a torrent of colors and tempests. As he turned his head to the others, muscles were drawn against the hard frame of his face. "How the hell did you not see an eighteen-wheeler coming at us?"

"I'm okay," Mavis repeated. He was shouting.

"Put *me* in the driver's seat," he continued. "I may be blind, but I'd probably do better next time a frigging bus tries to run up our ass."

"Errol," Mavis said, planting a hold on Gavin's thick upper arm. She reached around the front seat to pat Errol on the shoulder with the other hand. "Can you stop somewhere, please?"

"Yes," Zelda said with a firm nod. "I think some air would do us good."

She could feel Gavin straining against the fast line of respirations coming through him. She held his arm until the Caddy found their exit and they rolled onto the grassy shoulder of a cracked bucolic strip of highway. Admittedly, she was the first one out of the car. Hanging on to the open door, she watched Gavin pace past the interstate on-ramp sign, steps choppy, kicking up dust. He paused, his back to them, lifting his face to the sun.

She saw his shoulders drop. His head came down after them, chin against his chest. She held on to the door tighter, wishing her ear wasn't ring-

ing so she could go after him. The heat was intense. There was no breeze, but the air wasn't still.
It seemed to rise in heated waves, transparent and
trapped in a primordial shimmy between clay-
baked earth and hard, empty sky.

As Mavis counted the seconds it took him
to double back, she tried not to think about the
shimmy she'd felt in his palm against her temple.
He'd been on edge the entire ride. Why hadn't she
noticed sooner?

He'd hidden it. He didn't want her, or anybody
else, walking on eggshells around him. And he'd
told her, too, that he'd had several good days after
running. Maybe he'd let his guard down and had
just earned himself a tough lesson for it.

Gavin.

"He's coming back," Zelda murmured.

Mavis jumped a little, breaking mentally with
the longing thought process. Glancing around at
the older couple, she said, "He didn't mean it." She
directed the sentiment to Errol, especially.

Errol's eyes slanted down at the corners and
were so blue they looked watery. Reticent, as he
always was, he moved his mouth in a way that
showed her Gavin's outburst hadn't fazed him.

Mavis wished Gavin could see the understanding there, to know more of what lay behind it. But
an anonymous roadside was hardly the time or the
place for either man to bare his soul to the other—
especially since neither was the soul-baring type.

When she heard Gavin's footsteps closing in, she moved toward him. "Feel better?"

"Fine," he said, clipped. In the hard slant of the sun, she saw the first rasp of five-o'clock shadow on his cheeks. "The head?"

She lifted her hand to it again. "Intact."

"You sure?" he asked. He was back to searching, even if he was doing it now at a safe distance. "You don't need a hospital? I'm sure there's an urgent care place somewhere here in BFE."

"Mavis hit her head?" she heard Zelda say with surprise and concern.

Mavis batted off the apprehension. "I'm all right," she said. "I'd just like to get where we're going."

When Gavin only frowned at her, she moved to slip back into the car. He was there, too, quickly, cupping her under the shoulder to help lower her to the seat as if she were made of something ridiculous, like porcelain. The hopped-up covey of butterflies in her stomach roused into a frenzy.

Yep. Feelings, she noted, and closed her eyes to the obvious truth.

"SOMETHING'S UP WITH this place." Gavin braced one hand on the hood of the Cadillac. He'd lifted the screen of his sunglasses to view the field. "The light's wrong." Scanning the sky, he tried to breathe through the immense heat. "Smudgy. Yellow. Like old newspaper."

Mavis spoke from the trunk where she gathered the ghost-hunting gear. "The air quality's crap. The index will be a hundred and five before noontime."

He'd grasped the last part. He never thought he'd crave lying in the icy blue surf of Coronado or cold showers between assignments overseas again. He sniffed and got a lungful of hellfire and ozone. "So it's not just me."

"It's not just you." Mavis drew even with him as she adjusted her pack, passing equipment off to Errol. "It'll make for a fair lightning storm before dusk."

He tried to assess her. "You up for this?"

The question brought her head around sharply. "I told you I was fine, Gavin."

The tone bordered on tetchiness. He grabbed what gear she'd kept for herself to carry. "Let me take this."

"I'm fine," she argued.

"Mavis, you invited me," he told her. "I can't much observe. At least let me be the pack horse."

Zelda descended on them. "My friend Julian says we've got the run of the place. The house is open. There'll be some tours later for real estate agents to snap photographs of the house and grounds. We can use the bathrooms and whatever water we need from there."

"Is it air-conditioned?" Mavis wondered.

"Electrical's up and running," Zelda said. "Julian

says it's cool enough inside if we need a breather. He drew me a crude map of the grounds. There's plenty of pasture for us to cover and more woods, but he's highlighted the hot zones. Well. Campground. Cemetery."

"Cemetery," Gavin repeated.

"It's small and part of the lore, apparently," Zelda said. "There's some riding paths from ATV vehicles, but they've been abandoned and the undergrowth's taken over. We'll have to rough it. Julian does, however, have a golf cart. He gave me a walkie-talkie if we need a lift back to the house or car."

Gavin took the initiative, shouldering Mavis's pack before she could protest again. "How does this work?"

"We're the trained professionals," Mavis said. "Leave that to us."

"Okay, Venkman," Gavin said. He drew up short when he heard the wheeze of a low laugh. "Errol. Is that you?"

Zelda edged into Errol's personal space, winding long arms around his neck. "Give us a kiss, darlin', for luck."

Mavis groaned and set off for the large house at the mouth of the pasture. He waited for Zelda to finish sucking good vibes from her cabbage boy. She broke with a gusty sigh and offered Gavin a "Your turn!"

Gavin held up a hand. "I'm good." He followed

as Zelda began to trek off through the high grass. "What do you need luck for? Your job is to find nothing."

Answering from under the brim of her straw hat, Zelda fixed the strap of what looked to be a vintage Nikon over the front of her shockingly pink blouse. "Julian doesn't want us to find any anomalies. It seems some fast turnover is needed. He says our inspection report will look good with the rest."

"Next to Terminix's?"

"Sure." She beamed at him. Her sharp-angled facial structure was striking even in the shade of his disability. She somehow managed to look exquisite in this light. "Why not?"

"You two really do take this seriously," he said.

"We can't count you in on that. Not yet." Zelda patted him, low around the back of his beltline. "Give it time."

"You know I only signed on for one field trip?"

Zelda removed the round white-framed sunglasses from the neck of her blouse and placed them over her eyes. "We'll see about that, mister. Mavis!" she called. "The old well covering. Do you see it yet?"

"You're not going to split up?" Gavin asked.

"Hell no," Zelda said. "You never separate, especially outdoors. Say you encounter something amazing and there's no investigator to back up your claim. People would laugh themselves silly."

"I think we're pretty much running that risk

already." Mavis entered his field of vision and he slowed. "What is it, Frex?"

"I need my pack." She circled him, yanking down the zipper. "Bend backward. I can't see."

He tried to do what she told him. To his left, Zelda was taking shots of the field with the Nikon. "Shouldn't y'all be doing this under the cover of night?"

"Would you come out here after dark?" Zelda asked him, clicking away.

Gavin shrugged. Mavis made a discouraging noise behind him and he stilled. "I might, if it meant meeting Slimer."

"You ever buy a ticket for a hayride?" Zelda asked, amused.

"Oh, sure. Who doesn't love when the freaks come out for Halloween? No offense."

Mavis came around his front, ripping tape from an electrical roll. "Would it be uncouth to tape his mouth shut?"

"Seeing as it was you who brought him along..." Zelda chuckled to herself, stuffing the Nikon into her pack and pulling out a fussy-looking camcorder.

"What're you doing now?" he asked as Mavis rolled the tape around something small.

"Rigging you up." She bent, grabbing him by the pants pocket.

"Hey now." The warning held nothing of alarm. He didn't dance away from her as she clipped the device to the outer lip of his pocket. "We're not alone."

"You wish, don't you?" she murmured.

"Mmm." He touched the device and earned a slap on the wrist. "Do I at least get to know what it is?"

"It's a hands-free voice recorder." She straightened, holding his attention. "Which means when we count down from five, you'll need to be vewwy quiet, mister."

If it wasn't so damn hot and weird around here, he'd have smiled at her. "You're kind of cute when you mock me."

"Now I know why you wouldn't kiss Errol," Zelda said slyly. "Oh, I almost forgot. Julian said to look out for the wild horse."

"The *what*?" Gavin and Mavis said as one.

"It lives on the property," Zelda went on. "The previous owners abandoned it. There were two, apparently. This one survived. They've been trying to catch the poor thing, but it's feisty. He said there's not a wrangler in five counties who's been able to catch it."

"The owners just left it here to die?" Mavis cried. "That's criminal!"

Gavin studied the lines of her, sharp and real. She was always real. But in this light, in this heat, in these surreal circumstances, she looked realer.

"There'll be more people today," Zelda assured her. "Maybe they'll catch him."

"Then what?" Mavis demanded. "What's Julian going to do with him? Sell him to the highest bidder and send him up for glue?"

Gavin cautioned, "Don't get any more heated than necessary."

"Oh, so I'm supposed to *ignore* animal cruelty?" she asked, sidestepping the advisory.

"It's being seen to," Zelda said. "Let's work, hmm? I've got a hot date planned for tonight and we've already sunk half an hour into prep time."

CHAPTER SEVEN

THE CEMETERY WAS indeed small, the headstones sunken into unkempt grounds. Most of them were no longer legible.

"'Real Joe Willeker,'" Zelda read. "Makes you wonder where 'Fake Joe's' buried and what led to the misunderstanding."

Gavin tried to shake his unease. The only times he'd visited a grave site was when a buddy had died in arms. Boots was buried in a decorated service animal plot in Maryland. Benji was buried in the city of Monroeville where he'd spent the better part of his childhood. Gavin had been to both burials but had zero visitations to his name. "We done here?" He swatted a fly. The gnats were worse amid the deep foliage. The no-see-ums were biting.

"Mavis is finishing the perimeter. Anything?" Zelda called out.

"We'll have to listen later. Maybe audio picked something up," Mavis responded.

"I didn't hear anything." Gavin stared at the crown of her head as she bent to his waist again. "Really? In a cemetery, sweetheart? That's wicked."

"Ha ha, funny. I'm not your sweetheart," Mavis said half-heartedly.

"Some people see it as life-affirming—sex in cemeteries," Zelda piped up. "Not that I'd know."

"Sure." Gavin smirked. Mavis cursed below him, and he touched her shoulder. "Hey. You good?"

"Hot." Mavis straightened from undoing the recorder. She backed away, taking the pack with her. "I might sit for a spell. Zelda, do you have a drink?"

"Here," Zelda said, searching her bag. "You rest. We'll gather the equipment."

"I thought she said she was always cold," Gavin noted when Mavis walked off a pace with Zelda's water bottle.

"That's what worries me," Zelda admitted. She snapped the handheld tripod off the bottom of the camcorder. "Keep an eye on her for me, will you? As soon as I get everything packed, I'll radio Julian to send Errol with the golf cart."

"Unless it's a four-by, it won't make it through the boggy part of the trail," Gavin mumbled.

"I don't want her walking back," Zelda said, echoing his thoughts.

"I'll carry her."

"She won't like that." Zelda raised her voice slightly as Gavin began to follow in Mavis's footsteps. "But don't let that stop you."

He was drawn by Mavis's red bottoms. He

reached her as she settled at the base of a low-bearing tree. "You found one your size."

Mavis answered by lifting the water bottle to her mouth. Gavin squinted at the sky for a few seconds before shifting closer.

She waved a hand. "Look, it's hot enough…"

"Relax, Freckles. I'm blocking the sun off you." He bumped his forehead against one of the branches. Tilting his head curiously, he reached up for the small fruit hanging heavy from the leaves.

"Fig," she said.

"Kumquat," he retorted. When she drank again in response, he pulled the fruit free from the limb. He pitched it up a short ways and caught it.

"You should take some of those back to Briar," Mavis suggested. "Her fig jam is the best."

"Everything Briar makes is the best," Gavin said. "Especially her jams." He stuffed the fig in his pocket and contemplated how he would steal the rest needed for his stepmother's boiling pot. Something brushed his leg. He glanced down to see Mavis offering her black backpack to him for the figs. Grabbing it, he said, "You're reading my thoughts again. I'm starting to think you've got some sort of Spock mind meld thing going."

"I never figured you for a Trekkie."

"What? Man can't carry a gun *and* enjoy *Star Trek*?" He tsked at her, stuffing more figs in the pack. "You're a little offbeat for a labeler."

She sniffed. "Always hated that word. *Offbeat*.

Like everybody has to march to the same damn cadence in order to be accepted by society at large?"

He heard bitterness and stopped picking to
tilt his head and get a better angle on her. "Are
you going to rack my nuts if I ask if you're okay
again?"

"I might."

"I don't care. I'm worried about you, Bracken."

"Hush."

"Zelda and I have a wager on whether you'll let
me carry you back to base."

"No. I mean it. Be quiet. Shh!" Mavis came
quickly to her feet, her hand clapping over his
mouth.

His body drew up tight. From her. From wariness. He heard the low nicker in the trees beyond
him and spoke through her fingers. "There's a
horse behind me, isn't there?"

"Bag," she said. When he offered the pack, she
reached in to rummage through the contents. One
of Errol's fairy-tale-red apples appeared from the
depths. "Your knife." He frowned at her. She widened her eyes, palm up. "Your knife, Gavin."

Worry slowed his hand, but he palmed the butt
of the knife from the sheath on his belt.

She frowned at the long blade. "Who the hell
carries a knife like this?" At the indicative quirk
of his brow, she shook her head. "Never mind."

"Are its ears back?" he asked. "Is it foaming at
the mouth?"

"Neither," she said as she pared the apple. "It looks injured, around the foreleg."

After she sheathed the knife, finished, Gavin stayed her with a firm grasp above the elbow. "Remember that talk we had about approaching wounded predators in the wild?"

"I know horses," she told him, already moving around him in a slow circle. "If it bites, it bites."

"I'm more worried about you getting trampled." And he cursed because there was no talking her out of this. He pivoted enough to see the horse's form some twenty-odd feet from their position. It was still as a statue, its attention seized on them. "Careful, Frex," he said.

She took her time approaching, signaling Zelda across the cemetery to stay back. Gavin tried not to shift his feet. He wanted to pace. He'd shout if he was sure the animal wouldn't bolt toward Mavis. Plus, he wasn't sure he wouldn't trip headlong into a gravestone and spook it regardless. As the distance between Mavis and the horse closed to an arm's length, Gavin's fingers bit into the fig.

Mavis stopped, keeping moderately back. Gavin heard her speak to it. He recognized the Zen tone. The apple rose as an offering on her palm.

Gavin didn't breathe as the horse weighed her and the gift.

The sound of whirring droned over the quiet density of the woods. "Mavis," Gavin barked. "Back away."

The horse skirted forward as the sound of the battery-powered engine grew. Gavin took several steps until Mavis's back buffered his front. Drawing her in a quick backward retreat, he wound his arm over her chest as the animal's hooves struck the moist ground. Gathering speed, the horse careered across the cemetery, tail feathered high.

A white golf cart bumbled into view. Gavin checked the urge to yell at whoever was behind the wheel. Beneath his forearm, he could feel Mavis's heart thumping hard against her breastbone. Loosening his grip, he drew her around to face him. He opened his mouth.

She shook her head sharply. "Don't say anything," she said, shrugging free from his arms.

Gavin scowled at the line of her back as she walked toward the golf cart, then he looked off into the trees on the other side of the cemetery where the horse had vanished.

"You walkin' back, handsome?" Zelda said from the golf cart.

"I'm coming," he called. He lifted Mavis's pack to his shoulder and left the silent graves to themselves.

"THEY'VE CORNERED THE BRUTE."

Mavis frowned at the man in the power suit who stood at the balcony wall, hands planted across the high-gloss stones. The balcony jutted off the back of the first floor, but the house had been built over a raised basement, giving its edifice an imposing upsweep and offering an expansive view of the pasture. It might've been impressive had the whole house not had the entombed echo of an abandoned ruin. She might have been able to admire it if not for the sick feeling twining in the hard pit of her stomach. "Mr...."

"Julian, please," he said, turning to her with all the charm of an experienced businessman. His comb-over was neat, his hair silver and fine as a newborn's. "A friend of Zelda's is a friend of mine."

"Sure." Clutching her glass of water with both hands, she held it against her stomach. "I guess in the spirit of friendship I should ask how long you've been hiring wranglers to catch this horse."

"Oh, weeks. Two months, to tell the truth. It nearly scared the socks off me the first time I came to assess the place. It must've been alone just as long before we realized it was here. A terrible pity they left it the way they did."

Only because you see it as a nuisance, she thought. Choosing her words carefully, she pondered through the swell of a headache. "Yes, terrible."

"And the wranglers aren't hired," Julian told her, pivoting back to the view and the men running across the field in strategy. They'd nearly locked down a corral with the horse backed against the stable wall. No room to run. "They'll be paid if and when they secure it for transport."

"And from there?" Mavis asked. His back was to her, and she passed the cool sweating surface of the glass across her brow. "Where will they take him?"

"Wherever they please."

"You don't wish to be compensated?" Mavis asked. "To go against the house selling costs?"

"I don't know much about horses," Julian replied, "but I do know this one couldn't have been very valuable. Or else its owners wouldn't have left it."

A distressed whinny broke across the pasture. Mavis did her best not to grimace as the handlers tried to fit the horse roughly with a bridle. "You do realize it's hurt?"

"Is it?" Julian asked, mildly curious.

"I got close enough to see swelling around its front left splint."

"You know horses?"

"My parents own several," she explained. "I had a chestnut named Neptune. We did some show jumping."

"You're an expert in many areas, it seems."

She drank the rest of her water, then set the glass down on the balustrade. "What would it take for me to convince you to talk these men into transferring the horse across the bay to my parents' farm?"

The question scrubbed Julian's face blank. "Why would I do that?"

"Well, do you know these men?"

"No. They're hired hands."

"So can you tell me you trust them to give the animal the proper care and attention it needs?"

Julian pursed his lips, peering across the field from where shouting and cursing was audible. "I suppose not."

Mavis pressed harder, sizing him up. "This situation already smacks of an animal neglect case. You wouldn't want the horse's welfare to come back and haunt you. Would you, Julian?"

"The men will expect to be compensated. I did offer a reward."

"How much?" Mavis challenged.

A muscle in his face twitched. "Five."

"Hundred?" She narrowed her eyes as a beat of silence pressed between them. "Is that all?"

"I thought generous enough seeing as they're getting the animal in the bargain."

"I thought the animal wasn't worth much," she countered. As Julian rooted around for the appropriate reply, Mavis scanned him thoroughly, deciding that a friend like Julian was the kind she'd be better off passing up altogether. "Zelda! Could you bring me my bag, please?" To Julian, she added, "Will you accept a check? Or do you prefer cold hard cash?"

Julian cleared his throat. "A check will be fine."

"Good," she replied, and stepped forward to take the ballpoint pen from his lapel.

"WHERE'RE WE GOING EXACTLY?" Gavin asked as he moved with Mavis in determined strides across the pasture. The afternoon sun was high and harsh, bringing the temperature to its staggering climax. He felt his shoulders baking through the fabric of his T-shirt. A line of sweat sluiced down the center of his back.

"You wanted to help," Mavis reminded him. Was it just him or was she speaking through her teeth? Her focus was fixed on the skirmish in the stable yard. "I need to convince these men not only to give up the horse but to take it across the bay and deliver it to the farm."

"Why?"

"Because I just bought it." She ignored his answering oath. "They're expecting a reward for its capture."

"Will they get it?" Gavin asked her.

"We'll see," she said, and picked up her pace.

Gavin widened his strides as she broke into a half run. The reason for her hurry became evident. Men shouted. The animal was on a lead rope, but it reared and bucked, trying to break free. One man fell, likely kicked, and scrambled out from under the horse's hindquarters. Another man near the front called out, bitten.

Gavin gripped the top of the metal railing.

"Well, it might not look like much. But at least it's plucky."

Mavis gasped as the horse bellowed in protest. Gavin winced as the man on the lead rope dragged the animal's nose to the dirt, straining the lead until its body tipped. It hit the ground with a resounding thud.

"Bastards!" Mavis cried as she bent and slipped through the rungs of the gate.

"Mavis!" Gavin leaped over the top and sprinted to catch her.

She was already on the posse. "All of you! Stop what you're doing!"

They did stop, momentarily. They assessed her quickly, then went back to struggling as the horse gained its feet and resumed its fight for escape. "Who're you?" the man on the lead rope ground out.

"Mavis Bracken," she replied. "I'm the horse's owner."

"Yeah," the man replied with a laugh. "And I'm Jefferson Davis. Nice to frickin' meet ya."

"This isn't necessary," she said, trying to butt against him so she could take the lead rope for herself. "You've got him pinned. There's no reason for rough handling."

"How do we know it's not going to make a leap for it? The guy who was here last week said it jumped their fencing. We've worked this hard. I'm not taking chances. Get back so we can get him into the effing crate."

Gavin noticed the horse trailer squatting behind a large truck on the other side of the fence, ready for use. "And by crate you mean crate," he pointed out, sweeping his hat up to doff the sweat from his brow with the underside of the bill before settling it back on his head.

Mavis had planted her hands on her hips. "At least give it that bucket of feed over there. It's exhausted. It's hot. It's dirty. There's a good hose with well water running to it. The best thing to do now would be to give it a cool rubdown."

"Why don't you do it, clever clogs?" the wrangler replied. "And while you're at it, the rest of us are hot and dirty, too. We could use a rubdown just the same."

Gavin's arm lashed out to grip the man's collar. He didn't miss. "Say it again, dipshit," he said.

"Gavin," Mavis said, cautioning.

"Slower this time," Gavin said to him. "I don't think I heard you right."

"There's no need for any more aggression," Mavis pointed out.

"Just grab the rope, Frexy," Gavin directed without turning his head to her. He stared a hole between the man's eyes. He waited until Mavis took possession of the horse. Then he added, "You ever hear of soap, goober?" He threw the man back several paces.

"Gavin, really," Mavis called wearily.

"What? He smells like a garbage truck and a corpse flower had a baby." Grabbing the rope, too, he helped Mavis guide the horse to the other side of the corral, near the hose. He tied it off for her on a hook. Grabbing the feed bucket, he set it on the peg on the fence rail under the horse's nose. "Bite me, porcupine, and I'll lead you back to 'em."

"No, you won't," Mavis said, already dragging the nozzle over the horse's withers. A course of streaming water poured over its matted brown coat. "No, you won't," she repeated gently, circling her hand over the horse's neck.

Gavin willed himself to stop wishing that was his neck she were rubbing and held on to the halter. When Mavis moved away, he added in an undertone to the animal, "Kick the lady and I swear to God, pal..."

The horse eyed him balefully. It jerked its head against Gavin's hold, then settled down as the water caressed its back and hind legs, its ears lowering. The coarse sound of a nicker reached Gavin's ears. "She's good at that massage thing, right?" Gavin muttered. Despite himself, he moved his hand over the white diamond between the horse's eyes. "Atta boy."

"Girl," Mavis said from the horse's side.

"Yeah? That explains a thing or two."

"Like what?" came Mavis's prickly response.

He valued his tongue so he kept it safe inside his closed mouth.

"Try feeding her."

Gavin tugged on the rope. The horse jerked. "Come on," he said, scooping a hand into the bucket. "Nothing but figs to eat for weeks? Gotta be hungry." Laying his hand flat, he offered the feed in a slow gesture of goodwill, hoping he didn't lose a finger in the process.

The rub of whiskered lips grazed his callouses. Gavin raised a brow as the horse chowed. The feed disappeared. Gavin felt a slow smile crawling across his face and scooped another handful. The animal took the second offer without delay, putting scruples aside and giving way to hunger.

"Oh, good girl!" Mavis said.

Gavin looked up at Mavis, the hose dripping from her slackened arm. "How 'bout that?" he said, rubbing the damp hair on the horse's neck.

"She likes you," Mavis murmured.

"Poor lamb," he muttered, spreading the caress wider. "Her judgment's off."

"No. It's bang on."

His eyes charted back to Mavis as she moved to the barren trough lining the fence. He watched her bend over to sweep a line of dirt from the bottom. He traced the slope of her back and tried to etch the muscles of her calves more clearly. They were tight and round, probably from all that yoga.

The hose clattered to the dusty earth and Mavis

made a grab for the fence in front of her. "Ohh," she moaned. Her hair dropped over her face, veiling her profile. "Oh, no…"

"Mavis?" When her brow dropped to the edge of the trough and she didn't respond, Gavin rushed toward her. "Hey—"

Her knees hit the ground. The feed bucket toppled off its hook, littering grain everywhere. "Mavis?" He made a grab for her.

Her hand came up to meet his. Her body seized, and she began falling back to the grass.

Gavin caught her around the shoulders. *"Mavis!"* She didn't respond. His stomach flattened. He grabbed her by the chin.

A twitch went through her, small, followed closely by another. His mind traveled back to the Bradley overseas where Benji had slipped away. The sweat on Gavin's body became chilled. Fear jammed the back of his throat. He tasted it. His lungs burned.

He felt himself start to slide away, into the anxious spiral. He shook his head, trying to ground himself to the present. To Mavis. He patted her cheek with the back of his hand. "Mavis, baby. You gotta talk to me. Talk to me, damn it!"

"Out of my way! Out of my way!"

Something pink nearly knocked Gavin flat. Zelda pushed her big floppy hat at him. "Hold this, sug! Where's her pack?"

Her pack? How the hell should he know where

Mavis's pack was? Why did it *matter* where her pack was?

Zelda pinned him. Her hand clamped on to his upper arm. "Okay, first, *calm down*. Can you do that for me?"

"She's—"

"—having a seizure," Zelda informed him matter-of-factly. "You do know she's epileptic?"

Epilepsy. Yes, he had known that. Kyle had told him at some point or another, when Mavis was still a kid. Gavin had never been around to see the disorder take effect. In fact, it had been so many years since he'd heard it mentioned, it had slipped his mind.

"You, calm down," Zelda repeated. "What she needs now is calm. Take some deep breaths and help me turn her on her side."

While the first set of instructions had revealed the very large weight of terror sitting on his torso, this second set punched through because it required action.

He felt himself shake, then stilled the tremors and helped Zelda get Mavis onto one side. He made sure there was no shaking in his hand when he reached out to comb the hair back from Mavis's cheek. "She—She needs something under her head."

"Here."

Gavin looked around to the mouthy wrangler and the offered towel. "Thank you," Gavin said, taking it. Cradling Mavis's head in his hand, he lifted her just enough to position the bunched fabric underneath. He lowered her to the makeshift pillow.

A whistle cut across the yard. The wranglers who had crowded around them parted and Errol was there with Mavis's pack.

"Oh, thank goodness for you," Zelda praised him.

Errol wasted no time upending the open bag. Items tumbled free. Among the gear and personal items that littered the sparse grass, a medicine bottle caught Gavin's eye. He grabbed it, only for Miss Zelda to take it from him. Steady as a soldier, Zelda unscrewed the childproof lid, then shook out a capsule. "If we can get her to come to, we can do this a lot easier."

Gavin watched Mavis's eyes roll. When he saw the whites, cold took a bite out of him. "If she doesn't?"

"We can give her the medicine, but she's going to need emergency personnel."

"Jesus," he hissed. "Jesus Christ."

Someone latched onto his shoulder. It took Gavin a second to realize that it was Errol standing behind him. He chose not to shake off the grip.

It might have been the longest wait of his life. He'd done recon missions requiring whole nights, even days of waiting. He'd bobbed like a cork on listless seas in what amounted to little more than a dinghy waiting for the right ship to pass. Spent hours waiting for the right man to cross his scope on a classified task force.

He'd waited outside a curtain to hear the doctors at base pronounce what he already knew—that death had taken his brother-in-law.

Mavis's chest rose. He heard her exhale. Her lids came down over her eyes. Then, slowly, she blinked them back open.

"Mavis," he said, crouching farther into her range. "Freckles?"

Her brow furrowed. She was limp. She made a faint motion with her arm.

Zelda was there with the capsule. She set it on Mavis's tongue, then uncapped a water bottle. Cupping Mavis under the chin, she helped her swallow. "Welcome back," Zelda said, patting her on the cheek.

Mavis mumbled a reply.

Gavin sat back on his heels, cursing himself and the world at large. He gave in the rest of the way and sat on the grass, elbows to knees. He had half a mind to lower his head between them.

Errol motioned the wranglers farther back as Zelda helped Mavis take another swig of water. "We should get you inside. Do you feel okay to move?"

"W-Wait." Mavis's hand fumbled. It wasn't until it settled on Gavin's ankle that he realized she'd sought him. He saw finally that she was looking at him and suddenly wished she wouldn't. He was bone, splintered and white.

"How'd he handle it?" Mavis asked Zelda hoarsely.

"He'll be all right if we can get him off the ground, too," Zelda replied handily.

"I'm a'right," he grumbled. Still, his hand clenched over the back of hers. "Jesus, Bracken. Jesus."

"Sorry." Mavis closed her eyes again.

"Stay," he said sharply when she opened them again. "Stay with me. Okay?"

Mavis bobbed her chin in a short nod. "Okay."

A pang hit him, the urge to pick her up and get her the hell away from this place. Far enough away that they could forget about the whole crazy experience. Yet she looked fragile. If he touched her, she might break into dust, like plaster. Not to mention that his knees were nice and jellified from the spin he'd taken. No, lifting a human—as little as she was—probably wouldn't be a good idea.

He couldn't stop himself from touching her, though, light brushstrokes across the high point of her cheek. Her brows came down. She patted his leg. "It's okay."

Gavin shook his head. "What—What can I do for you?" Swearing at himself, he pressed his teeth together. "I need to know what to do."

She blinked—long enough for him to worry. Then she licked her lips and looked beyond him.

Gavin glanced around and saw the horse graz-ing nearby, keeping a wary eye on the proceed-ings. Reading her thoughts, he blew out a breath.

Of course. She was worried about the nag. She was Mavis. She had a thing for beasts, whether they barked, cursed, bit or kicked.

And they tended to love her in return.

To hell with it. Gavin shifted to his knees. Lean-ing over her and sliding one arm underneath her knees, he cupped the other arm beneath her shoul-ders.

He was rock steady when he lifted her. His knees stayed in place as he came to his feet.

"You're going to carry her all the way?" Zelda asked, impressed.

Gavin didn't answer. Mavis's mango perfume was in his nose. Raising his voice to the gathered hands, he moved faster. "If that animal isn't loaded into that trailer in the next few minutes, it's my foot in your ass!"

Mavis mumbled his name.

Obediently, Gavin jerked his chin in the horse's direction. "And if I find one scratch on Mollie Mc-Carty, my foot will be the least of your problems!"

Errol had fallen into pace with him. He gave a low whistle. Gavin heard the approaching whirr of Julian's golf cart. He nodded in decision, letting Errol lead the way to the gate.

The golf cart bumbled up to it and the man in the suit peered at them from the covered cab. As

Gavin moved sideways through the slim parting of the gate with Mavis, careful not to jostle her, he heard the noise of the portable fan keeping Julian cozy.

"No trouble here, I hope, Zelda?" Julian asked.

Gavin all but growled. He looked to Errol, who nodded back in a minute gesture before closing the distance to the golf cart. Gavin watched wistfully as the man grabbed the banker by the fancy label and tossed him bodily from the driver's seat to take his place behind the wheel.

Gavin walked smoothly through the satisfying cloud of dust Julian kicked up as he scrambled to his feet again. He might've trod on the man's toes as he rounded the back of the cart. Cradling Mavis to his chest, he settled onto the rear bench seat, shifting her so he would absorb any bumps along the trail. Glancing around, he jerked his chin at Zelda. "Comin'?"

"Absolutely," the woman said, sliding onto the seat next to Errol. As Errol put the cart in reverse, she spoke to the slack-jawed man in the headlights. "Sorry, Julian. There seems to be limited seating. But we do thank you for your hospitality."

Julian stammered appropriately. "I—I—I…"

Errol put the golf cart in drive and did an adept 180. Gavin would've found it satisfying to watch Julian disappear in a cloud of dry dust. But Mavis wasn't shrugging him off. She'd chosen him to lean on.

They could both do with some leaning at this point, he was willing to admit, and tucked the crown of her head beneath his chin.

HOME. SOMETIMES, IT wasn't the river. Sometimes—a lot of times, it was a restored farmhouse in a private country wood.

The Cadillac splashed across the shell-lined drive. The afternoon storm the skies had promised pounded overhead. Rain fell in lashing strokes against the car. The lights of the house swam through the windshield, and the wipers shrieked to keep up with the deluge.

In a low mutter from the front seat, Zelda weighed whether to wait for a break in the weather. Mavis met Errol's assessing look in the rearview mirror and turned away. She looked down at the center line between her and Gavin and the hard hand that had been locked over hers from the moment they had left the house in Mobile.

The whole drive he'd been silent. She'd felt him scoping her as they crossed the long bayway that bridged Mobile County with the Eastern Shore. His tension was palpable. His concern evident. He hadn't asked if she was okay again. He'd just watched—waiting for her to bat an eye wrong.

Waiting to jump into a heartbeat's action.

Errol braked and put the car in Park. Gavin didn't let go of Mavis's hand. She didn't remove it.

Mavis pursed her lips. "It's not letting up," she said.

Zelda swiveled to her. "What did you say, dear?"

"The rain," Mavis said, raising her voice enough to be heard over the drubbing. "It's going to go on like this for a while. And y'all need to get home." She touched the door handle.

Gavin quickly moved against his door. "I'm going with you."

She frowned at him, but he'd already opened it, cutting off any argument.

"Wait!" Zelda cried. She produced a small umbrella. "Take this. It won't keep you both dry, but at least Mavis might—"

Gavin took it quickly and left the vehicle.

Mavis gasped as she stood up next to the Caddy. The rain was like blunt nettles. She was drenched before Gavin made it around the trunk to shut her door for her. "There's no need for that," she half shouted at him when he raised the umbrella over her head.

His arm fit over her shoulders. He ushered her up the front walkway to her parents' covered porch. She ducked her head. It fit nicely in the groove between his chest and triceps. Mavis fumbled with her bag, fishing for keys. Swiping the hair back from her brow, she ran her palm fast over her face to stop it from dripping. Sniffing, she dug deeper.

When she was still unsuccessful, she groaned.

"You don't have to wait. You can go back to the car—" The words seized as arms spanned her, pulling her in.

Gavin hugged her firmly from behind. Mavis's mouth dropped open when his face turned against her damp neck and burrowed.

Arms lifting uncertainly, Mavis struggled to breathe. Not because he was cutting off her air supply, but she'd never known what to do with open affection from anyone but her parents or brother, and even that she preferred at a minimum. Words. She liked words. Sensible, intellectual conversation was all the stimulus she needed on a regular basis.

Or rather, it had been, until these arms. His chest pressed tight against her back and his scar-riddled nose lodged against her rapid-fire pulse.

Not that she knew what to do, exactly. An exhale shuddered out of her when his lips grazed the curve of her neck and shoulder...then pursed, brushing a kiss there. It was a nerve center. Her body lit up.

She pulled air into her lungs, siphoning it carefully around the jittering, knocking ball in the center of her chest. He'd begun to rock her. When she gripped his forearm and squeezed, she told herself it was for balance but knew it was a lie. She told herself other lies. She was tired—which is why she tipped the back of her head to his ready shoulder. She was *really* tired when she closed her eyes and absorbed him, the sensations that he brought to her skin.

Her eyes popped open. Too much. Too fast. Too soon. She wiggled slightly, tensing. His arms loosened.

Mavis pivoted slowly to face him. Her mouth was open in explanation when she finally found it in her to raise her gaze to his.

His mouth collided midway with hers. It might've been an accident…had he not groaned in satisfaction. Had she not gone up on her toes in reaction. *An accident*, she lied.

She felt the cotton of his T-shirt straining against the insides of her fists. She broke away in shock. She'd taken hold of him by the neckline and had practically bent him to her. Shaking her head, she planted the soles of her shoes to the porch and sought the coupling of clever words she often relied on.

It failed. She failed—to speak, pull away. His arms spanned the middle of her back. They felt good folded there. Heat curled against her center at the press of his navel to hers. In an instant, it grew, burning blue as a sapphire. And it brought on a large bolt of fear.

Too hot. Too close. Too real. *It's too real*, she told herself. Nudging back, she placed her arms against his chest.

He let her go, just as quickly as he'd swept her in.

She tried again, to say something intelligible at least. Again, she settled for a lie. "I'm… I'm tired."

He scanned her, mute. His mouth was full. She wondered if it felt pinched and puckered like her own. His eyes looked dark under the covering of the porch. They practically glittered. He reached.

She wouldn't stop him. *Oh God.* If this was their beginning, where was the end?

With him gone, her broken and nothing.

He reached around her and pushed the door open. Then he retreated.

The disappointment struck. Yet another surprise.

"You'll take care," he said. It wasn't a question or a request.

She didn't chafe at the command as she normally would. She was messed up. She was messed up over him, and she couldn't blame it on the day. She couldn't blame it on the concern she'd seen etched as deep as his scars. She couldn't blame him at all. She'd started this. She'd initiated it all by touching him under the bougainvillea. By taking his demons into her own hands, hoping she could knead them and tame him—hoping she could bring him back to himself.

She backstepped over the threshold. She heard her mother's voice. More arms around her, these familiar.

"Won't you come in, Gavin?" Adrian invited.

Yes, please, Mavis thought. Then she shook her

head at the automatic answer. What was living inside her...no. *Too soon. Too much.*

Gavin saw the motion of denial. His hooded eyes rested on her without ceasing. "Thanks, Adrian, but I ought to be getting back and Mavis ought to get some sleep."

"Thank you," Adrian said. "Zelda told me over the phone what you did. How you helped. I'm grateful. We're grateful to you. Please come by for dinner. Sunday."

Gavin. Gavin at the table. Like before. Only not like before. So much had changed, but he'd be sitting in his chair again, the one that had been his despite the navy-imposed and self-chosen absences...

Mavis couldn't think of anything she wanted more. "Come," she agreed, aware of the fact that he was looking at her still.

Gavin nodded quickly at her bidding. "Sunday."

"Wonderful," Adrian said, smiling.

"Let me know," he said, talking to Mavis again. Only to Mavis. "If there's anything you need."

You, in all your shattered bits and pieces. Mavis would've stepped back if not for her mother's supportive arm around her waist. "I'm fine," she said instead. "I'll see you?"

"You'll see me," he promised, the significance doubled by his unyieldingness. He nodded to Mavis's mother before backing away.

Mavis didn't breathe until he was out of sight.

Then she didn't dwell on it, or him, until she was alone. It was shining through her. If she thought about it, her mother, her father, they would see it. They would know how far Gavin Savitt was lodged inside her. And how much it would cost her to remove him when this was all over.

CHAPTER EIGHT

GAVIN DIDN'T SLEEP the night after they returned from Mobile, or the next. The third night he managed to grab something resembling rest between the bright flash-bang of dreams that woke him once or twice before dawn.

So the series of knocks clattering against the other side of his bedroom door at seven thirty made him think about the pistol he kept on the back side of the headboard. He'd been trained to shoot in the dark. He could work without eyes, he mused, then deal with the mess later. *After* sleep.

Already a headache throbbed at his temples. It would be a shitty day, he thought, before Prometheus began nosing his leg to rouse him. The mattress moved as he stepped over Gavin's prone form and jumped from the foot of the bed. Gavin heard him rooting beneath the door.

Before Prometheus could claw his way out, Gavin planted his feet on the floor and scrubbed his stubbled cheeks. At the sound of the fourth set of knocks, he growled and leaped to answer.

"What?" he gruffed, throwing the door wide.

Mavis stood on the other side.

"Damn," he said instantly. He'd worn nothing but Fruit of the Looms to bed and hadn't thought to grab shorts or a shirt between the bed and the door.

She took several seconds to blink at his indecent state. Without a word, she did an about-face. "I'll wait," she said.

"For…" He drew the word out.

She touched her chin to her shoulder, careful not to look. "For you to cover up."

"I was sleeping," he told her.

"Sorry," she said, scrubbing Prometheus's ruff with both hands when he vied for her attention. "It's daylight. I thought you'd be up."

Well, he was now. It was a good thing she'd turned around.

When he didn't move, she added, "I need to talk to you."

About the other night. About the other night when he kissed her. Or she kissed him. He hadn't known where it started, exactly, or who had started it…

He'd take the blame. He'd wrapped himself around her like a bandage, hating the fact that it wasn't enough. To cure her. To remove the vicious memory of her eyes rolled to the back of her head…

It wasn't enough, he'd thought, and he'd kissed her. As ill-advised as it had been, he'd taken Mavis's mouth on her parents' front porch and he wasn't even sure he was sorry about it.

No, he pondered, visually tracing the line of her shoulders. She was wearing a loose black sleeveless T-shirt. Under the close crop of her haircut, he saw the halter tie of a matching bikini. Freckles dotted the points of her shoulders.

He wasn't sorry.

He backtracked into his room without bothering to close the door. He located a clean shirt and yanked it over his head. He'd stopped wearing clothes to bed a while ago. It was no use with night sweats. Jerking a pair of running shorts up to his waist, he padded back to the door. Cinching them, he said, "Go on."

"Are you decent?"

"I'm suitable for the eyes," he said. Though even that was a stretch.

She scanned his attire, settling on the shorts. "Do you have swim trunks?"

"I might."

"Put those on instead," she instructed. "And meet me downstairs in five."

He rolled his eyes as Prometheus trailed her to the stairs. "I had plans to go back to bed."

Gripping the banister, she tossed back, "I'm talking to you, whether it's here or down there. Your choice."

Gavin groaned because he knew there was no way she was entering his quarters. Not with the shades down and the sheets in disarray.

He padded into the bathroom. It was a small

room, but the ceiling was lifted and hanging plants helped it breathe. Gavin washed his face and gargled Listerine. Running his knuckles over his cheek, he scowled. No time for shaving this morning. He ran his hand over the top of his head. Later, he'd call Harmony for a haircut. His sister had a steady hand and a barber's eye.

He left the shirt on and traded the running shorts for a pair of buff-colored trunks he'd almost forgotten that he had packed. He kicked his duffel bag into the corner where it'd lived since he moved to Zelda's. It had been weeks since he arrived here and she had yet to announce an expiration on the invitation, and he had yet to unpack. No clothes in the bureau. No shoes in the closet. So far, the only items he kept at hand were toiletries, and those were limited.

He'd been surprisingly comfortable at Zelda's, for the most part. He'd slept more hours in this room than he had in the one he'd occupied as a boy at the inn. However, he wouldn't kid himself into believing this had in any way, shape or form become home. None of it took away from the clock in his head that was winding down in expectation of the moment he would move on.

He might admire the long-standing residency that Zelda, his parents, and the Brackens and Mavis held in the town, the solid legacies they'd carved…but he'd be a fool to think he could plant himself as they had. Plunk down roots, buy land, stop being a drifter.

It wasn't so much wanderlust anymore that kept him going, he admitted. What led him away was more the burden he created for the ones here. If there was one thing he refused to be, it was burdensome.

He didn't know when he would leave, where he would go or how exactly he would part with the people he'd grown reattached to.

There was one person in particular whom saying goodbye to could be likened to torture.

He'd hate disappointing Mavis. But if he suspected for just one moment that he was burdening her...

Since meeting Mavis, Gavin had found that he could live with being blind. He could live with having no direction. He'd survived that way thus far. But he couldn't live with encumbering her with his issues.

Swallowing some pain pills for the dull thumping on the left side of his skull, Gavin left his room and started down the stairs to the first floor. The old treads creaked and whined in places. There was one toward the middle of the first set that was shorter than the rest. It'd tripped him up a couple times after he'd moved in. He avoided it altogether, moving smoothly to the second set that turned sharply to the right to meet the house's entry point.

He pulled up short at the figure waiting at the

bottom. Back to the railing, she favored his right side, as always.

Now that there was some light, he noticed that her sleeveless shirt had a grinning Day of the Dead skull. Also, it was so elongated that it either hid her shorts or masked the fact that she wore none.

As he came down the last bit of stairs, ducking the low part of the ceiling, he couldn't fight half an amused smile. "Where's your red today?" he asked, scanning her closely. She'd taken her mango scent up a few notches. Or else he was that much more aware. Like a territorial mammal sniffing out its mate.

The word *mate* birdied the good part of his brain off a cliff edge. The only thing that tethered it back was the double kick of his pulse on his eardrums.

He'd been intimate with women. He thought he might have been in love a time or two in his past, but he'd never associated *any* female with the word *mate*.

Mavis reluctantly reached over the rail to the trestle table. When she revealed the straw-colored panama hat and the thick red ribbon plaited around its middle, Gavin couldn't fight the single laugh that shot from his chest. He lifted his hand to the brim. Mavis let him take it.

He swiveled the hat over his fingertips. If the kiss had troubled her, would she have bothered bringing the hat with the ribbon? Would she have bothered to show up for him at all?

Silent questions grew thick between them. Finally, unable to bear another moment's hesitation, she took the hat and the hand underneath it. "Come on," she said, tugging.

"Where're we going?" he asked. He buttoned up quickly when they were met by a small group of women in the foyer with yoga mats either arriving to class or leaving. Several of them greeted Mavis. She didn't waste much time on small talk, steering him through the contingent to the wide sliding doors rife with golden light.

Gavin dug his sunglasses out of the pocket of his swim trunks. He followed Mavis through the door to the grassy lawn. He heard the breeze moving through the wispy branches of the wide weeping willow. Ducking under the limbs, he kept his neck low.

She sailed easily underneath, headed for the clean lines of the dock.

"Are you embodying the spirit of mystery more than usual today, or do you plan on telling me what you're up to?" He tipped his gaze to the robin's-egg-blue sky. The light wasn't nearly as harsh as it had been in Mobile, even if the water's fishy odor was strong. The angle of the sun was long and light. "Damn, it's early."

"You're a navy man," she said, letting him go. Her tall Grecian sandals twined up her calves, almost to the knee. They slapped against the planks of the dock as she made her way to a small boat.

"I was." He watched without much shame as she bent down to untie the dock lines. "Why? You need a captain for this...vessel?"

"Not yet, Prometheus," Mavis said when the dog tried to step into the boat. "Not yet. You're going to need counterweight." Waving an arm at Gavin, she said, "Come."

"No," he said, snatching the dock line from her.

"No, you're not getting in first? Or no, you're not coming?"

She probably meant to sound sarcastic, as always, but he heard the waver under it all. Fighting not to touch her, he took the hat from her fist and placed it on her head. "Ladies first."

Taking his offered arm for balance, she stepped into the canoe, then clambered over the first seat to sit at the bow.

"Go 'head, beastie," Gavin said, tapping Prometheus on the back. The canine arced lithely from the dock's edge to the middle of the boat, which pitched into a drunken rock. Mavis grabbed for the sides and Gavin crouched quickly to grab on, too. "Still dry?" he asked wryly when the rocking subsided.

"Still dry," Mavis confirmed.

"Oars?" Gavin nodded approval when she lifted two for inspection. "Casting off."

"Careful," she said as he shoved off the dock with his feet, hands on either side of the boat.

At his smooth transition from dock to boat, she groaned. "Cat."

As they strayed from Zelda's with the current, he remained standing long enough to peel the shirt from his shoulders before settling on the center seat and taking the oar Mavis offered. If he'd felt at home anywhere, ever, it was on the water. "Where to, Frexy?"

"Downstream," she claimed, shifting so her back was to him. She positioned her oar across her lap before falling into the rhythm he set, dipping in and out. Without looking back, she alternated strokes. When he dipped port, she dipped starboard. The arm action was so deft and intentional, he no longer had to wonder where her shoveling muscles hailed from.

The weather wasn't just favorable, he realized as they set a course; it was gorgeous.

They paddled around a series of corkscrew bends. The gentle laps of sun and exercise and the sound of the water sluicing around them...even the tug of tidal resistance against his oar relaxed him. The quiet call of small birds and the shouts from people along the river's grassy bank helped erase the pounding in his head. He and Mavis fell into a companionable, working silence as they explored the river's snakelike parameters.

The river widened; the current quickened. Gavin caught the white flash of a shiny mullet as it made its oxygen-seeking leap from the depths. Prometheus barked at it. He barked louder at the reed-like motion on the shore from an unfazed heron.

"Osprey," Mavis cried out, stopping her oar long enough to grab the lid of her hat and jut her nose to the sky. "See it?"

Gavin could make out the shadow and predatory glide of the large river hawk near the tops of the trees. "Affirmative."

"I think I see its nest," she said, dipping her oar to port to bring them closer. "Up there. Top of that bald tree."

Gavin squinted. Osprey nests were high, large and normally easy to spot if you knew where to look. He shook his head, unable to see it for the backdrop of other trees. He fell back into rhythm with Mavis and shook off the puff of gloom.

Not today, he thought. There wasn't room enough in this boat, what with him and the dog. Gavin wouldn't let it crowd its way between him and Mavis. Somehow she'd known he needed this today. She always seemed to know exactly what he needed. That was the miracle of her.

Mate. Miracle. He doubted she'd go for either classification so he did his best to stop thinking. *Onward.* Onward was better than the way he'd come. And it was the first time in months he had admitted as much.

Hell. She was part of that, too, wasn't she?

Mavis. It was Mavis at every turn. *Sunk*, he mused, dipping his paddle deeper as the current

picked up and the river stretched. *Sink. Sank. Sunk.*
Like an old B-24 in blue Adriatic water covered
from tip to tail in rust and barnacles.

It was a good thing he liked water.

The sun picked up on the chain of freckles on
Mavis's neck and shoulders. Her arms. He could
lean forward and lay his mouth over each dot, draw
lines between, map her out until he knew precisely
what her constellation would add up to. Androm-
eda? Aquila? Cassiopeia?

Gavin felt a cool kiss around his ankles. His oar
stilled over the river's surface when he glanced
down. "Uh...we're leaking."

Mavis looked back at the water gathering at the
bottom of the boat. "Oh, that. We're nearly there.
We'll dump it once we hit land. The canoe should
be good for the paddle back."

Gavin swiveled his head to the left and right,
combing the trees.

"What are you doing?" she asked.

"Looking for Dilbert," he said.

Mavis chuckled in that hummingbird way that
went straight to his blood. "Row, Nemo, row."

The murkiness started to bleed from the river
and the scent of marsh hit Gavin's nose. Soon, the
river would funnel into Weeks Bay. Beyond that, it
would thread like a needle into the mouth of Bon
Secour before meeting Mobile Bay and, beyond
Fort Morgan and the barrier islands, Gulf waves.

Mavis chose to disembark before they found the

river's end. She steered to a sandy spot on the starboard bank. The boat bumped ashore. Prometheus took his leave first, leaping over the canoe's port side, drenching Gavin in the process. He gave a startled laugh when the mongrel arced like a noisy porpoise in and out of the water.

"Don't let your shirt get too wet," Mavis pointed out. She'd tossed her oar onto the sand and tucked a small basket under one arm.

Gavin frowned at the T-shirt he'd hung across the bench. Lifting it, he saw that the tails were already damp.

"We'll hang it," she said, grabbing it by the neck.

Gavin stood to take her arm as she threw one leg over the bow. When both her feet had touched down on the grass- and sand-strewn turf, he reached up to adjust the hat on her head, keeping her shaded. Her eyes met his briefly before she moved off to drape his shirt over a fallen tree.

"Where'd the mutt go?" Gavin wondered, trying to find Prometheus among the thatch of undergrowth encroaching on their beach.

"Marking trees. Chasing snakes…" She spread a towel on the flattest patch of ground. "Whatever it is menfolk do when they make camp." Setting the basket in the center of the towel, she returned to the boat. "Let's flip it. It can dry while we eat."

"You brought breakfast."

"It's more brunch at this point." Mavis grunted as she yanked the canoe deeper into shore.

"I've got this," Gavin said, nudging her aside so he could heft the boat and upend it over his head.

She sighed as he walked the canoe to shore. "Brute male strength is so irritating."

"Chalk it up to my long list of faults." He set the boat on a bed of dry leaves, hoping it would drain properly. "No discernable holes," he said, tipping his sunglasses up to check the hull.

"There's a crack," Mavis claimed. "Just a sliver. I fix it, but the patch never holds."

"She's yours?" he asked of the canoe.

"Kyle and I are both water signs, for a reason. He lives for a sail," she said, picking up the discarded oars. "I live for a good paddle."

He ran his tongue over his teeth and looked pointedly away from the oars. "I'm trying to figure out what you're wearing under that shirt."

Her scoff didn't ring true. "Try cooling off instead."

Gavin was going to have to, at this rate. The fresh air and exertion had helped him leave what he'd seen behind closed eyes in his curtained room at Zelda's. Now here they were, just the three of them. No river houses in sight. No boats. A long towel spread between them.

Gavin took off his sunglasses, tossed them onto the basket. Before she'd finished laying the oars against the canoe's hull, he was knee-deep in river. Without much of a thought, he pushed off the silty bottom with his feet and dived all the way under.

Mavis wasn't worried. Why should she be? SEALs could hold their breath for an ungodly amount of time. As she opened the basket to arrange its contents on the towel, the seconds ticked by on the inside of her head, growing louder.

She wasn't going to wring her hands over him. Gavin was an excellent swimmer. At the farm, as boys, he and Kyle had swum often—Kyle more leisurely and focused; Gavin restless and pacing, like a shark.

The idiots. She used to despise their games. Who could tread water the longest? Who could sit on the bottom of the pond the longest? There were times she thought their heads would never break the surface again. One time when she nearly dived in to save them, they'd come up laughing, making her realize that the game had changed and they'd been counting to see how long it would take her to come in after them.

She stopped following them to the pond after that.

Gavin's head popped up near the other bank, spraying mist. Mavis set the glass in her hand down before she could lob it at him.

Slowly, he swam back. First freestyle. Then he flipped over and paddled backward. As he swam closer, turning over again, her fingers loosened around the glass.

She hadn't seen him relaxed since he'd been back. Not completely. The edge was always there, relentless even when calm took hold. She'd memorized how it wormed along his taut jaw and wove itself in invisible streams at the creases of his eyes. Shadows, too. His was a face full of shadows.

Not now. Repose had taken hold and for the first time in a decade, Mavis saw the old Gavin. The young Gavin.

She swallowed. Her heart knelled against her breastbone, rocking and ringing as if to proclaim itself out loud.

Stupid, she thought, and went back to prepping brunch. This path she'd somehow chosen toward him. *Stupid, Mavis.* She'd told herself she would be his friend, that she was ready to be his confidante, his buffer.

Colliding headlong with him as she had three days ago on the porch…it was foolish and dangerous and so not what *he* needed.

Not that she'd planned this. What kind of a hot mess could've planned this? He was Gavin. She was Mavis. It didn't matter what life had wrought for either of them. It didn't matter that they seemed to understand each other on an existential plane…

Somehow, her fate seemed tied to his in an irrevocable manner that was both frightening and irreversible. She wasn't scared of what went on inside his head. She wasn't scared of where the journey might take them.

She was scared, however, that she could see fighting his battles beside him long into the future. She was scared that she wanted that—to be beside him.

He was a runner. He never stayed in one place. Always moving. Always roving. Swim or die, he seemed to say every time he moved on.

It was an act of survival. It was as ingrained in him as the mystery of all of it. Even as she embraced it as part and parcel of who he was, she admitted that it might be the one thing about Gavin that terrified her most.

Prometheus cut through the undergrowth, tongue lolling playfully, panting. Mavis silently thanked him for cutting through the fabric of her thoughts and tossed him a Milk-Bone. He yanked it out of the air with his teeth, making quick work of the snack. Mavis ran her finger through the clean water she'd poured into his water bowl next to the towel, pleased when he moved to it to freshen his palate.

His fur was warm from the sun when she ruffled it above his collar. Fingers sinking in, she lowered her cheek to the flat top of his head when he came up for air, answering the touch by pushing lovingly against it. "You're with me," she murmured. She hated the ache inside her. She hated how it made her question—everything. "Right?"

Sitting back on her heels, she braced herself as Gavin stood. The river sluiced off him, a glossy coat. It tuned her in further to his potency. Muscle and bone didn't so much cohabitate, as each fought for ground, bringing his struggles to the surface. The survivor—warrior Gavin—was there in rippling arms, pectorals, abdominals. His thick quads were outlined by his buff-colored trunks pasted wet against his skin. She couldn't even look near his waist where his distinct V-cut was on parade.

Embattled Gavin—haunted Gavin—was there, too, and it was loud in the strain of his rib cage and the knots of his collarbone and high shoulders.

As he splashed to shore, he ran his hand over his face, then back and forth over the crown of his shorn head. Mavis's attention snagged on the fangs of the wolf. The wildness of it, the primal nature…it suited.

He wasn't tame. He snarled. He spooked. He made the hairs on the back of her neck stand sharply on end. He was a wild thing that appealed to everything offbeat inside her. He made her answer in places she didn't normally have to think about on a regular basis. She chastised herself and nearly thought better of the gesture she'd brought him here to make. Frowning, she lifted the hot foil-lined packet between her hands as his wet feet dredged into the sand. "Here."

"What's this?" he asked, taking the gift with a measure of caution.

"An animal sacrifice." She shook her head as he unwrapped the foil with a rustle and settled slowly on the towel next to her.

"Ah," he uttered, and she heard the moment the grin hit his face. "You," he added with affection.

"I did promise," she said, and sniffed. The smell of braised beef hit her squarely in the stomach and she turned her nose. "Eat it quick before Prometheus catches a whiff or I decide it needs a proper burial."

"Mmm," he answered, mouth full. "Oh, gawd!"

Mavis held up a hand. "The sex bomb noises aren't helping." Seriously not helping. Her gorge wasn't the issue anymore. More, the cinder and burn sweeping outward from the star-bright point of her navel.

"But it's *so good*!" He polished off the burger quickly, licking his fingers and crumpling the empty foil. He gripped her arm, the one closest to him, tugging her around to him. Big hands framed her cheeks as he said, "*You* are a dark, strange goddess but I'm willing to worship you any way you'll let me."

"Hmm," she said, trying to sound noncommittal. He released her and she turned halfway away, filling their tea glasses with lemon water from the well-capped pitcher she'd brought in the basket. Composing herself appropriately.

He ran his tongue over his teeth. "Are you ever going to tell me?" he asked.

Her brows lowered. "Tell you what?"

"How you got into the business with Zelda. You

said you'd tell me, eventually, if I stopped thinking of it as a racket."

"Have you?" she probed, raising the lip of the glass to her mouth.

He nodded, decisive. "Sure. I mean, I don't know if I believe that there's something there. I do know that you believe in what you're doing. So does Zelda. You're pros."

Mavis nearly smiled at the admission. "Thank you," she said. At the tilt of his head, she added, "For saying it."

"Do I get to hear the story now?" he asked.

She took another sip. "You've probably heard it before. It's no secret." Sitting up straighter, she cleared her throat. "My interest in the paranormal found me. Kyle was fifteen. He knew how to drive but only had a learner's permit at that point. He wanted to drive Dad's Mustang into town. Dad was in the passenger seat. I was in the back. We came up to an intersection. The light turned green, but before Kyle could hit the accelerator, Dad yelled at him not to. It wasn't a second later that a tractor trailer blew through the red light and hit the car in front of us.

"Traffic stopped, as you'd expect. Everybody got out to help. Dad told Kyle and me to stay back as he ran to see if anyone was hurt. I remember Kyle dialing 911 on his cell phone, speaking to the operator. He had his hand on my shoulder, like he wanted me to turn away, but you know how it is when you see something like that. You can't help but look."

Gavin nodded sagely. When he stayed silent, listening, she went on. "The driver's door of the tractor trailer was open. It's as vivid to me now as it was then. I saw the driver climb down from the cab. He was wearing a blue shirt. He didn't look injured at all. I think he even looked up at me. Then he turned and walked away into the crowd of people standing around. It didn't occur to me that nobody stopped him, nobody…"

She paused in the telling to wet her throat. Gavin frowned at the lull. "You're going to tell me he didn't really get out of the truck. Aren't you?"

Mavis brushed her knuckles across her chin to wipe away a bead of excess water. "We were at dinner the next night. Nobody had spoken about what happened, at least not around me. Dad said something about a diabetic coma. I wanted to know what that was. He told me. Then Kyle asked, 'That's what the driver had?' It took me a moment, but the way Kyle said it bothered me. Past tense. I asked, 'What do you mean he "had" it? He's all right, isn't he?' I knew by the look on Mom's face that that wasn't the case. It was Kyle who finally told me that he never made it out of the truck."

Gavin's stare was trained on her profile. She could feel it washing over her features. "How old were you?"

"Five," she said. "Close enough to my birthday

to feel six. But five." At Gavin's next beat of quiet, she spread her fingers wide. "I've gone over it in my head a thousand times or more. There's a good chance I didn't see what I think I saw. It was the closest to death I'd ever been at that point so there's a possibility I imagined it, to cover the shock."

Gavin shook his head. "That doesn't sound like you."

She turned her gaze to him, finally. "It doesn't?"

"No. I remember all those times Kyle and I would camp out in the woods. We'd hear you in the bushes when we told ghost stories. No matter how scary we made them, you'd never run. We could never make you scream. You've always absorbed things. That's one thing I noticed. You and your owl eyes—always absorbing everything and everyone around you."

"Is that why you thought I was spooky?" she wondered.

"You could say that," he replied.

She studied him, pursing her lips. "You don't think I'm crazy?"

"I never thought you were crazy," he told her. "A little weird, but in a good way. An interesting way."

She smiled with more ease than she would have thought possible after telling her story. "Good answer."

His eyes skimmed across her lips. She caught the gleam in them, the beginnings of an answering grin before he glanced around at her picnic basket. "Didn't you pack anything to eat?" She nodded and he picked it up by the handle.

"Thank you," she said, and opened it to find her brunch. "Anything else you want to know while we're here?" *Alone*.

"Plenty," he admitted. "Like what's the deal between Zelda and Errol?"

"What do you mean?" Mavis opened another foil-wrapped packet. The veggie wrap didn't smell nearly as offensive as his cheeseburger. She dived in, realizing how hungry she was.

"Well," he said thoughtfully, stretching his legs and hooking one ankle over the other, "when we got back to the river house after our field trip to Mobile three days ago, Zelda was out of sorts. Errol quietly volunteered to make us grub. Zucchini lasagna."

"How was it?" Mavis asked curiously.

"I've had worse."

"You should try his vegetarian meat loaf," Mavis suggested, taking a large bite from her wrap. "It's his specialty."

He held up a hand. "Help me out here. How the hell do you make meat loaf vegetarian? The meat part's baked into the title."

Mavis crumpled the foil into a ball. She chewed, swallowed and answered, "Chalk it up to a man trying to impress a female…even if it means giving up that vital crutch all red-blooded American men seem so desperately attached to." At his frown, she expounded. "Cow."

"Huh."

"Someday you'll have to explain to me the correlation between virility and beef," she told him.

Gavin's jaw worked for a moment. He leaned in slightly, lowering his voice. "You worry me, Frexy. Did your parents not tell you the deal about the birds and bees?"

She elbowed him in the side, enough to make him straighten up. Being close to him wasn't helping her train of thought.

"Anyway, after the meal," he said quickly, "Zelda thanked Errol profusely, and asked if I was in good form. When I answered yes, she made it pretty clear that she was dragging Errol off to her wing of the house."

"And?" Mavis asked.

"And he was at breakfast the next morning," Gavin finished.

Mavis shrugged. "So?"

He scratched the tip of his nose. "So, they're clearly doing some bed-hoppin'…"

"And you—a red-blooded American man who is no stranger to sexual escapades—is scandalized by the idea of a single man and a single woman having relations because *why*?" When he made a face, she rolled her eyes. "Tell me it isn't their age."

"I don't have a problem with old people doing

it," he claimed, "just so long as I don't try to picture it in my head."

"Why would you picture it?" she asked. "Are you a pervert?"

"Not that kind of pervert," he said.

"Then what's the deal?"

"They've been doing this for how long?"

"I don't know," Mavis replied. "The whole thing started six months or so after I moved to the river."

"And how long have they been having sleepovers?" he wondered.

"As long as they've been together," Mavis said.

"And they live in separate houses?" he asked. "Zelda's not the conventional sort so I wouldn't be surprised if she opposed the marriage route, especially since she's...however old she is. She still won't tell me."

"She has a flair for mystery," Mavis said.

"Like you," he acknowledged.

Look who's talking, frogman. "You know how old I am."

"In the physical sense. But you're an old soul. That's been clear a hell of a lot longer than I can reckon."

His eyes grazed her features again, as if he were memorizing them. Mavis cleared her throat. The starry point at her center was swelling at an alarming rate. "You're right about one thing—Zelda doesn't believe in marriage. She tried it once, when she was younger."

"I take it it didn't last long."

"About thirteen months. He wanted to bring home the bacon and leave her at home to do the washin', dryin' and child-rearin'. Also, he wanted to give her an allowance."

"Sounds quaint and domestic." Gavin gave a false shudder. "No wonder she ran."

"As for her and Errol's arrangement," Mavis continued, "it suits them. They both can operate independently. If ever one needed to take care of the other, things would change. But for now, Zelda's home is the river house. It's her business. It's her life, one I think she had to reinvent in a lot of ways. It took guts for her to go back there after her father passed on. Her mother ran off with the mailman when she was little."

"The mailman?"

Mavis nodded. "The mailman. Her father remarried quickly. Her stepmother was a woman of the church with two little girls of her own. While they never toed the line, Zelda was—as you'd expect—different. Rebellious. Outspoken. The stepmother put all her energy into convincing her father that she was evil."

"Seriously?"

"She went so far as to try to get the reverend to affirm that Zelda was possessed by the devil," Mavis revealed.

"And Zelda's father believed this?"

"It's unclear what he believed," Mavis said, "but

he didn't do much about it. Zelda ran away before she was sixteen."

"Where to?"

"Where else?" Mavis said, smiling. "To join the circus. She was a trapeze artist."

"You don't say."

"She toured for several years, wound up in Vegas where she joined an acrobatic troupe. Before Cirque du Soleil, there were Zelda and her fellow artists. Then her father died. He left the family money to the stepmother and her daughters, but he bequeathed the river house to Zelda. She didn't have to come back. She had a good job, good money and good standing—none of which she'd ever had at home. But she was like me; even when her stepmother was taunting the shakes out of her, she could never stop loving the river. She swept back home, making an entrance in a pink stretch limo and a gold lamé cape."

"Like Elvis?"

Mavis held up a silencing hand. "Don't bring up Elvis. She'll spend hours regaling you about how he stole her look after their torrid affair."

Gavin chuckled deeply. "Okay. Don't bring up Elvis."

"The stepmother had decided to stay on at the house, figuring Zelda wouldn't dare show up again."

"But she did." Gavin tipped his chin. "Thatta girl."

"Zelda said the stepmother packed her bags

quicker than Jesus could part the waters and she never heard from her again. Anybody on the river will tell you what happened next. She dissolved the family antiques business, took every last scrap of furniture she could find and piled it on the front lawn and burned it all to cinders. Some say she danced on the ashes."

"Naked?"

She eyed him balefully. "That's when she planted the willow and started her own business. She's been here ever since."

"And Errol?" he asked.

"He and his wife moved here after the war."

"What war?" he asked.

"'Nam."

"What branch was he?" Gavin asked contemplatively.

"Army," she said. "He volunteered to fight, lied about his age to do so…"

Gavin grew quiet.

It was her turn to watch him. "I won't tell you how it went. I think you already know. He and his wife lived in the city. Once he was discharged, apparently it became clear to her fairly quick-like that he needed a change—of scenery and pace. So they came here. They bought a house with an apple tree. She died sometime in the nineties, leaving him alone."

"Until Zelda," he guessed.

"When she and I started investigating, a lot of

people laughed," Mavis explained. "*Most* people laughed. A lot of callers wanted to hire us for the spectacle. Errol was one of our first clients. The first one to take it as seriously as we did. And the reason he won't move to the river house with Zelda is because his house was the first place we discovered legitimate EMF anomalies."

His shoulders moved as he released a breath. "The wife. He thinks she still lives there."

Mavis licked her lips in reply. She realized the foil was still balled in her hand and tossed it into the basket with the pitcher.

"How does Zelda feel about sharing?"

"Oh, she doesn't mind. Aurelie, his wife, had dibs on him first, after all. Though when they do the sleepover bit, it's not often at his place."

"I should think not."

Mavis noted his discomfort on the subject. Maybe Gavin did believe, after all. She wrapped her hand around one of the glasses she'd filled. "Cheers," she offered.

"To what?" he asked.

"To a large step in an uncharted direction." When he frowned, she elaborated. "You did something three days ago—something you weren't comfortable doing. But you did it regardless, and whether you choose to join Errol, Zelda and me again in the field, I'd just like to say congratulations."

"Why?" he said, frown deepening.

"Well, when I do something that scares me…" Mavis waited a beat for Gavin to deny that he'd felt any sort of fear on their jaunt to Mobile. He didn't. Pleased with him, she continued. "… I tend to confront pieces of myself I wouldn't have otherwise known. Which I think is exactly what you need right now, especially since you don't know exactly what you want to do with the rest of your life. And at this point there's nothing wrong with that." He groaned in disagreement and she shook her head. "Your life's been turned upside down. There's nothing wrong with recalculating, recalibrating and taking the time to know your-self again—discovering what else there is in life. I know that's what you want."

"Do you?"

It was a direct question, posed in a direct man-ner. "It's okay if whatever path you choose doesn't bring the same sense of satisfaction as being a SEAL did," Mavis said. "And I don't care where it leads you when you find it. Just… I want you to find it."

"You do?"

"Yes." Mavis nodded in certainty. She tapped her glass against his, brought the lip to her mouth and sipped. "It's water," she added when he sipped, too. "Sorry. Champagne's not my style."

"I hate champagne." His voice broke, gruff and brambly. He hung the glass in both hands between raised knees. A muscle in his jaw hammered visibly against the strong bone there. "Mavis, how are you?"

She tipped the drink to her mouth once more. "You held out asking longer than I thought you would."

"You hate the question, and I'm pretty certain you could shave off a vital part of my anatomy with a look."

"Sometimes I wish that were my superpower," she granted. She pushed her foot through the sand, letting it mold against her calf. "How do I look to you?"

She felt him honing the points of her profile yet again. "Riveting. But then, you always look riveting and I can't see you nearly as well as I'd like. So humor me, before I start shaking you for answers."

The vulnerability he exposed by saying as much gripped her as fiercely as the strength and fortitude he wielded like sword and shield. She'd never met anyone more human, she thought, and she had to curl her fingers into sand to hold off on touching him. "My grandmother told my mother for years the best thing for me was the indoors, particularly after an episode like the one in Mobile. That's what she called them. *Episodes.*"

Gavin's foot brushed alongside hers, unintentionally. He moved it, but the small bit of contact wobbled Mavis off course. She gathered a breath and peppered chastening thoughts at her id. "She… seemed to think I'd be better off living in a bubble, that I never should've left the incubator. I was something feeble to be kept under glass and looked after closely.

"It was Dad who listened. He wasn't around when Kyle was a baby, so everything was new to him. The seizures terrified him. He didn't trust himself to make decisions about my care. He hardly trusted himself to hold me. So while Mom said I needed to build stamina and play like any normal child would and Edith said the opposite, he listened to the latter because it made more sense. It was one of the few painful parts of their marriage. Mom went by instinct; he heeded caution for perhaps the only time in his life. It wasn't until years later that I told him I used to follow Kyle out into the woods when I should've been napping. Mom knew and turned a blind eye because it worked—it helped me. There's something about fresh air. Trees and grass. Sky and earth. It heals. Edith moved off the farm before I was ten because Dad started to see what Mom saw. He'd take me out riding. It'd be years before he let me have my own horse or ride alone. But he'd take me out on the front of his saddle and we'd ride for hours."

The memories of her father, James's, wide chest snug against her shoulders and the vibration of his gentle, sonorous tones brought warmth deeper than the sun ever could reach. "He knows I'm like him—hardheaded, independent, and I like to make my own way. But days like the one in Mobile bring his irrational fears swarming back."

"Can't blame him."

She peered at Gavin's frown and stifled the urge to soothe it. "I told you water's always called to me. I've always loved the river. It's never the same. It's never still. It's like the moon; it changes, every night. When I saw that river house for sale, I knew I had to have it." Rolling her eyes, she raised her glass. "Not before Dad and Kyle got a hold of it, of course. The sale had barely closed and they were already repairing and updating everything down to the kitchen tiles. There was mold in one of the bathrooms. They gutted it. The outside stairs weren't to code. The deck was falling down. Every week or so, Dad still shows up for breakfast or dinner. Really, he's looking it over, every speck of it. Still trying to pacify those irrational fears. In silent ways, at least."

"He's a good man who loves you," Gavin stated plainly. "Any real man'd do the same."

Love her or look after her? Mavis wondered. Tucking that away for later, she leaned back on one hand and said, "It all comes back to the river. Since I moved from the farm to the water, I've had less 'episodes.' Bad days have been fewer and further between. You, Dad and my grandmother can argue all you like about what happened a few days ago. But days like this…" A cool breeze licked over her, caressing skin slicked lightly with the dew of perspiration. She turned her face into it and closed her eyes. "… I wouldn't miss for the world."

When he didn't agree, she raised a brow and tipped her head back so she had a panoramic view of the sky. "You might as well ask me to crawl back into that incubator."

"I'm not asking you."

He might as well have been whispering. Still, she could hear he was troubled. And she sighed. Because *men*… Releasing restraint, she shared the warmth with him, placing her cheek on the sculpted muscle of his arm and twining her arm around his waist. She stroked his spine in small circles, then, giving in, spanned her fingers wide and traced his vertebrae—those tired bones that'd held him up through everything. "I wish it hadn't happened with you there to see it."

"Don't do that, Frexy," he muttered. He lowered his head to her hair. She felt the air from his lungs push through. "Don't apologize to me." A curse. "I was useless."

"No."

He kept chiding himself. "I was no use to you when you needed me. It's what I am. It's what I will always be. You wanna talk about irrational fear? It's crept in on me every day, every mission since…"

Mavis's brows veered together when he stopped abruptly. She lifted her cheek to study him. "Since when?" At his short uttered refusal, she slowed the caress on his spine, moving her palm in a horizontal glide over his waist. "You want to tell me."

"No. I don't," he said sharply.

"Yes, you do. Or else you wouldn't have started. I'm here." She said it because, *again*, he needed to hear it. "Tell me, once and never again, unless it's what you need."

"That's what you want?" He was grim. Eyes flat, they drilled straight into the ground between his feet. "You've already seen more of my cards than anybody. You want to see the ugly ones, too?"

"Why shouldn't I?"

"In my experience, only professionals want that. And they're paid, Mavis."

She made sure to steady her hand before placing it over the base of his neck. "I want you to tell me. I want you to tell me all the things you're afraid to tell anyone else."

"I'd rather make out."

The quick stab at amusement couldn't sway her. "Gavin."

His defeated breath deflated him swiftly. "They ask you, after every mission. You go into a room, sometimes with your buddies. Sometimes without. They make you break it all down, piece by piece, until every detail of the op has been transcribed, every decision scrutinized, every motive questioned and upheld. Toward the end, they ask: Would you do anything different? Would you have waited a second longer to pull the trigger? Would you have rushed the door a minute sooner? Would turning counterclockwise instead of clockwise have made you more effective? I used to think it was ludicrous because my answer was always the same. Hell, no, I wouldn't do anything different because I always did the thing I should've. I did everything they trained me to."

He pinched the skin between his chin and neck where sweat had begun to gather. Just like in the Cadillac, Mavis could see it beading along his temple, collecting around the slight hollow adjacent to his ear. "One day, the answer changed. My training never failed me. Somehow, it was something inside me that disconnected. I hit a patch of mental ice and went off the skids."

"What happened?" she asked.

Pain washed over his face, then trickled away, taking his color with it. "Benji."

Of course. *Benji.* Gavin had been the acting medic on the squad Benji was assigned to when he was killed. If stories were true, Gavin had carried him out of firing range. He'd tried to save his life.

It made sense. Benjamin Zaccoe's fate haunted Kyle, too. It was Benji's ghost and the sense of duty that Kyle felt that had kept him from pursuing Harmony sooner. It was Benji who had kept Harmony single until she and Kyle had decided to take their friendship to the next level. As gross as it was to have a longtime bestie and a brother infatuated with each other, even Mavis had to admit

that Kyle and Harmony's collision was inevitable.
"You feel responsible for what happened to Benji?"

Gavin's brow rucked. "You're damn right I'm responsible."

She picked through what she knew of Benji's death carefully. "Kyle told everyone Benji couldn't have been saved."

"A surgeon could've saved him."

"Gavin, you aren't a surgeon."

"No," he said. The muscles of his face quavered. "No. I'm not."

Mavis's mouth numbed. A dinner at the farm came back to her, over a decade past. The conversation around the table she remembered crisply, as if she'd heard it yesterday.

"So, Gavin," Adrian said, peering across the centerpiece to the person occupying the chair opposite her own. "Have you decided what you would like to do once you graduate?"

Gavin's mouth twisted into a half smile as he cut his steak with fork and knife. "I thought about joining Kyle at Emory so I could bug the hell out of him, but my grades won't make the cut."

"You haven't thought about what you want to do?" Adrian asked, less judgmental than curious. "You don't know what you want to be when you leave school?"

Gavin's smile turned inward. "I don't know. I'd like to see some of the world, I guess." At James's affirmative nod and grunt from the head of the table, Gavin went on, encouraged. "School's not easy to get into and it'd take forever to finish the way I want. But... I don't know... I kind of always wanted to be a doctor."

Mavis's chin sailed up. "You? Really?" she asked before she could close her mouth. Every face turned in her direction. Adrian raised a brow, quietly reproachful. Reprimanding herself, Mavis fell silent again.

Gavin cleared his throat. "Yeah." He'd lost what hype the conversation had managed to drum out of him. "I guess."

"What field?" Adrian asked kindly. "Pediatrics? Psychology?"

"Plastic surgery?" Kyle snorted.

"Hush," Adrian chided shortly.

"A surgeon," Gavin granted. "Though nothing superficial. I want to do the gritty stuff. Maybe be a corps surgeon."

"That's admirable," James noted.

Gavin didn't seem to know what to do with the compliment from James. He nodded and went back to cutting his steak.

"You'll never do it," Kyle opined. He yelped and stared broodingly at Adrian for kicking him under the table. "What? If Gav's going to do anything military, he's going to be on the front line with a gun in his hands. He treats every day like a training exercise already. Not that you'll ever make it

*through basic. You'll punch out the first instructor
who calls you a worthless piece of—"*

"Kyle," Adrian said in warning.

*Mavis eyed her brother. "That's better than cry-
ing, which is what you'd do."*

*Gavin barked an astonished laugh. When he
turned to her, he smiled at her in a way that wasn't
irritating or smug like all the times before.*

*She recognized affection even if she'd stopped
giving it. Unsure what to do with it and the awareness that flickered like a wakening light bulb under
her skin, she looked quickly away again and spent
the rest of the night pretending that her family
didn't have company for dinner after all.*

She couldn't deny even after all these years that
he'd surprised her that day. She'd never bothered
to dig underneath the surface of the troublemaker
she knew him to be and unearth all the potential
he'd hidden there. Intelligence. Self-effacement.
Goals with far-reaching scope.

The tumult burned off him. She could feel it
through his arm. "Even if you had been a surgeon,
who says you would've been in the same place at
the same time when he was shot?" she asked. "The
chances are nearly nonexistent."

"Nearly," he groaned, distant.

She tightened her grip. "You could've been the
greatest surgeon in the navy and you probably still
wouldn't have saved him. There's no coming back
from an injury like that. Is there?"

"You're saying he wasn't meant to be saved."

Mavis didn't know how to answer. Not when she could feel the tremor going through him. "Kyle's going to kill me for this, but I heard him say once that he wished it had been him that day."

"In my place?"

"In Benji's."

"He didn't say that."

"Have you not thought the same?" she challenged. "Benji had everything going for him—wife, baby on the way…"

"And what did I have?" he echoed. "Family I avoided more often than not? Some frenemies from high school, aside from Kyle, who didn't like me anyway? Would the impact back here at home have been smaller if it had been me?"

"You believe that." Suspicions confirmed, Mavis took the care to breathe slowly, coolly. Her hand flattened. She lifted it from him. "You actually believe that."

"Didn't I tell you," he stated, "if you dug deep enough you wouldn't like what you found?"

"You think Cole and Briar would've been better off?" she asked. "What about Harmony? You think you're less than equal to Benji in her eyes? If you asked Benji, would he have thought his place in the world bigger than yours?"

"I can't ask him. Can I?"

"What about me?" she demanded.

Gavin's countenance cleared. One by one, the

shadows strayed off, leaving only questions. "What about you?"

Her heart pounded. The twin surges of rage and need had made breathing unnecessary. She couldn't draw a single breath. "It would've mattered to me," she concluded. Something damp singed the back of her eyes. She blinked three times in the space of seconds. "You matter."

"I didn't then."

Dropping to a whisper, she asked, "How do *you* know?" She waded against wisdom and spoke, freely. "I'm glad you're here. I'm glad you're here with me."

He stared at her, questions eclipsed by awe. "Ah," he breathed, "I'm going to kiss you."

He took her face in his hands again. They were gentle this time, tipping her chin up so that the angle was right.

Mavis began to shake her head. If he kissed her, he'd lay all the reasons he shouldn't to waste and she'd no longer care if either of them could handle it. Even though she *knew* she couldn't.

"Shh." It soothed from him to her. He pressed his brow to hers. His mouth skimmed the tip of her nose in a whispered kiss. "You can't talk like that…and not expect a man to kiss you. Especially a broken one like me."

"I don't see broken."

"No." He laughed in one hushed burst. "You don't, do you?" The line of his mouth wasn't steady. A wince worked over it, unguarded. "I think you know me. What I am. You might know me better than I know myself. And fuck if that doesn't scare me, Freckles."

He was right, maybe. She couldn't take it, knowing what she knew. She couldn't stand it, knowing he wrestled his soul every night. *Not alone anymore*. The sentiment blazed like a comet, incinerating doubt. *I won't let you do this alone anymore*.

Their lips met. He moaned. Her eyes drew closed. She felt a crease form between them as his lips closed over her upper lip. His teeth grazed once. Then again. All the muscles of her neck and shoulders went lax in approval, sensations rooted deep in sinew. Jaw loosened, she let him confront her, mouth to open mouth, and had never felt so eager or needy.

She pulled back, enough for his hands to slide away. Gripping his shoulders, she climbed to her knees, taking the high ground. She mirrored him, embracing his face and kissing him.

"Mmm," he said. His arm slid over her waist, looping all the way around her back. He pulled her close.

She licked him, his lips parted in a sneer that was as involuntary as it was wolfish. She licked him once more, encouraging. She found the tip of his tongue with her own and traced it in one teasing stroke. Under her palms, she felt a shudder. It went through him, from bottom to top. Gripping harder, he jerked his chin back. His gaze locked on hers, hard and green. His fingers raked, spread, through her hair. He cupped the back of her head and beckoned her to him again.

It'd be so easy to rock him back to the surface of the towel and take more, deeper.

She withdrew because she felt her tremor go up against his. The urgency between them had built to the height of anticipation. She remembered he was vulnerable—more so than she might've been. Slow was the name of their game. It had to be.

He didn't follow her lead. Holding her close, he laid an open kiss to her cheek. His chest rose on a prolonged inhale. When he released it, it resonated, gruff. A predatory sound that drew her skin taut everywhere.

"You're prickly," he murmured against her cheek, "but sweet. Like a pineapple."

She dragged the tips of her nails gently over the nape of his neck. He was salty and deep. Like the Dead Sea. Even there, she sensed, she'd swim until her limbs felt like noodles and she had no course but to sink. He tipped his mouth beneath her chin to a place that was ultrasensitive and she closed her eyes. The tremor had grown into a consenting shimmy. "Give me a minute. I…think I might have something to say."

Both his arms roped around her waist. "Nah, baby. We just got started."

"Yes. But… Gavin, you're not exactly grounded right now."

"Right now, I feel like a freaking sequoia."

Risking it, she lowered her eyes so she could study his features. There was want there, yes, and need great enough she felt the bite of it along the ranks of her inner thighs. A smile stitched the seam of his lips together. She caught herself teasing it with the edge of her thumb and dropped her hands from him completely. "You shouldn't smile," she admitted. If only he knew how much him smiling, sincerely, laid her bare. "Not when I'm trying to be sensible."

"I've never wanted to be less sensible."

Mavis gulped air. "That's my point. This…all this…it's nice for now. But what happens in the end?"

"When I leave?"

Mavis lifted a shoulder. "Isn't that what you'll do, eventually? You've been very clear. No promises."

Gavin relinquished half their link, bringing one hand up to his face to rub his lips briefly before propping it behind him and leaning away.

She shifted to her hip, feeling as flattened as he looked. "I'm not fishing for assurances you're not comfortable giving. I've told you. I know you don't know your place in the world anymore and I'm aware of who you are—who you've always been. You'll go looking elsewhere for it if you can't find it here. You're—"

"A drifter," he concluded, gaze dull and far off. "I run."

She groped for his hand and gripped it tight. "I want you."

The truth bomb snatched his head around, back to hers. His brows hitched, surprised. Impressed.

Mavis nodded. "That isn't something I'm capable of ignoring anymore."

"Anymore," he murmured. His jaw softened. "How long *have* you been ignoring it, exactly?"

"I don't think it's relevant."

"Oh, I think it might be," he said, mischievous.

"The point is…" she said, trying to strengthen her resolve when she felt weak. *So weak.* "If we pursue this—whatever happens, I won't stop you if you need to run. If you need room, just tell me, before. That way I can… I can try to…"

Using their entwined hands, he pulled her to him again. "Okay," he murmured. He turned his nose against the place beneath her ear and held her fast against his heart, nodding. "Okay, Frexy."

She stopped talking, thinking—everything. Quickly, her arms banded around his shoulders. Closing her eyes, she burrowed against hot skin, muscle and bone, doing her best to hold firm.

Then he said the one thing that could undo her entirely.

"I promise." Husky, sure miracles tripped off his tongue. "I promise you'll be the first to know."

She shuddered again. It might've been a silent sob, but she ignored it. Indulging the need to grin like an idiot, she ran her hands up and down his back. "You promised."

"There's a first for everything. Right?"

She skimmed a kiss across his lips in reward. Then another in gratitude. And another...because she wanted another. *Stop smiling. Stop. He'll think you're insane.* "What're we going to tell our parents?"

"At this rate, I don't care," he said, adjusting his weight. She gave a sharp gasp when he hitched her all the way onto his lap. "What I want to know is, do you always kiss dirty?"

She beamed. His hands were underneath her now, emboldening her to answer. "Is there another way?"

"Aw." He laughed, bringing his mouth up to hers. "Aren't you perfect?"

CHAPTER NINE

"ARE YOU SURE we should be doing this?" Mavis asked as she and Gavin approached the farmhouse the following Sunday. Prometheus trotted ahead of them on the familiar path. A frisson of disquiet skated up her spine. Her family was inside, most likely with Harmony and Bea.

"Not getting cold feet, are you, Frexy?" Gavin wondered.

Mavis didn't want Gavin knowing how close he was to the truth so she gave his hand a squeeze. He'd hung his ball cap on her head somewhere along the drive from the river. She was glad of its shadow right now.

She'd never introduced a guy to her family. Not because she feared the wide-reaching channels of information that branched from the Brackens to Gavin's family back to the Leightons and others. And not just because her brother was a SEAL who would've intimidated any of her past romantic prospects on sight. She hadn't introduced a man to her family because she'd made a vow not to do so after the painful incident with Aaron

Quarters. Its solemnity had been restored after the affair with William Leighton.

So it was simple. She didn't introduce a man to her parents unless he introduced her to his first.

Gavin had always been good at breaking barriers. The windows of the house loomed. Anybody could have been watching from inside yet Mavis kept her hand in his.

They were really doing this.

Honesty, he'd said. Putting everything on the table so they didn't have to sneak around the people they respected and loved the most.

Kyle's absence at the table would make the bombshell slightly less explosive, though repercussions would come swiftly from that department. Harmony's inability to keep a secret was notorious.

But Mavis knew how to handle her brother. It was only by reminding him that he'd made a move on Gavin's sister two months ago. Kyle and Harmony's flirtation had even gone on in secret until Mavis inadvertently walked in on a make-out session.

Her parents… Mavis frowned at the windows. James and Adrian were more of a mystery. She didn't know how either of them would react. They both liked Gavin. He'd been welcome at the table since their time at the farm began. Despite his bad reputation in school, Adrian had always given him the benefit of the doubt, and James had approached him from a position of understanding. He, too, had been the small-town rabble-rouser once.

Whether they trusted a rabble-rouser with their daughter, Mavis couldn't be sure.

Plus, there was the important fact that Mavis just wasn't willing to give away much about her and Gavin's relationship. She wanted to guard what had grown between them and guard it fiercely.

Whatever was between her and Gavin remained undefined, fragile, and she feared that a hard enough wind—blown from the direction of James, Adrian or Kyle or some correlation of the three—might knock it over before it could gather strength.

She wasn't ashamed. She was protective. She'd told Gavin her own truth—she wanted *this*. She wanted *him*. She wanted however much he could give before he felt he had to move on and find himself.

She wanted to give him the strength and confidence to do so. She hadn't planned for anything romantic. Yet if being with her helped him find a way to stand taller against his demons, she no longer saw why they shouldn't be together. Her regard and her feelings for him grew every chance they had. The closer she got, the closer she wanted to get.

As they climbed the steps to the porch where Prometheus waited, panting and patient, Gavin passed his free hand over his head. "I should've brought something for your mother."

"She sees plenty of flowers; she's a florist," Mavis reminded him. "And she doesn't keep wine or liquor in the house. What option does that leave for a proper hostess gift?"

"I don't know. A pineapple?"

Mavis moved into his path before he could open the door. "Wait. Just a second."

"Is this where you change my mind and turn back?"

His eyes swept quickly over her face. This close, he could see. He potentially saw everything. The niggling doubts. The expansive need. She fought the urge to look away. Touching her fingers to his shirt, she murmured, "I'm not getting cold feet. Though I do think you're crazy for wanting to tell *everyone*."

"Because they'll overreact."

"No." She shook her head. "You want to tell them because not telling them means hiding. And as close as everyone is in this town, that'll be pure exhausting."

"Damn right."

"I think, deep down, it's… Don't hate me for this." She screwed up her face. "Honorable?"

Gavin hissed in reaction.

She nearly smiled. "I think after all this time you still respect my parents, as much as you respect Cole and Briar. Am I right?"

"Maybe I just want to creep out my sister and get good and thrashed by your brother," he said.

"It adds up." Fisting his shirt in both hands, she tapped her knuckles against his chest. "It adds up so much I'm inclined to think it's awfully big of you, Petty Officer."

He shook his head slightly. "Don't do that."

"Does being called 'petty officer' again make you as uncomfortable as 'Freckles' makes me?"

"If by uncomfortable, you mean 'really want to kiss you,' then yeah." He smiled, slow and warm enough to make her knees ache in tune with her chest. "I'm painfully uncomfortable."

His mouth brushed hers in a barely there tease that nearly brought her to her toes. Her palms flattened against his chest. They hummed there as he slid his lips across hers to the corner of her mouth where they firmed in a gentle kiss.

She held on, the silence holding her, and lifted to the points of her boots. Her mouth skimmed the lowest scar, just below his cheekbone. She tilted her head, following the rough tissue half an inch along the seam.

His fingers bit into the skin between her high-waisted jeans and her crop top. She felt him give against her. She absorbed him like a sun-kissed breeze.

He held her tight, tighter, for another minute. The far-off sound of clanking made Prometheus rattle off a series of barks and trot off the edge of the porch to investigate.

Mavis eased back. "It's Dad," she whispered, unable to gather volume. "Probably in the barn."

"Mmm." The mumble was rife with regret.

"More," she promised, glancing at him through her lashes as she gripped the handle of the door. "Later."

"Soon," he added.

She nodded. Then she went into the house because to stay on the porch with him meant making out. They hadn't done that since the river, and stopping what they'd done at the river had nearly killed her.

Alone, she promised herself. She'd be alone with him soon and they'd see how wild things could grow. As soon as they sorted whatever complications their families were sure to hand them. "Mom?" she called.

"What?" Adrian shouted from the back of the house. "Who's there?"

Mavis shut the door behind them. "Uh. It's me. Your daughter."

"Oh. Mavis. Thank God. I'm in the kitchen!"

Mavis frowned as she moved through the house. Gavin stayed behind her, his hand spanning the curve of her hip.

The house was cozily arranged with flowers spilling out of every container. Plaid blankets were folded over armchairs. Textured rugs bled over hardwood floors marked by character. The hearth was laid with logs even if they wouldn't be lit until fall weather chose to set in. The rooms smelled like pine and wood polish. They were cool, but warmth was abundant—in the color palette, the multitude of family photos framed on walls and tables, and the sense that this was a place where people embraced each other fully.

The earth-tone kitchen with its honey-oak cabinetry boasted enough room for entertaining. It opened into the dining area with a brawny table around which claw-foot chairs were cluttered. Mavis noted that it wasn't yet laid with chinaware or the traditional floral arrangement. "Mom?"

"Up here."

Mavis looked around. Her brows nearly hit her hairline when she saw Adrian standing on the kitchen counter, armed with a feather duster, a sponge and a can of Lysol. "What're you doing?"

"Cleaning like the dickens," Adrian answered briskly. Her arm worked in furious circles.

Mavis narrowed her eyes. "Is, um…is anything wrong?"

"Yes," Adrian said with a decisive nod. "Oh, yes. It's coming."

Mavis moved toward her, wondering how to get her down. "*What's* coming?"

"The fifth horseman of the apocalypse," Adrian said, finally glancing around. She was wild-eyed. Her hair was in unusual disarray and her cheeks were flushed. "No, the Antichrist. Think of your worst nightmare, doll it up in freakishly white Keds and a fur-trimmed vest that some poor bunny had to die to make, and you've got it!"

Mavis's eyes widened slowly. "Oh, crud."

"Who's she talking about?" Gavin asked in an undertone, as if he were afraid to spook Adrian.

"Shit on a broomstick," Mavis said. No wonder Adrian was so agitated. Mavis turned to him. "My grandmother's coming."

It struck him, too, visibly. "Oh."

James entered from the back door, letting Prometheus in with him. "Horses are shod. They've got plenty of hay. Mavis." He gave her a peck on the head. "That beauty from Mobile's starting to get friendly with Fury. They've been nosing along the fence for the better part of the afternoon. If the vet approves, we could have a new foal next spring. And you," he said, pointing up to his wife. "Thanks for making that run into town for feed. Come down from there, li'l mama, so I can kiss you."

With a nimbleness that caught Mavis further off guard, Adrian bounded down from the countertop, abandoning the cleaning in her rush. She grabbed her husband by the arms. "Run."

James let out a half laugh. Then stopped and pressed a hand to her cheek. "Adrian…"

"My mother is coming, James. You need to run."

His mouth fell. "Say that again?" he said numbly.

"She just called," Adrian confirmed. "She'll be here. Tonight. Get the hell out of here while you still can. Take Mavis with you. The last time Edith was here, she threatened to get her exorcised."

"What, really?" Gavin asked.

Mavis sighed, pinching the space between her eyes.

James finally found his feet, sidestepping Adrian and heading straight for the exit.

Gavin dropped his voice and leaned toward Mavis's ear. "Is he? Running?"

James stopped, doubled back and, in the spirit of a man beyond comprehension, yanked the door to the refrigerator open.

Adrian wrung her hands as James stood at the fridge. Both seemed to be in a complex state of indecision. Mavis looked from one parent to the other, trying to decide which to approach first. As her father simply stared at the organized shelves, she cautiously moved to him. "Dad?" He didn't answer. She tried again. "Dad? Can I help you with something?"

He stood, brow knit, scowl engaged. "It's not here." He shook his head, as if he didn't understand.

"What's not here?" she asked.

"There's no beer in this fridge."

Mavis closed her eyes and fought not to drag her fingers through her hair. "Dad..."

The refrigerator door shut. James's voice rang with desperation. "Why is there no beer in this refrigerator?"

"Dad!" Mavis said, raising her voice to match his. "You're in AA! Neither you nor Mom has brought beer into this house as long as I've been alive!"

"I bought a drink at an Irish pub the day after you were born," he admitted. The confession tumbled out, absently. His eyes glazed. "I didn't drink it. Just sat there staring at it while the bartender told me some story about a good girl named Brandy and some asshole who couldn't commit."

"Isn't that a song?" Gavin asked from the other side of the room, where he and Prometheus were trying to lie low.

"What a lovely story," Mavis interjected. She grabbed James by the collar and yanked him toward the table. "This way." Once she'd arranged him, sprawled, in his usual chair at the head of the table, she went to Adrian, tugging the feather duster away with some resistance. "Mom, go upstairs. Take a bubble bath, meditate, whatever. She's coming. You might as well pull yourself together."

"I haven't done the top of the breakfront," Adrian protested even as Mavis led her out by the elbow. "Or the chandelier. And the potatoes!

You know how she is about potatoes. Mavis, *who's going to cook the potatoes?*"

"Let me worry about all that," Mavis insisted. She nearly had to chase Adrian up the stairs with the feather duster. She waited for several moments at the bottom to make sure her mother wouldn't come back down. Then she met Gavin at the entrance to the kitchen. "I'm sorry…"

"Not tonight," he agreed. "What can I do?"

"Call Zelda."

"Zelda?"

"We need to fill every chair at the dinner table," she explained. "Ask if she's available for dinner. Tell her to bring Errol, if possible. Tell her there's likely to be a little theater—that'll entice her. Second…" Mavis went to the side table and opened a drawer. She drew out a pack of cards and handed them to him. "You'll find the poker chips in the breakfront," she informed him. "Let Dad take every dime you've got. It'll give him something to think about—besides Budweiser and matriarchal woes."

"What are you going to do?" he asked her.

She'd already rolled up her proverbial sleeves. Picking up a spray bottle and a dishrag, she said, "Clean. Cook. Whatever I have to do to get this place polished enough to satisfy one über-discerning, nausea-inducing grandmother."

He frowned. "Good luck with that."

The back door opened. Mavis expected to see

Harmony. The person walking in gave her the second cold shock of the day. "What are *you* doing here?"

Kyle stopped as he tucked a long-stemmed bouquet under one arm and half embraced Prometheus, who leaped at him in greeting. "I live here," he stated plainly.

"Son!" James crossed the room in a long gait. He hauled Kyle to him with one strong arm, clasping him in a taut hug. There he clung like a wet blanket.

"Dad." Kyle chuckled, thumping him on the back once…then again when James didn't let go. His brows lowered as he eyed Mavis over James's plaid-covered shoulder. "Everything okay?"

"Edith's coming to dinner," Mavis said, snapping on a pair of rubber working gloves that went all the way to the elbow.

"Son of a…" The sentiment died off when Kyle's eyes shifted to Gavin. "You're still here?"

"Yep," Gavin said, placing one hand on Prometheus's head after the dog trotted back to his side. "Still here."

Mavis fought not to reach for Gavin like she wanted to. Instead, she extracted her father from Kyle's arms. "Dad. I told you. Sit down. Gavin's going to play cards with you."

"You hate gambling," James reminded her.

"Yes, well," she grumbled as she made sure they

both took their seats, "I'll pretend you're knitting or something."

"Mom doesn't know I'm here yet," Kyle said, snatching off his ball cap and peering through the door. "I could sneak off to Harmony's…"

"Oh, no you don't," she said, resisting the urge to grab him by the beard and haul him away from the exit. "Edith likes you. You're the buffer. You can be the one to greet her." She took the flowers. "With these!"

"Yeah, those were for Harmony," he stated in protest.

"Wah wah wah," Mavis chided. "Go upstairs. Comb your hair. Shave. Then come back. Since you're here, I've got a list of chores for you, too."

Kyle groused all the way to the fridge. He opened the door.

"There's no beer in there, son," James called from the table.

"Yes, Daddy," Mavis said. "We *know*." At Kyle's deep-riddled frown, she motioned with silent urgency. *"Go!"*

As her brother finally did as he was told, she ran her fingers through her hair to straighten it. Kyle's arrival in addition to Edith's slapped one conundrum on top of the other.

Mavis couldn't fight the feeling that with Edith, the conundrums would arrive in droves and soon be stacked like pancakes.

"So. James." Edith took her time choosing a leaf of lettuce from her bowl. She stabbed it with her fork. "I hear you're just getting out of prison again."

A muted groan went up among half the occupants of the table. James, however, answered without much of a hitch. "Yes," he admitted. "I am."

"He was framed, Mother," Adrian spoke up.

"Naturally," Edith decided, folding her too-thin mouth. Her too-thin brows rose in a cleaving manner, sleek as daggers. She measured her son-in-law width-to-width. "Charles here was once a bail bondsman." A hand rose in the direction of the man beside her who had escorted her from their retirement village in Florida. "He once dealt with criminals such as yourself."

Adrian sighed. "James isn't a criminal."

"Charles," Edith said, undeterred. "Tell the family how you caught that large man wanted for stealing a truckful of avocados."

Charles cleared his throat, raising his napkin from his lap to his mouth where he patted his chin. "Well, it's an interesting story—"

"Mavis." Edith leaned forward to see around Zelda and Errol to Mavis, who'd been seated farthest away. "Are you still seeing that William Leighton fellow?"

Gavin raised his brows, hoping they sliced much in the way Edith's did.

Mavis glanced quickly from Edith to him and back. "I… No. That's…over. Very over."

"A pity," Edith said. Her fork hovered midway to her mouth. "That one would've done you well. He struck me as charming and levelheaded. Who are you seeing now?"

Mavis avoided looking at Gavin altogether, spooning spaghetti onto her fork with fierce concentration. "Nobody you'd find charming and levelheaded, I expect," she muttered.

Gavin gave a grunt of laughter. He silenced himself quickly when Edith narrowed her gaze on him. She sniffed at him, then at Prometheus, who hadn't won a seat at the table but had propped his snout on the edge between Gavin and Harmony, eyes swinging, wide and brown, to each attendee. Gavin heard him whine as Edith's stare singed, and gave him a supportive pat.

"I think Charles should tell the story about the man and the avocado truck," Zelda opined. "My goodness, does it sound entertaining."

Charles opened his mouth, lighting up at the prospect, but Edith cut him off with a look. Gavin watched him deflate and wondered whether to pity the man or go on with his amusement.

"Zelda," Edith said, eyeing her latest quarry. "You don't look a day over seventy."

Kyle coughed into his napkin.

Zelda cackled merrily. "And I was just thinking how well you look in that tone of rust," she said, gesturing to Edith's schoolmarm sweater. "Yard sale or clearance, dear?"

Edith frowned at her before looking to her next victim. "Adrian."

Gavin placed his arm around Adrian, who was seated to his left and sinking fast into her chair. "Yes?" she asked.

"These potatoes are quite tasty, for once. What did you do to them?"

Adrian blinked several times at the woman. Gavin tapped her on the back. She shook her head then said, "The potatoes. Yes. Actually, these are Mavis's—"

"Say thank you, Mom," Mavis overrode her. Her eyes widened for emphasis.

"Yes," James chimed. He was in Gavin's blind spot, but his tone grew more intimate as he added, "Say thank you."

Adrian exchanged a glance with him, then took a breath, reached for her water glass and said, "Thank you. Mother."

The sound of utensils filled the quiet. Gavin cleared his throat and tilted his head toward Adrian's. "Did that hurt?" he wondered in an undertone.

She drank deeply, then touched his sleeve, whispering, "Catch me if I pass out."

He gave her a nod. An arm wound around her waist. Gavin caught the turn of James's head as he pulled her in against his side and he ceded the lady to her husband.

"Kyle," Edith said.

"Yes'm?" Kyle said.

"When is the wedding?" She gestured with her fork between him and Harmony.

Harmony froze with a mouthful of potatoes. Bea, next to her, perked up. "Wedding! There's going to be *a wedding*?"

Harmony looked to Kyle. "Is there?"

Kyle was flabbergasted. "I hadn't exactly gotten around to…"

"Well, why not?" Edith said, rapping her knuckles on the tablecloth. "Neither of you are getting any younger. You're both in two of the most dangerous lines of work I can fathom. And by my estimate, it's been three weeks since you visited me in Fort Lauderdale. Did you lose it already?"

"No," Kyle said, chastened. "No. I didn't lose it. I just got home this afternoon."

Edith waited, expectant. When she didn't cease, Kyle pushed his chair back from the table.

Adrian cried out when he dropped to a knee.

Gavin shook his head. "You're doing this now?"

"You knew?" Harmony asked him. To Kyle, she said, "You told *him* before me?"

"I was hoping for surprise. I was also hoping to do this just the two of us…maybe in bed."

"Get on with it already," Mavis advised.

"All right," Kyle said, shifting uncomfortably. "Christ." He took the ring out of the box and said, "Harmony Savitt, you'd make me the happiest

SOB on earth if you plant this big-ass diamond ring on your finger and let me be your husband."

Bea's loud whisper spilled into the void. "What's does SOB spell?"

"Oh, brother," Mavis said, burying her face in her hands as Edith threw her napkin onto her place mat and prepared to rise.

Harmony beamed. Her fingers spread as she shook her hands in front of her. "Yes! Oh, *yes!*" And she took his face in her hands and planted an unreserved kiss on his mouth.

"Ew," Gavin said as everyone else, besides Edith, applauded. Prometheus's tail thumped the floor heartily in response to the excitement. Charles gave a robust "Bravo!" before earning another quelling look from his companion.

Bea jumped between the intendeds. "Can I wear it?" she asked of the ring.

Kyle smiled at her indulgently. "Of course you can, sweet pea."

"For heaven's sake, don't let the child lose it," Edith snapped. "It was your great-grandmother's!"

"It looks perfect on you," Harmony cooed to her daughter. She hugged her.

"What do you think, Uncle Gavin?" Bea asked after twirling around for the others to see.

Gavin tipped his head back to see the too-big band with its overt stone hanging precariously from the child's thumb. "You might have some growing, but 'til then—man, will it ever make a good weapon for any boy who tries to mess with you."

Harmony had settled on Kyle's lap now that he was back in his chair. "I'd still like to know why Gavin knew before anybody else."

Kyle looked to Gavin cautiously. "Because when I told him about you and me, he tried to tear my guts out."

Harmony tutted. "Uncle Gavin's right, Bea. Boys are stupid. Stay as far away from them as long as you can stand."

"You never said."

Gavin caught the words from Mavis, as quiet as they were. He offered an apologetic smile. The news that Kyle planned to ask Harmony to marry him had initiated a hesitant truce between him and Gavin, especially after Kyle announced his trip to Florida to see Edith about a family ring before he returned to training. Gavin had tried to put it out of his head. It'd take some getting used to, the idea of Harmony and Kyle shacking up for life. Kyle would be his brother-in-law and, despite any issues that lay between them, they'd forever be mixed up in each other's lives.

Gavin had a feeling some of those issues would be difficult to kill off completely. Especially if he followed instinct and pressed his relationship with Mavis out into the open where they didn't have to hide.

"Go on, Edith," Kyle invited, grinning from ear

to ear. *The SOB.* "Ask us again when the wedding is."

Edith only pursed her lips as she watched Bea wander from person to person to show off her newest accessory.

"When is the wedding?" Adrian obliged him. Her arms were around James. They grinned as one.

"Next month," Kyle announced briskly.

Harmony all but buzzed at the haste. "That soon?"

"Apparently, we're not getting any younger." Kyle's eyes softened on her. "I figure we could do it here, at the farm."

"Oh," Harmony sighed. "That sounds perfect."

Gavin looked away quickly as Harmony kissed Kyle hard enough to rock their chair back.

Adrian started buzzing, too. "Yes! Perfect! We could have it out in the woods somewhere. Or in the field of wildflowers. Or...we could fix up the barn!"

"Really, Adrian." Edith shook her head. "A *barn*?"

"I love that idea!" Harmony shrieked.

Edith's jaw hit the floor. "I suppose you'll ride in on a cow."

"An ass," Gavin supplied. "Big and braying."

Harmony swatted him in response. "I want burlap. And tartan."

Edith's horror wove into the corners of her mouth. "How quaint."

Kyle rubbed his lips together. "I was thinking we could celebrate now, plan later…"

"We only have a month," Adrian said.

Harmony chimed in. "We should call Mom. And Liv. And Roxie. Roxie could plan the whole thing in a jiff—"

"So plan now," Kyle recalculated. "Celebrate later. Before you get too far into the planning process, there's one more thing we need to raise our glasses to." He shifted sideways toward Gavin. "You wanna do the honors?"

Gavin's stomach tightened, knowing instantly what he was referring to. "No. I don't think so."

"What is he talking about?" Mavis asked.

"It's nothing," Gavin said quickly.

Kyle frowned at him. "A Silver Star ain't nothing."

Another collective gasp rose from the table. Gavin felt the needles of attention drive straight into his hide and he squirmed.

"Gavin," Adrian said. She gripped his arm. "Oh, Gavin. That's *wonderful*."

He began to shake his head before Zelda cut in. "A Silver Star. That sounds spectacular."

Kyle accommodated her with an explanation. "It's one of the highest personal decorations for valor in the US military. I was talking to my CO and he just happened to mention Gavin had picked one up about a month before he returned here."

"I believe Errol has a Silver Star," Zelda remembered. "Don't you, *mon saucisson*?"

"What conflict were you in, sir?" Charles asked of Errol.

"Charles, you've left potatoes on your plate," Edith sneered. "For God's sake, eat them."

"Do you drink, Charles?" James asked. Adrian cuffed him on the thigh. "Ow!" he cried out.

"A month?"

Again, Gavin raised his eyes to Mavis. He worked his jaw and gave another shrug. Scooting his chair back, he raised himself to his feet. "It's just a formality." As he edged away from the table, he shot Kyle straight through with a glare.

Unfazed, his friend added, "I took the liberty of telling your dad for you, too."

Gavin stopped. The glare was honed.

Kyle swallowed a mouthful of water from his glass. "Honesty sure is refreshing, ain't it?"

Gavin's jaw cracked. He told himself to take a breath. *Steady.* But all eyes were on him, and blood was rising up his throat. He felt an eyelid twitch. His mouth opened and words tumbled out. "I kissed your sister." Grinning what he knew to be a good, grim grin, he raised two fingers to his brow in mock salute. "You're right; that is refreshing."

CHAPTER TEN

MAVIS BIT HER TONGUE. She bit it hard as she drove back to Zelda's.

In the passenger seat, Gavin sat in trained silence. He hadn't spoken since dinner.

Unless, of course, Mavis counted the sheer amount of swearing he'd done when he'd come to. She wondered how long it had been since a fellow teammate had choked him.

She wondered how long it took other SEALs to come to ordinarily after being choked out by a teammate. The minutes she'd spent waiting for him to resurface had felt like half an eternity. She'd used it well, berating Kyle. Berating Gavin. To deaf ears, on both accounts.

Gritting her teeth, she punched the accelerator and drove faster. After he came to and Adrian took him into the other room to be sure he was all right, she'd heard an earful. Oh, yes. They'd taken turns—the family. Suffice it to say the only person at the table to decide congratulations were in order was Zelda. The rest, besides Errol, had formed their own opinion.

Kyle had seethed. "Please tell me this is just to

get back at Harmony and me. Or is he taking advantage of you? You tell me if he's taking advantage of you. I'll—"

James had interrupted, but only to ask, "Is a relationship the best thing for him? For either of you? When I was in AA, we had a no-relations policy—"

"He seems a rather troubled sort of young man," Charles had expressed for, it seemed, even he felt it right to intervene.

"He's a troublemaker," Edith told him. "Has been since he was a juvenile. I never knew why Adrian let Kyle bring him around. I'm shocked he never wound up in some home for boys. Mavis, I'd say you were well suited to each other, but you've never known what's good for you. Just like your mother…"

Above all the dismay, Harmony had settled with, "What if it ends badly? He might…never come back."

When Mavis had finally gotten Gavin to the car, her mother stopped her. "You're not sleeping with him? I don't think that's a good idea. It'll only… complicate matters."

So, to sum up, Mavis had snapped at her mother, growled at her father, nearly screamed with frustration at her grandmother and her man-sheep, ignored her best friend entirely and thought very, very seriously about mangling her elder brother.

Mavis bore down on the steering wheel. She

couldn't forget the expression of horror on Adrian's face as chairs upended and the table tipped. A beveled glass dish dumped the remains of the potatoes in Edith's lap. All the china and drinkware Mavis had arranged meticulously so Adrian wouldn't have to worry…

Mavis fought not to cut her eyes to Gavin when she heard him whistling under his breath. After several minutes, though, her brow furrowed. "What *is* that?"

"What?" he asked.

"That song," she said. "What is it?"

"It's 'Brandy.'"

Mavis frowned at him as he began to whistle again, this time loud enough to get Prometheus's attention from the back seat. The dog made a throaty noise that normally preceded an episode of howling. She groaned. "Dear God."

"William."

"William who?" she asked warily.

"William Leighton," Gavin said thoughtfully. "I thought it would've been the other one. The Greenpeace dude with floppy hair and sandals. What's his name? Fergus? Finnigan?"

"Finnian," Mavis all but growled.

"That's him."

"You won't hurt him," Mavis stated plainly. "William. He didn't do anything."

"Did he put his hands on you, Frexy?"

"Yes, but so have you. And I know you don't

think it's wrong because it wasn't until you wouldn't apologize for it or say that it was wrong that my brother tackled you into the table."

Gavin fell quiet. A studious silence.

Mavis rapped the heel of her hand against the wheel. "It was a *million* years ago. It was brief. Harmony figured it out. She blabbed about it in front of Edith. They were the only ones who knew anything about it before tonight."

"Why?" Gavin wanted to know. "It went on between you two for a while, didn't it?"

"Yes," she said, tight-lipped. She didn't want to go down this road—the shame she felt about the way it turned out.

The itch between her shoulder blades became intolerable. She shrugged. "Look…he didn't want anyone to know. I know he cared about me. Normally you think that caring enough about someone to be more than friends for months at a time means at least telling the people who mean the most to you about it. So I put a stop to it before I could get any more attached."

"That's why attachments aren't your thing," Gavin realized.

"I don't know." She made the turn onto their road. "I'm not the type who likes roses. I think sonnets are cheesy. And PDA from people like Mom and Dad and Harmony and Kyle makes me squirm to no end. But…when I'm with someone… when I care about someone that much…it matters. It matters enough that I don't think it should be hidden. Which is why no guy's ever met my parents."

Gavin riddled it through quickly. "You need him to be the one to brag on you first."

Mavis rolled past her house. Gravity pulled the car down the slope of the road to Zelda's. She let her foot relax off the pedal.

"You were going to let me tell them."

She saw the snatched glow of his eyes as they passed a streetlight. The low words worked their way into her chest and rooted there firmly. She looked away. "Yeah, well. I like you." Had she not made that clear by the river?

It wasn't until they could see the turn to Zelda's driveway that he spoke again. "You're right."

"About?" she asked, pulling onto the shoulder in front of the lotus-painted mailbox.

"If William felt anything like what I do…he wouldn't have left you guessing."

Mavis's hand fumbled on the shifter. She gripped it and put the car in Park. She didn't have to touch her fingers to her throat to feel her pulse. She licked her lips. "Why didn't you tell me about your commendation?" she asked.

He scoffed. "It's like I said. Just a formality."

"Gavin—"

"It should've been Kyle's," he shot off. "I didn't earn the thing. He did. The higher-ups looked at the paperwork and saw what they wanted to see.

I didn't get to the helo the night the RPG hit. *He* got me there. For some reason, they decided Purple Heart wasn't enough so now I've got the Silver Star *and* guilt. I wouldn't have walked away alive from that op if it hadn't been for your brother, and he walked away with nothing."

Mavis frowned. "He doesn't care about medals any more than you do."

"It doesn't matter," he muttered, pressing his fingers over his eyes. "He's out there still fighting for his country and his family and I'm not. But at least the higher-ups can sleep at night. I may be useless, but they know I've got a bunch of shiny souvenirs as company."

Mavis hesitated only a moment. She pressed her hand to his wrist. After several seconds, his fingers folded, touching the tips of hers.

He heaved a quiet sigh before he asked, "How pissed at me are you? About tonight?"

Mavis thought about it—about everyone knowing. About the sheer amount of opinion she'd had to contend with. "Well," she said, "you accomplished what you set out to accomplish from the beginning. It wasn't great, the fallout or the way you went about it…"

"What can I say?" he said with a slight smirk. "I'm a man of action."

"Why did you have to provoke him?" she wondered. "I can deal with everyone knowing about us. But why did you have to bait Kyle? If not for the fight, Mom at least would've walked away from the dinner unscathed."

"Don't you think it's about time your parents and everybody else stopped worrying so much about what your grandmother says?" he asked.

"Yes," she admitted. "But it's complicated, especially for Mom. She managed to make a good life for herself. A great life. She wants Edith to acknowledge that."

"Nobody should have that kind of power over somebody else's life," Gavin said.

Mavis took note of the bitterness in his voice. "Those who shape who we are aren't easily set aside."

"I don't want that to make sense."

"I know," she said. She touched her brow to his shoulder.

His fingers wedged between hers as their palms slid into place. His lips pressed against the parting of her hair.

He might never come back... Harmony's fears echoed endlessly in the caverns of Mavis's head. She could deny it all she wanted, but they were fast becoming her own. She wanted him close. She'd wanted that for weeks, even when she wasn't willing to admit it. Curiosity. Desire. Now...she could add near panic to the mix.

She could put the car back in gear, do a u-ie... take him home. Keep him close.

Or she could trust, in him and the promise he had made at the riverside.

Self-preservation wasn't so much about getting hurt. It was concern that she might find that thing she'd never had outside of her family, and that Gavin, outside of the SEALs, had never had at all. A place, a person, that fit and the inexplicable fear that it could be taken away.

Nothing lasts forever. He'd stamped it on his body, as if he might forget.

"Is that Zelda's Alfa Romeo?"

Through the windshield, Mavis saw the tail of a red car in the drive. "No. She keeps it in the garage."

"Then whose is that?" he asked.

"I don't know." She sat up a little straighter. "Looks more like a Bentley."

"A Bentley. You're sure?"

"Pretty sure." She frowned at him, suspicious at the drop in his tone. "You know someone with a red Bentley?"

"Only one." He'd already shifted away from her. "Prometheus should go with you tonight."

Thrown off guard, Mavis glanced back at the canine snoozing soundly on the back seat. "No. I don't want you to be without him."

"I'm fine," Gavin said.

"It's hard enough for me not to stay with you tonight," she admitted, drawing his attention back. "But I'm not sure either of us is ready for that."

"Don't trust me to keep my mitts to myself?" he asked.

"I don't trust myself not to keep mine off you," she said. When his jaw loosened, she shrugged. "How's that for a truth bomb?"

"Deadly." He took his hand off the handle of the door. With it, he cupped her chin. "I'm gonna have to ask you to hold that thought."

Mavis eyed the red Bentley. "It doesn't look like I've got a choice."

Gavin's sigh blew across her face. She felt the tension fighting against the need—his and her own. "I'll deal with this. Take the boy home. Let him get some rest there…"

She waited for him to say more. The tension was working its way through the duct tape and stitches. It nearly came to the surface, but he shut it in. Shut her out of whatever consequences the Bentley brought. "Don't be a stranger," she told him.

He let out a humorless laugh as he leaned for the door again. "I don't know that you and I have ever been strangers, Frexy."

So don't start now. Mavis bit her tongue, hard, recalling that no matter how far she thought they might've come, there were pieces of Gavin she didn't and might never know.

She tried not to touch her nose to the cotton of his shirt and breathe him in as he twisted around to give Prometheus a pat. She saw his ball cap on the console between them. "Here," she said when he was done.

He donned it. "I'll call you," he said in an undertone, his face truly in shadow now.

She nodded without words as he opened the door. The scent of river filled the car in his absence and lingered when he closed it. She watched the streetlight shift across the line of his back. The night closed around his silhouette.

Mavis eyed the Bentley. It didn't take much guesswork to assume who'd ridden in on that splashy horse. There was only one person who could wreak more havoc in a single night than the dysfunctional rift between Gavin and Kyle, or her dill pickle of a grandmother. As Mavis put the car in Drive, she couldn't erase the unease that she had abandoned Gavin to his demons.

"She's gone."

Gavin turned away from the pinpricks of red taillights fading fast in the distance and probed the inkiness of the porch. The light near the door wasn't on, meaning Zelda must have gone to Errol's for the night. He'd known someone was lurking there. He didn't have to smell the luxurious Parisian perfume to know the culprit.

He kept his mouth shut as he moved to the door. The streetlights had probably revealed what had gone on in the cab as Mavis lingered. Gavin could only assume what his mother knew. So he assumed the worst and took the lone key out of his pocket. Feeling around, he found the dead bolt and slid it out of place without much trouble.

The door creaked open and Tiffany said, "You certainly know your way around the place."

"I live here," he stated.

"Yes," she said, still nothing more than a ghost in the dark. "With the old lady."

"Careful tossing words like *old* around," he advised. "They might stick to you."

Tiffany chuckled. It was a small sound, a familiar one.

The laugh of a parent should've been comforting. This wasn't. Not because it was cruel, or callous. Because it was without humor. Gavin couldn't remember the last time he'd heard Tiffany laugh, raw—from the gut. He wondered if he knew what her real laugh sounded like.

He moved over the threshold. She spoke again, closer. "Aren't you going to invite me in?"

He blocked the way. His body against one side of the door casing and his hand on the other, arm and body barring entry into Zelda's place of Zen. A place that had become sacred to him. "It's not my house."

"You have a key," she indicated. "What? Has she banned visitors of the female variety?"

"The only thing Zelda bans is bad karma and energy." With a flick of his wrist, he flipped the switch next to the jamb for the porch light.

Tiffany turned her eyes from the glare. Gavin studied her. The hair was a little shorter. The heels were, too. Nevertheless, she cut an impressive figure, carved by a sundress scooped lower than the average woman her age would've dared. She liked to think she was anything but average, which explained the Bentley. The diamonds around her neck. The chain of fools she'd left throughout the years. The endless string of lawsuits she'd set off.

Zelda would take one look at Tiffany's aura and cry, "Begone!" The image amused Gavin so much he was moved enough to smile almost.

She spread the fingers of one hand, sending the gold bangles on her wrist flashing. "So we're going to stand here like this?"

"Not necessarily," he said thoughtfully. "You could leave."

"You want me to go."

He leaned further against the jamb. She wouldn't leave, he knew. Not until she was satisfied. Crossing his arms, he said, "You wanna waste time on questions we both know the answers to?"

She sucked air through her nostrils. A warning sign, if he'd been interested in warning signs. He wasn't. "Where's what's-his-name?" he asked, wondering how far he could still push her. "The investor guy with the jet? Did he dump you?"

"I left him," she said tightly.

"Figures," he said. "He might've been decent."

"When it comes to men, there's no such thing as decent. You know that."

He scratched his chin. "Yeah, as a species, we're deplorable. Your PI says hi, by the way." At her scoff, he smirked. "You must've been desperate. You couldn't have trawled for anything greener in the Gulf."

"Well, once my sources informed me you were back here, I had to act fast."

"Why's that?" he asked. And here they came to the point.

"I pity you," she told him. With a tilt of her head, she moved a hair closer to the dividing threshold. "You always come back looking for something you'll never find." Her hand lifted to the other side of the jamb he was holding. "It's sweet and sad at the same time."

He waited. He wanted her to say it and be done with it. Her reasons had always been the same. They'd always been a hair too close to the truth.

"Gavin, you know Fairhope is no place for somebody like you," she summarized.

She tried to sound kind. The faux softness fell on him like a rough quilt. He fought to brush it off. "You would know," he said, the words grating from the bottom.

After a moment, she nodded. "Yes. We're the same, you and I."

He shook his head automatically before he

stopped himself, readjusted. Pressing back from the jamb, he stood apart from her.

"I learned a while ago that I could never make a life here," she pointed out. "Your father, the innkeeper—they had me ostracized. I can hardly think about it now without…"

Gavin rolled his eyes. "Listen, Meryl, it's been a long day. As much as I'd like to watch your next great performance, why don't you go ahead and thank the Academy so we can call it a night, eh?"

"Don't be callous like him."

He groaned, shifting his weight in impatience. "Pot, kettle."

"You're a bully," she said heatedly. "*Just* like him."

"Say what you will about me," Gavin said. His spine had grown rigid. "As for him, you have no right."

"I have plenty of right," she said. "Ten years of abuse gave me that right."

He leaned toward her again, homing in on her hard features. "The man never laid a hand on you. Everybody knows now that he's not the kind of person you made him out to be during the divorce. But you? You *are* the kind of mother who'd put her kid on the stand and lie to put a man of good standing away."

"You don't remember what it was like," she claimed. "You were little."

"I remember everything," he told her. "I remember him coming in late off a narcotics case, you meeting him at the door. I remember you slapping him across the face, screaming because he'd missed another dinner. You chastised him constantly for trying to save the world and be a hero, leaving you alone."

"You did the same," she said. "You abandoned me. You went off to godforsaken places so you could kill people in the name of God and country. Just another thug with a gun."

"I found purpose, Mom," he said. "I found a calling. Something better, I think, than sitting on what was left of the Howard family fortune and casting stones at people who don't deserve it because nothing else makes you happy."

"And look where it's led you," she said, her voice rising. "Look at you, Gavin! You can't see. You've lost your so-called calling. You couldn't make it on your own so you ran back to your father. Have you found purpose here, Gavin, or just a handful of people obligated to lead you from point A to point B?"

Gavin stared.

"It's worse now," she went on. "You're a veteran. You've got issues. Vets like you make people nervous. There's just no telling what might set you off, what you're capable of. It's why you need to come to your senses and get out of this town. It'll get to you, just like it got me. It'll chase you off, like a coyote or worse. You'll wind up in a lineup."

Gavin shook his head again. Despite the night sweats and flashbacks keeping him edgy enough to confront the reality that PTSD would never not be a part of him, he wasn't hostile or trigger-happy. "What are you suggesting?" he wanted to know.

"Come with me," she said, gently. More gently than he knew her capable of being. "I have a place. It's in St. Augustine. Remember that trip we took to St. Augustine? You loved the Atlantic. Those were good times between you and me. It can be like that again. Even if you can't hold down a job, I can take care of you. We can be a family again."

He felt the space between his brows seam tight. "You've ruined every relationship I've ever had. You tried to put space between me and Dad, me and Briar, Harmony. The Brackens. Every girl I dated in high school and college. Do you think that's what family does to one another?"

"I wanted to protect you," she said. "I didn't want you to get hurt, as I've been."

"The mama bear protecting her cub. *That's* your excuse? I've spent the last decade looking over my shoulder for the PIs you hired so you'd know there was nobody close enough to me to piss you off. Because if Tiffany Howard isn't happy, *nobody* is. Am I right, Jezebel?"

Her eyes had narrowed to slits. "You know," she said, "maybe Benji's father was right about you."

Taken aback, Gavin stood straighter. "What about Benji's father?"

"After the funeral," she said. "At that little wake you and the rest of the SEALs had in his name. From what I hear, Benji's old man drank enough beers, then started pointing fingers in your direction. He called you out for making Benji re-up. He wanted to get married, settle down. 'A SEAL never backs down from a fight.' That's what you said, or something along those lines. So Benji reenlisted and wound up getting himself killed right after the wedding. Now his daughter has no daddy. What did his father call you, exactly? A warmonger?"

Gavin felt sick, all right. And blind. Blinder than he'd felt since learning to cope with his shoddy vision. He cursed inwardly as his stomach tightened into a fist and his emotions began to hammer... He swallowed, tasted bile on the back of his tongue. "How do you know about that?"

"I told you," she said, quietly. "I have my sources."

"Go," he told her plainly. "I want you gone."

"You can't get rid of me completely," she pointed out. "Unless, of course, you think about picking up your gun again."

The jamb was under his fist again. The wood bit into the callouses. "You're sick and warped, a hell of a lot more than I am."

"You'd like to think so, wouldn't you?" Tiffany challenged.

"He said go."

The voice came out of the dark. Gavin peered

over Tiffany's head. Mavis materialized in black, Prometheus at her side. "No," she said as Tiffany opened her mouth to argue. "You've said enough. Now you're going to come away from there quietly so Prometheus and I can walk you to your car."

Tiffany's silence could have been misconstrued as shock. However, Gavin could hear the busy whir of her personal scanner trying to get a read. "I know you," Tiffany said. "You're the Brackens' youngest."

Mavis wisely chose not to answer. When Prometheus nudged her knee, she merely reached down to him.

Tiffany turned back to Gavin. He could see enough to recognize the incisive gleam on her face. He shook his head in warning. But what good had his threats ever been?

Hitching her bag onto her shoulder, she moved away from the door, as she had been told. As she descended from the porch, Gavin followed, closing the door to Zelda's behind him.

Mavis led the way across the lawn in long strides.

Tiffany waited until they were halfway to the Bentley before speaking. "You'd be better off letting him go."

"Excuse me?" Mavis said.

"He'll disappoint you," Tiffany explained. "It's what he does."

"Haven't you talked yourself out already?" Mavis wondered.

"He didn't leave all of those women he saw through the years because of me," Tiffany told her. "I might've interfered once or twice. But there were others he left on his own. He was always the one to go. Don't think because you're close to the place he can't seem to leave behind that he won't leave *you*. Even if he doesn't burden you in the short run, he'll eventually abandon you like he did them."

Gavin jumped the gun and reached the driver's-side door of the Bentley first. He opened it wide. "Get in," he said.

As Mavis stood by, waiting, Tiffany looked from her to him. She shook her head. "I fail to understand what you see in each other." To Gavin she said, "Her family's pleased about your arrangement, I assume?"

"Get in," he said again in answer.

"Just a slip of a thing," Tiffany said thoughtfully, tossing her bag into the passenger seat. "Usually he likes the taller ones. Blonder and skinnier, too."

Gavin reached for Tiffany's arm, but Mavis said, "Don't. She'll probably go to the police, tell them you manhandled her or something. And you wanna know what I fail to understand?" she asked Tiffany directly. "Why you can't let him live life the way he thinks is right. Do you really believe what he needs right now is another dose of your toxins?"

"I'm his mother," Tiffany told her. "You're a piece of the pattern. Another temporary solution to a problem he'll never solve. An itch he'll scratch, then handily forget. You won't fix him. Neither will you keep him. Do yourself a favor, sweet pea—don't assume you're anything close to what he needs. Trust me, you don't need him."

Mavis frowned at her, nonplussed. "How would you know what I need?"

"The last thing any woman needs is the burden of a man who can't support himself, much less her. The man carries the load, right? You want to convince me you can fight your battles *and* his?"

"I could," Mavis said without hitch. She shifted her stance, feet spreading, arms crossing. "And you know what, witch? I pity you."

"You pity me?" Tiffany said with amusement.

"Yes," Mavis said, nodding. "It's none of my business what made you this way or why you've worked so hard to make things difficult for Cole and Briar. But Gavin's your *son*. By not compromising on your anger, you've managed to turn him so far away from you that you'll never know what it's like to have him on your side. Good luck living with that. Not to mention, yourself."

Gavin patted the top of the door. "Last call." When Tiffany continued to measure Mavis, he said, "The car, Mom. *Get in* the car."

"One last thing," Tiffany asserted. To Mavis again, she said, "When it's over, do you think he'll ever come back here, even for Cole and Briar and Harmony, when he knows you're here, too?"

"Do I need to count?" Gavin said. "Don't make me count."

"Don't make him count," Mavis reiterated, quiet. "Leave him now, in peace."

"Oh, there's no rest for the wicked," Tiffany said, and had the gall to smile as she slipped into the driver's seat.

"No sympathy for the devil, either," Gavin told her, and closed the door. He stepped back only slightly to keep the tires from going over his toes.

The engine revved. Gavin heard the gears shift. The car began to roll away. He heard the whir of the driver's window. Tiffany's head poked out. "Good luck with your mission," she called to Mavis.

Gavin's jaw creaked under tension as he watched his mother's grin disappear. He listened until he could no longer hear the Bentley.

A hand slid into the bend of his elbow. Unable to look at Mavis yet, he did his best to exhale. "I'm sorry," he said bluntly.

"She's…" Mavis stopped, at a loss. "I heard she was terrible, but I've never seen it in action." He heard her swallow. "She's soulless."

Gavin moved away; Prometheus trotted after him. Gavin paced to the end of the driveway before doubling back toward her.

"You don't believe any of that, do you?" Mavis asked. "What she said—it's *crap*."

"Not all of it," he said. "I did leave some of those women without her help."

"Because she spent your whole childhood planting a voice inside your head," Mavis said vehemently. "*Her* voice."

He gritted his teeth. "Believe what you want. Not everything I do leads back to her."

"Give me an example," she challenged.

You. Gavin bit his tongue. He'd known better than to touch Mavis, taste her. He'd known if he did, there'd be consequences for both of them. "Why did you come back? If she didn't know before, she knows now."

"About us?" Mavis shrugged. "What difference does it make? She can't hurt me. I don't care how much she tries." She closed the space between them. "I'm not going anywhere. It'll take a heck of a lot more than Tiffany Howard to make me budge, Gavin."

"What about Kyle?" he asked. The night was growing darker and denser, just like the hollow feeling inside his chest. "Your mom and dad. Harmony. Your grandmother…"

"It's my life, my choices," she said. "You and I are together because at this point in our lives we choose each other. I won't back down from my choice."

Gavin wanted to look at her, pinpoint every one

of her familiar features in the shadows, but his mother had already probed her enough. He looked over her head.

"Will you?" she asked. "Is this…not what you want after all?"

Okay, he didn't just want to look at her. He wanted to touch her, reassure her with everything he was—even if that wasn't much.

Mavis bit her lip. "I wish… I wish she could see you. The way I do."

"Mavis," he said, trying to stop her.

"Your mother's a fool. A damn fool."

"I won't argue that," he muttered.

Her arms twined around his waist. "Tell me you don't believe her," she said, down to a murmur.

He found himself skimming his palm over the silky black surface of her hair, wanting to absorb her. Her sureness.

He could be honest, with both of them. "I know it'd be better for you if I left."

"You let me be the judge of that," she advised.

"The moment you're burdened by me," he said, slowly, "I'm out of here."

She didn't agree. No. Instead, she raised herself to her toes.

Gavin's eyes closed and his breath hitched as her kiss washed breathily over his lips and blew him away. He cradled the side of her head, absorbing heat and certitude. Answers cropped up inside him, bright like candles. His hand moved around to the back of her head, no more able to snuff them out than he was to convince her to walk away.

CHAPTER ELEVEN

THE NEXT AFTERNOON, Gavin hitched a ride in Errol's Caddy. He listened to the drone of good tires and the light twang of bluegrass tuned to a low murmur. Errol's herringbone driving cap was pulled low, his eyes narrow against the refraction of light off passing cars. There were more lines on the man's face than Gavin could count. No scars, just experience.

Gavin could speak up about what he knew, his own experiences. However, he didn't much feel like going unanswered. So his lips stayed sealed as they passed into city limits. From there, the Cadillac took them through the beehive of downtown, through the fruit-and-nut section where houses were old and trees were older. Finally, the bay. It boiled with color under the low sun.

Gavin asked Errol to let him out near the pier. He thanked the man and watched him drive off before starting the long walk to the inn.

Some of the store- and house fronts had changed along Scenic 98, but not enough to muddle Gavin's memory. He knew the treads of this street, this walk, like that worn-in pattern on an old pair of jeans. It sounded busier than it had in his youth—cars whishing, people roving, dogs barking. But to him, it hadn't changed. He reached up to touch a snag of Spanish moss that trailed off the nearest tree just before he made the turn for Hanna's.

The drive was rocky and gravelly. It was packed with cars. Gavin avoided the front entry with its wide porch and ivy-strewn columns and wove a path through the quiet space of the gardens. A new wing had been added over the last year. It had opened to fanfare over the summer. Briar's business was doing outstanding.

Hummingbirds buzzed like drones around the feeder near the kitchen door. They didn't shy away at his approach. Gavin tried to count their jewel-green bellies as he passed under them, but they darted too quickly.

He'd always thought of Briar that way. Darting from task to task, always in efficient motion.

He stood on the stoop, peered through the door. The screen was clean, like the pane behind it. He saw Briar's outline.

Gavin took a breath before parting the screen from the door. He reached for the knob, then stopped. Hesitant, he raised his fist and knocked lightly.

Briar stopped. She stepped back from the prep counter, gathering the apron in her hands. He heard her heels clicking against the floor before she snatched it open. "Gavin!" She smiled wide and touched his shoulder. "You didn't have to knock. Come in, come in."

He took off his ball cap as he let the screen tap against the jamb and she closed the door to keep the cool air in. "I would've come through the front, but there seemed to be something going on in there."

"It's just the orchestra practicing for a wedding on Sunday," Briar explained.

"A whole orchestra?"

"Well, it's the Frenchleys' girl. They seem to know everyone from here to Arizona and about half of them are invited."

Gavin made a noise. "Who'd wanna know that many people, much less invite them to their wedding?"

"Your father said the same thing," she said. "Are you hungry? Have a seat. I just took a fresh batch of scones out of the oven. You better get them before Gerald visits this afternoon. The bride's father is a fan of the tavern brew. He's ordered a keg to keep the reception hopping. Gerald and William will be dropping it off this evening."

"Good for them," he said. The Leightons' draft had long been one of his favorites. He shook his head when she pulled a chair back from under the round table at the center of the kitchen. "I don't want to get under your feet. You're busy with wedding prep and all. I just came to talk with Dad about something."

"You're never under my feet," she protested. "I wish you'd come more often." When he only nodded, she rubbed his shoulder. "I'll go see if I can hunt up Cole. First, though… I've been meaning to get this out to Zelda's for you." She passed a mason jar to him from the counter. "Fig jam," she told him. "I put it together last week with those figs you brought. There's a few more jars, if you or Zelda want them. I thought about sending some to Mavis—"

"With all you've got going on…" he said slowly, turning the jar this way and that. It was tied prettily with a square of gingham and twine and labeled. "You still found time to do this?"

"Well, yes."

Ah, damn. Gavin swallowed. It'd been a long time since he could remember what it was like being six years old in this kitchen, waiting eagerly to see what Briar pulled out of her double ovens. She'd always given him food and warmth in multitudes. He'd been the contentious kid with the Mohawk and the bad attitude and she'd been the stepmother who'd had his back in quiet ways.

He sighed, pulling her against his side. His arm spanned her narrow shoulders so he could hold her a moment. Touching his chin to her head, he breathed cinnamon and flour, lavender…and home. "Thanks."

She patted his stomach. "It's no trouble, Gavin,"

she murmured. Her voice sounded thick. "It never has been."

"I'm starting to get that," he remarked. "Sorry it's taken so long."

"You're just fine," she told him. As he released her, she turned to the door. "I'll get Cole."

Gavin saw her swipe the back of her wrist over her eyes and looked pointedly away. The scones were cooling on a cookie sheet on the range. Unable to resist, he snatched one and had just scarfed another when Cole entered. "I'll take one of those."

Gavin extended a scone. "Busy?"

"I've been told to rest and have a cup of coffee with my son, and that suits me just fine," Cole said. He ate the scone in one bite, then went to the coffeepot. When he lifted it in invitation, Gavin shook his head.

Cole poured the coffee into a mug. He set it on the table. They both pulled out chairs and sat.

"How've you been?" Gavin asked. He and Cole hadn't had a decent conversation since the day at the Leightons' orchard when his father had caved under the afternoon heat.

"Okay," Cole said as he stirred creamer in his coffee. "Briar's on me about hiring a landscaper, at least until the weather cools."

"Will you?" Gavin asked.

Cole shrugged. "I don't see much point in waiting until winter to landscape. The annuals die off, the perennials hibernate. There's nothing to do then on the lawn even with the grass turning. I can't do any of it too early in the a.m. It disturbs the guests. I've taken to doing most of the work in the late afternoons."

"Would you consider hiring a yard boy to help you?" Gavin wondered. "To get what needs doing done in less time?"

Cole thought about it. "It's an idea. Why? You know somebody who'd be interested?"

Gavin shifted on the chair's thin cushion. "Me."

Cole lowered the mug from his mouth. "You?"

"Yeah. Why not?" Gavin asked. "I'm handy with a mower. I can weed, mulch and take care of any heavy lifting you need. I'm cheap, too, just so long as Briar's willing to feed me something non-vegetarian before I head back to Zelda's."

As Gavin spoke, a grin slowly crept around the corners of Cole's mouth. "Is this just for the summer? Or are you thinking long term as well?"

Gavin decided to tread carefully here. "For now, let's say it's for the season. We can reevaluate after it's over. You may not want me for another."

"I can't think of anything I want more," Cole asserted.

Gavin cleared his throat. He took another scone and rolled his shoulders forward as he braced his elbows on the table. "You might say something different when I accidentally kill off a gardenia bush and Briar stops cooking for either of us."

Cole's laugh filled the room and worked into the

dry, mottled cracks of the grim mood Gavin had had trouble casting off since the evening before.

"I heard Briar and I missed an interesting dinner last night," Cole said.

Gavin groaned in answer.

"Adrian said that Edith was there so I'm sure you've had your fair share of lecturing. I will ask, though, if you know what you're doing—with Mavis."

No, Gavin thought. Then, *yes*…then *no* again. He settled for a frown. "I want to be sure," he said honestly. "She deserves someone who's sure."

Cole watched him for several moments. "Is Mavis who you wanted to talk to me about?"

Gavin sighed, letting his chest rise and fall until he'd released the laden breath completely. "Yes and no. Mostly, it's about Mom."

Cole gripped the mug but didn't raise it again. "Oh?"

Gavin nodded. "There've been things through the years I never told you. Things about her and what she's done."

"To keep you away." Cole's voice dipped into a deep sound.

"She couldn't have done that on her own," Gavin commented. "I made the choice not to come back, or not to stay whenever I did come back."

"But your mom had her say, too," Cole inferred. He'd once been a detective, a good one who could sniff out troubles near and far from home.

"She hasn't needed a say," Gavin pointed out. "Not for some time."

Cole muttered a curse. "That woman spit enough poison while you were young. She hasn't had to show up to keep you under compliance."

"I didn't think she had a hold of me," Gavin thought aloud, "until last night when she showed up at Zelda's."

"I was under her hold once," Cole reminded him. "I know how hard it is to break it."

Here Gavin turned the focus on Cole, measuring him closely. "How'd you do it? How'd you keep her from coming back here, hassling you?"

Cole thought about it. "First, I'll need to tell you a story—one that might not make you look too well on me."

"Try me," Gavin charged.

"Thirty years ago, I didn't come to Fairhope or Hanna's Inn by chance," Cole explained. "I came here because Tiffany told me I should."

"This was after the divorce?" When Cole nodded, Gavin scowled. "Why would you do that?"

"I had nothing," Cole said, spreading the fingers of one hand. "She'd taken everything I cared out."

Gavin put the pieces in place himself. "She dangled it over your head, so you'd do exactly what she wanted."

"All I wanted was to be a father again," Cole pointed out. "She promised me visitation if I infiltrated Hanna's Inn and got the information she needed to buy it out from under the Brownings."

"Did you do it?" Gavin asked.

Cole looked away. "I did enough that it's a wonder Briar chose to forgive me eventually. It's hard to live with it, still, knowing how deeply I felt for her while I betrayed her. Trust me when I tell you I know the power Tiffany can wield over someone's life when she puts her mind to it."

"How did it stop?" Gavin asked. "You did stop it. She never comes anywhere near the inn or the two of you."

"There was a break-in during that time," Cole told him, "in the front office. The window was smashed, the place was trashed, and there were enough elements missing for me to draw a link to Tiffany. I leveraged it against her. And when she tried to push back, Olivia and Adrian threatened to tip off local authorities. Tiffany doesn't come around anymore because she knows if she does, they'll make sure she goes to jail."

Gavin absorbed the revelations, tracing the pattern in the place mat under his hand. Could he do the same—leverage enough against Tiffany to get her to back down?

"She managed to fight back after all of it, nonetheless," Cole added.

"How?"

"Through you."

Gavin read the truth in his father's eyes. His lips

parted when he realized what a pawn he'd been all this time.

He'd never been an outsider. Cole and Briar had embraced him. Yet Tiffany robbed him of a happy home, just as she'd tried to rob Cole.

She'd succeeded the second time around, Gavin thought bitterly. He'd doubted his father and let her win.

Gavin folded his arms. "One more question."

"Anything," Cole replied willingly.

Gavin nodded at the readiness behind his father's acceptance. "Do you know a good lawyer?"

"It just so happens I do." Cole dipped his chin. "If you're thinking about fighting the good fight, I'm here to help you every step of the way."

Cole offered readily, and for once Gavin accepted without thinking. "Why don't we get started? Tonight."

CHAPTER TWELVE

MAVIS TOOK HER TIME. She'd started teaching a restorative yoga class bright and early on weekdays. She'd spent two busy mornings in a row at her father's garage, Bracken Mechanics, where she often handled the bookkeeping. Yesterday afternoon, she'd gone on a field excursion with Zelda and Errol. They'd spent an hour or so scanning the inside of a 1930s townhouse with their EMF readers. She'd then stayed up all night listening to audio recordings and screening new voice mails from potential clients.

She had definitely earned a few hours in the Bracken stable with her new mare, Mollie. The name had stuck since the day in Mobile when they met.

Mavis ran a comb over Mollie's mane, brushing out the snags. Now that the horse was eating right and had been cared for, her coat held a lovely sheen. Moving her hand over it, she worked the comb over Mollie's neck gently. During their small getting-to-know-each-other sessions, Mavis had found that the mare found song comforting. Her ears were no longer peeled. They stood at ease together. Her eyes, no longer wide, had lost their wariness as Mavis hummed into the restful lull.

She stopped humming, however, when she realized what song she'd chosen.

Mavis frowned, stepping back from the horse to pick the horsehair from the comb's bristles. She tried to think of another song, but "Brandy" was on a constant refrain in her head. Maybe because Gavin had been gone for nearly a week.

He'd kept his promise to her. They'd had a conversation before he left. He'd told her he was leaving, though he didn't know for how long. She'd asked where he was going.

"There's something I need to take care of."

When she tried for more details, he had asked, "Mavis, do you trust me?"

"Yes," she answered.

Two days had been fine. Three was acceptable. Four days with no word from him and she had caught herself biting her nails. Now five and she hadn't slept and her stomach churned because she knew the pull he must be feeling—the instinctual tug to head for open seas. All this on the heels of Tiffany's visit didn't bode well for his return, either.

"I'll handle it," he'd said when she brought up Tiffany, and nothing more.

Mavis tapped the comb against the surface of the stool before returning to her chore, humming something new.

The footsteps coming through the stable fell hard and with enough economy for her to know her father was there before she saw him. "I thought you were at the airfield," she said when he reached the gate to Mollie's stall.

"It's after five," James said. "Quittin' time, baby girl."

Mavis peeked at the face of her wristwatch. *Hmm*, she thought. *Time flies when you're doing your damnedest not to mope.* She went back to brushing Mollie's withers.

James waited a full minute or two before he asked, "Are we not talking?"

Mavis lifted a shoulder, let it fall. "I thought you had enough say at dinner the other night."

He blew out a breath. "All right." She heard him shuffle his feet. "What I said the other night... about him..."

Mavis waited, stopping once more to clean the comb.

She'd started back on Mollie's face when James began again. "Emotions can cloud our thinking," he ventured, carefully. "Especially when it comes to the people who matter. Gavin matters, much more than I think William Leighton mattered or any of the other fellows you tried to hide from us."

Mavis frowned, grazing the star point between Mollie's eyes with her fingertips.

James made a gruff noise in his throat, as if he were frustrated with himself. "It doesn't matter that I've been sober over thirty years. To this day, I'm still an alcoholic. And I remember, like it was yesterday, how the grip of withdrawal made me reach for your mother. I saw her as a lifeline, and in a lot of ways, she was. I'm ashamed to say it, even after all this time, but in some ways, I did use her. I loved her, but I used her just the same."

Mavis crossed her arms over her chest, planting her feet as she faced James for the first time. "First of all, let's leave *love* out of it. It's not helpful. Okay? Second, you realize Gavin isn't an addict? He suffers from PTSD, and unresolved grief on top of some mental abuse, thanks to his mom. *Not* addiction. There's a big difference."

The light from the window at the back of the stall caught James's beard, bringing all the silver notes to the surface and making him look more salt than pepper. His eyes were alive with blue, however, and they were lined with apprehension for her. "Neither PTSD nor addiction has symptoms that can be healed overnight. It doesn't matter how much you love the person…"

"That's twice you've dropped the L-word," Mavis warned.

"Yes," James said simply.

I'm not emotional. The words came and went quickly, yet they were anything but fleeting. It was a terrible denial. An even worse lie.

"Don't let the truth chase you around like it did me," James went on. "Eight years. I stayed away eight long years. That's eight years I could've watched Kyle grow up, like I watched you."

"You were getting clean," Mavis reminded him.

"I was running," James admitted. "Just like Gavin."

Mavis felt as jumbled as a jigsaw puzzle with missing pieces. Mollie shifted restlessly beside her and she reached out to soothe her. Contact with the horse made her relax by a fraction. She realized then how tense she really was. "What is it that you want me to do, Dad?" she asked. "When he comes back—" if *he comes back* "—you want me to walk away?"

"I don't know," James said. He ran a hand through his hair, still as thick as it had been when she was a girl. "Between what he's got going on and the unresolved issues between him and your brother…it's a pickle, and it involves every one of us."

"His issues with Kyle are theirs," Mavis replied. "They can work it out between them."

"What if they don't?" James wondered out loud. "What if it goes on? It'd make the long game tough between you and Gavin."

Mavis couldn't think about the long game. Why she'd considered it in the first place… Well, she was starting to wonder.

"Unless…" James's facial muscles twitched, hinting at discomfort. "Unless you say the two of you never thought about the long game, that your relationship is temporary."

"You know, people choose each other because they need each other even if it's not lifelong commitment like you and Mom," Mavis explained. "It can be temporary and still mean something."

"I know," he said. "I thought about your mom every day I wasn't a part of her life."

"Maybe I see something in him," she argued, "like Mom saw something in you back then. He is mine, maybe for a short time—maybe for a shorter time than the summer you had with Mom initially—but that doesn't make what Gavin and I have less real."

James shook his head. "I'm not asking you to be ashamed. Your mother and me… We're the last people who'd punish you for lov—" She winced and he quickly revised. "For feeling that deeply for someone. We love you, Mavis Blythe, and you ought to know that there's nothing you've done in this life that has ever disappointed us. We just want you to be careful."

"He's not here," she said, the statement sneaking through. She stopped short of letting the wall inside her fall down under the force of what was behind it. The stool behind her drew her attention as she turned away and set the comb down. She rubbed her hands together. "I don't know if he's coming back, so you, Mom, Kyle and everybody else can stop worrying about it."

"I don't want him gone," James said. "Not if it makes you unhappy."

"I told him he could go," she revealed. "From the beginning, we agreed that if he needed to run then I wouldn't stop him, so long as he let me know beforehand. That way, I wouldn't have to find out from somebody else."

"That doesn't make it hurt any less," James said. "Does it, baby girl?"

She rubbed her hands on the front of her jeans and faced him again. "I can't talk about this anymore, Dad. I'm sorry."

James noted the tilt of her chin, the stubbornness behind it, and hopefully none of the resignation. "And I can't argue with you anymore. Not when you look more like your mother than ever. I hurt her once, the way he's hurt you. It's almost like history's repeating itself, and that's not an easy thing to watch."

Mavis looked at the wall. "She did okay without you."

He raised a brow. "It took a lot of truth to get her to come around to me again. And hugs, but those I had to sneak in so she didn't break a vase over my head."

She felt a smile along the fault lines of her mouth and wanted to hold on to it. "Are you trying to tell me you want a hug?"

"Would it make you angrier?" he asked, cautious.

"I'm not angry at you." Giving in, she walked

to the gate and let him swing it open. "Even so, I don't have a vase."

James didn't so much hug her as scoop her against his chest. How he managed to hold her firmly and softly she didn't know. When she took them, his hugs were always the same—just right.

"We don't do this enough," James said, and held her a smidge tighter before releasing her.

Mavis stepped back, brushing the hair from her face. Maybe it was easier for other people to be affectionate with those closest to them. For her, this meant more. "Don't worry so much about me. I'm fine, just like Mollie here."

"If there's one thing I've learned, it's that women are made of tougher stuff." He tapped the edge of her nose. "Dinner?"

"Kyle?" she asked.

"He'll be there. And you'll have to talk to him eventually, too."

"Sure," she acknowledged. "First I think it'd be best all around if I curb the urge to clock him."

"With a vase?"

"In my dreams, it's been more like one of Edith's old dinner dishes," she said.

"The ones with the peonies?"

"No, the ones with the quails she made us eat off of at Christmastime. I broke one once, so it's not like it's a complete set."

James threw an arm around her shoulders. Jerking his chin in the direction of the tree line, he said,

"Heard your hound 'round back yonder. Chasing the cats again."

Mavis raised her voice and called, "Prometheus!"

Someone answered back, but it wasn't the dog. "I found you! Put on your party boots, my friend. We're going out a-drinkin'!"

They stopped and pivoted as one to Harmony. She'd taken the walking path with Bea from the mother-in-law suite where they lived. After the wedding, Kyle would live there, too.

Bea skipped ahead of her mother, wildflowers tumbling one by one out of her fist. She threw herself at James. He laughed and boosted her to his shoulder for a ride.

"Um, what?" Mavis asked, wiggling the toe of Bea's sneaker as James made a circle around her.

"I said…" Harmony said, closer. Her hands were hidden in her back pockets and she had a gleam in her eyes that said *trouble*. "You, me, the tavern, drinks. *Too*-night. Your Mom said she and your dad could watch Bea."

"Dad and I just agreed to dinner," Mavis said, looking around for the man. He'd escaped into the house.

"You can do dinner at the farm any night of the week and so can I," Harmony reminded her. "But it's not every night that both Bea and Kyle are occupied elsewhere. Plus, your brother will have me married by next season. My bachelorette days are numbered, again. Let's go! Let's have some fun! Two single gals raisin' hell."

"You and your daughter raise hell all on your own on a day-to-day basis. Isn't that enough?"

Harmony shifted up on the balls of her feet, speaking out of the corner of her mouth. "It seems you've had a taste for hell-raising lately, too. Your shake-up with Gavin surpassed us. I'd be kind of proud of you…"

"If it wasn't him," Mavis finished. "I'm not going out." She decided firmly and made a move to follow James.

Harmony moved smoothly into her path. "I need you."

Mavis grimaced. "Don't do that."

"I mean it," Harmony insisted. "A bride can't celebrate her engagement without her maid of honor."

Mavis blinked. "You…want me to do that again?"

"Uh, yeah," Harmony said, as if it were obvious. In a second, she was back to serious. "You're my best friend. I want you standing beside me when I make an honest man out of Kyle."

"You're not going to make me wear aquamarine again, are you?" Mavis asked, wrinkling her nose. "Because once was enough."

"My aqua phase ended long ago," Harmony granted.

"Thank you, sweet baby Jesus."

"Besides. A little birdie told me you look much better in red."

Mavis frowned. "Little birdie?"

Harmony pursed her lips. "Okay, a big birdie. A big, *smitten* birdie."

"Smitten," Mavis said. Gavin had been coined a lot of things but *smitten* wasn't one of them.

"I might've cornered him," Harmony admitted, "at the inn, before he took off."

"You didn't think to mention it?" Mavis asked.

A thoughtful pause filled the void, along with a light breeze and echoes of a nicker from the stable. "To tell the truth," Harmony said, "what he had to say for himself took a few days to sink in."

Mavis opened her mouth to ask. Just as fast, she let it close.

"I went swinging at him," Harmony explained. "Verbally 'cause I figured he was still sore from Kyle's dinner interrogation."

"Ambush," Mavis amended. "Even you have to agree. It was a cheap ambush."

"Kyle got his licks from my end," Harmony acknowledged. "It helped Gavin out when he admitted he hadn't gotten you entirely out of your drawers." At Mavis's steaming silence, Harmony demurred. "I was confused. When we were kids, I thought you hated him."

"He irritated me," Mavis said plainly. "He was my big brother's best friend. I didn't think to look beyond that until a few weeks ago."

"You haven't carried a torch for him like I did for Kyle all those years."

"No."

Harmony closed her eyes briefly, relieved. "So what changed?"

"I was like a lot of other people we know," Mavis told her. "I never looked at much but what was on Gavin's surface, or what he projected."

"Even you," Harmony said with surprise. "The observer."

"He didn't want anybody to see the real things. He didn't want me to see, either, but when he came back, I don't think he was at the point anymore where he could hide them."

"Why did he pick you?" Harmony asked. "Me, Mom and Dad have been banging on that door for as long as I can remember."

"I don't know," Mavis said truthfully. "But I'm glad he did. I'm not sure I would've left him alone had he not chosen me. I'd still be banging at the door, same as you."

"I didn't get much out of him before he left," Harmony continued. "But he did say that he was glad, too. And he wasn't sorry for any of it."

Mavis frowned over the flurry of emotions. It took over, from her navel to her clavicle.

"I'm just going to say it." Harmony licked her lips, prepping herself. "If I didn't know any better, I'd say my brother's a little bit in love with you."

Mavis grimaced. "Everybody needs to *stop* saying that."

"Tight-lipped men just happen to be something I know a thing or two about." Mavis shook her head, but Harmony kept on, relentless. "He's never known what to do with love at its purest. He loves Mom and Dad. He loves me and Bea. He loved Benji. And that's part of what's been chasing him all this time. I know it." Before Mavis could escape to the house, Harmony grabbed her. "Mavis. *Please*. I need to know."

"Know what?" Mavis asked, frustrated that her heart was pounding under the scrutiny. "What is it you want to hear?"

"If he'd decided to stay, if he *was* in love with you…how long could you see it going? That's all."

That's all? Yeah, right. "You won't tell a soul I said this," Mavis warned.

Harmony lifted two fingers, eyes wide. "Scout's honor."

"I would've stuck as long as he needed me."

As Mavis breathed heavily into the quiet, Harmony let the answer dig in. Shock painted her. "God. Mavis."

"But it's over, as far as I know now," Mavis said quickly. "Right now, that's irrelevant."

Harmony surprised her by grabbing her into a fast hug. When Mavis stiffened, Harmony tightened her hold. "You need this. You can lie to everybody else, but *I* know you need this."

The statement was rife with truth. Mavis remembered how Harmony had loved Kyle for years. Well over a decade. Since she was a girl and he was practically a man, as far out of reach as the moon. So she didn't step back from the embrace.

"I wish you could have told me," Harmony whispered. "So what that he's my brother? You could've talked to me."

Mavis tried to take a gulp of air. "Can't breathe."

Harmony patted her on the back, consoling. "It's going to be all right."

"No. I can't *breathe*."

"Sorry." Harmony let go of her.

Mavis took air in. Pushed it out. "I'm not emotional."

"You might be an island," Harmony observed, "but chances are, your place is crawling with pineapples."

Ugh. Pineapples.

Harmony tilted her head. "You feel like getting drunk?"

Mavis let out a startled laugh. "You might talk me into it."

"Good," Harmony nodded. "After this, I could drink enough for both of us."

"You usually do," Mavis said as they walked to the farmhouse.

"That's the spirit."

"DON'T TALK TO ME," Mavis told Kyle the moment he appeared at Tavern of the Graces.

"Yeah," Harmony chimed, already three sheets to the wind. She raised her margarita. "Single girls for life!"

Kyle grinned. "Says the future Mrs. Bracken."

Harmony brightened. "*Oooh*. That's the first time I've heard it. Say it again!"

He obliged her, drawing closer. His mouth didn't so much meld with hers as clash with it, heatedly.

"Oh, good," Mavis groaned. "You're doing that." She picked up her half-drunk margarita and rattled the ice that remained. Catching William's eye from behind the bar, she lifted it in indication. She was going to need another, she thought, tipping it back for a watery swallow.

"Mm-mm," Harmony purred as she and Kyle parted. "I'm looking forward to that more on a day-to-day basis."

"Like you two don't do it enough already?" Mavis drawled.

"What's she so aggro about, anyway?" Kyle asked his intended.

Harmony rolled her eyes at him. "You know what you did."

"Are you still mad about dinner?" he asked Mavis.

Mavis narrowed her eyes on him. "No, I'm mad about what brought dinner to a screeching halt."

"Sorry."

She snorted. "That's it? 'Sorry'?"

"Well, what do you want?" he wanted to know.

"You choked him out," Mavis stated, "like you were still recruits and it was time for initiation!"

"It was a reflex," Kyle said.

"You might want to work on that," Mavis pointed out, turning away to face the bar again.

"He's using you, anyway."

Mavis started to count to ten. She gave up at four. Swiveling, she confronted him. "I know when you look at me you have this irritating habit of seeing a six-year-old with hair like a porcupine. But just this once, could you *maybe* open yourself up to reality? I'm twenty-eight. I have all my adult teeth. Even if I do still have freckles and haven't grown an inch since fifteen, I've been to college, I've held down three to four jobs for most of my professional life. I've met my fair share of people—men included. Not one of them was a saint and neither am I."

His face had gone blank. "Where are you going with this?"

"I know what it is to use someone," she replied sharply. "I've cut lovers off because they tried to get closer than I wanted them. If anyone's a competent judge of whether your buddy was using me or not, it's me."

"Give me one reason he wasn't," Kyle said. "Because I can't figure it out."

"Why is that?" she asked. "Am I not what a man would want?"

"Don't put words in my mouth, Mavis," he warned.

"It was more," she threw at him. "He needed me and I needed him."

"And now he's gone again," Kyle picked up. "He's disappointed the people who love him *again*, and he hurt you in the process. Don't paint him as the innocent party in this. That's not what he is."

"He made me no promises. I told him not to. I knew it would end this way."

"Yes," Kyle said with a nod. "Because that's *who he is.*"

"I think you're wrong," she told him. "I saw things in him. I saw fear and defeat, grief and loss and everything in between. I saw someone who wants to stay. He *wants* to belong to something. He doesn't think he deserves it. There've been too many who've told him he's a lone wolf. The restless troublemaker who needs to move on so all the tidy notions people have about small-town life can keep on existing. That voice in his head, you know who it is."

"He and Tiffany haven't spoken in years."

"They spoke the day before he left," Mavis told him. "I got to hear for myself the things she tells him. You're there, too—in his head."

"Do you know how hard I worked to get him

to come here in the first place?" Kyle said, raising his voice.

"Yes," she granted. "You brought him back. But he touches me and you're the one chasing him off into the night like a frigging dingo."

"He shouldn't have touched you," Kyle said, undeterred. He raised his beard-stubbled chin. "He *knows* he shouldn't have touched you."

"Like you shouldn't have touched Harmony," she batted back at him.

"Maybe not, in the beginning," he said. "But Harmony and I... With us, things could never be temporary. It was all or nothing. You and Gavin both knew whatever this was wouldn't last. And he went ahead with it anyway. That's where he used you."

She lifted a finger. "I'll remind you of one thing before you and I drop this forever."

"Forever?" he said doubtfully.

"Forever," she reiterated, piercing him with a glare. "When you and Harmony were first sneaking around this summer and I was the lucky party who stumbled in on the fact, what did I do?"

Kyle became reflective. "You called me a frog-faced good-for-nothing and hoped I'd get myself trampled by wild heifers. Then you gave me a nurple and told me to mind where I pointed my nether joints." His gaze rested on her again. "Hard to forget."

"After that," she said, "when the initial shock

and 'ew' factor had worn off somewhat, I kept it a secret when you both wanted it secret. More, I didn't keep you apart."

Kyle spoke levelly. "So...you're asking me to believe that what happened between you and Gavin is equal to what's between me and Harmony?"

Mavis glanced from him to Harmony. Her friend's eyes were wide on hers. Mavis shook her head. "I don't know."

Kyle surveyed her, his stare passing left and right over her before settling. "I'll say one last thing."

Mavis couldn't contain a quiet sigh of relief.

"If it was me where he is and Harmony where you are...*nothing* would be keeping me away at this point. You see, that's where I doubt he's in the same place you are, emotionally."

"I'm not emotional," she denied.

He stared at her, grim. He raised his beer to his mouth. "I've never seen you so emotional. Why do you think I'm so worked up about this?"

"It doesn't matter," she said, and shrugged, because she didn't know what else to say or do. Gavin was still gone.

"Your heart isn't any different from the rest of ours," Harmony said kindly. She glanced up at Kyle. "Neither is his."

"Hey, Kyle," Olivia called from across the bar. She jerked her thumb to the stage. "You're up!"

Kyle took a breath. "We'll finish this later."

"I'm good with now," Mavis replied.

He took off his hat and placed it backward over Harmony's braided red updo. "Your cousin talked me into hitting the karaoke."

Harmony crooned. "What're you going to sing for me? No Beyoncé. Liv's saving that for me. Do 'Beast of Burden.' I *love* when you do Jagger."

"As you wish." He kissed the skin along the ridge of her shoulder soundly before pointing sternly at Mavis. "No throwing peanuts at me like last time."

Mavis shrugged, nonchalant. "There's a reason they leave the singing to me."

Olivia met Kyle at the head of the room. A grand introduction and overtures of homecoming followed. Mavis raised her glass as Harmony bounced on her stool, clapping like a lunatic. "That's my husband, y'all!" she hollered.

Mavis shook her head. "Your single girl status has been wiped."

"Kyle, do the hip roll!" Harmony guffawed when he did as she suggested.

Mavis turned away from the display and found a fresh margarita waiting on the bar. William stood behind it, polishing an empty pint with a cloth. "Round two," he supplied.

She wrapped both hands around the glass. "Your timing is impeccable."

William gave her a sideways smile, set the clean

pint aside and reached for another. "That's why I'm the new boss."

"That's right," Mavis said. Olivia had only recently handed over the tavern reins to her eldest son. She and Gerald now were in charge of special events alone. She raised her glass again. "Well deserved."

"Why, thank you," he said with a bow of his head. "Only took a decade to wear the lady down."

Chin propped in her hand, Mavis looked at him thoughtfully. He was the reedy kind of tall. He had green eyes, a slow grin and a voice like a baritone. Plaid was his go-to shirt pattern, much like her father. He liked to pair it, oddly enough, with board shorts and flip-flops. Blond and tan, he'd become a maverick behind his parents' bar not because legacy dictated it but because he came by bartending naturally. Observing was Mavis's gift; listening was his—and mixing.

He'd once made her palms sweat and her glands sing. And after all this time, there was sentiment there. As well as a little awkwardness. And now that *everyone* knew what they'd carefully buried, the awkwardness had doubled down. Bringing the margarita closer, Mavis scooped salt off the rim with her fingertip. She stuck it in her mouth. Her insecurities from years ago flared like a sore tendon. "Out of curiosity," she said cautiously, "how did she take the news…about you and me?"

William raised both brows. "At first, she didn't

believe it because she thinks she's better at reading Finnian and me than she actually is. When it finally sank in, she was impressed that I pulled it off—sorry. That *we* pulled it off, together, for so long. Also that Finn was able to keep his mouth shut about it."

Mavis thought about that. Finnian was a notorious blabbermouth. "Yeah. How'd he manage that?"

"I paid him," William said, ducking his head as if he were still ashamed.

Mavis laughed out loud. "You did not."

"I learned early that the only thing that can shut my brother up is money," William pointed out.

She ran her tongue over her teeth. "Any other feelings from the home front, about us?" she asked.

"Well, she did say that the subterfuge wasn't necessary. She likes you. I think she's a little upset with me for letting you get away."

Mavis took a sip from the margarita. "I thought it was what you wanted."

"What?" he asked, his hand hovering over the next pint in the queue.

She set the glass down, carefully. "Wasn't it?"

William braced both his hands on the edge of the counter, scrutinizing. "I thought it was what *you* wanted. That's why you ended it."

Well, hell. Mavis sighed. "Oh, brother."

He continued to stare, blank-faced.

She shook her head. "If you wanted to keep on, why did you let me end it?"

"Because I was a dumbass," he said blandly. "I was young. I didn't know the first thing about holding on to a woman. I figured you wanted something else. So I let you go."

"Oh, I wanted something else all right," she grumbled. Then she winced. "You didn't…pine for me. Did you?"

William glanced over her head. He lifted his shoulder, eyes tracking their way back to her slowly. "Maybe a little."

Mavis put her face in her palm. She cursed out loud.

"I don't like the word *pine*," he said, using the cloth to wipe down the space of the bar between them. "I like to think it was a little more dignified than that. Like *brooding*."

"You pined!" She was going to need another margarita. "And you never said a word?"

"I cared enough to let you go," he noted. "That's what you do. 'Love 'em and let 'em go'? It felt adult, at least. I figured if what we had was right, you'd find your way back at some point."

She'd often wondered why some other woman hadn't married him already. She wanted to believe, more than anything, that it wasn't because of her. However, William had just blown up a whole decade's worth of insecurities and assumptions. Now she didn't know what to believe.

"Don't hate me for this," he said, treading gingerly. "But…would now be a bad time to ask if you're available?"

She blinked. "No. Yes. No." She held up a hand to stop herself. "Okay, it's clear I don't know the answer to that, either."

"Are you—pining?" William asked. "Over him?"

Gavin. Of course he knew about Gavin. Everybody from here to Shreveport knew about her and Gavin, the same as everyone knew about her and William.

He nodded, gleaning the answer for himself. He went back to wiping, though the bar was noticeably clean. "It's, uh, none of my business."

Mavis frowned deeply. "You'd be the first to say as much."

"Can I ask how you're doing?"

"Fine."

"Mmm-hmm," he said. He was doing his listening thing, she knew.

She jerked her thumb over her shoulder. "Look, just do yourself a solid and stay away from the lunkhead onstage," she advised. "I'd prefer to keep seeing more than the top of your head."

"The top of my head?"

"After he buries you," she said, and paused for impact. "Alive."

William glanced askance at the singing amateur. "Oh."

She spread her fingers. "What'd you expect getting involved with the commando's sister?"

He scratched his forehead with one finger. "Seemed like a good idea at the time. I don't know. What'd you want to be with me for?"

"It felt safe." It tumbled out before she realized she was saying it. When he homed in on her again, she looked away for the first time. "I...felt safe with you," she finished lamely.

It took a moment. William's mouth moved to a smile.

She lifted a finger at him. "Not another word."

"Okay," he said easily. He looked down. The smile grew.

Dear God, would *somebody* marry him? He was decent—likely the most decent guy she'd ever known. "Liv's still got her double shotty," she said. "Keep it loaded and take it to bed with you."

"You don't have to worry about me and your brother," William said with something of confidence.

That was something. "If only," she said out loud.

William's part-time bartender shouted at him from across the bar and rattled off a large order of draft beers. He logged the information in his mind, tossed the cloth into the sink behind him and moved to fill the requests. He took a glass off the mirrored shelf above the long row of chrome-and-gold taps, chose one and began to build the draft with only a small bit of foam on top. "Do you think we'll hear you sing tonight?" he called back to Mavis.

She glanced at her near-empty margarita. "Make me another when you've got a minute and time will tell."

"Easy there," he advised. "You never were great at holding tequila."

"My homegirl's getting married, and I'd like to forget some stuff, at least until tomorrow."

"All right then," William acquiesced. "Round three, coming up."

No sooner had he moved down the row of taps than a large hand clapped over her shoulder. "It's your turn."

Mavis squinted at Kyle. "Huh?"

"I've humiliated myself," he indicated. "You'll kill up there and humiliate me further. Win-win on your part."

"I like where I'm at," she claimed, and started to turn back to the bar.

"Don't make me start," Kyle advised. When she only doubled back to frown at him, he began to chant, "Mavis. Mavis. Mavis—"

She straightened when Harmony and several other tavern regulars struck up the tune. "Stop it."

Kyle raised his voice, pumping his fist. "Mavis! Mavis! Mavis!"

The chant went up through the bar like wildfire. She scowled when she heard William taking up the call to arms, too.

Kyle grinned. "Come on! Give the people what they want!"

"Later," she said, low, as she rose from the stool, "I'm going to throw a quail plate at your head."

Kyle answered by tossing her unceremoniously over his shoulder.

Mavis thought about clawing him as he hustled her through bystanders to the stage. They parted for him. When he set her on her feet, he pecked a kiss to the center of her forehead and backed off quickly before she could bludgeon him. "Mavis Bracken, ladies and gentlemen," he said into the mic before darting off.

Mavis pushed the hair from her face. As the music queued, she stepped to the microphone. She cleared her throat and raised her hand to the crowd. "Hi." Lyrics flashed on the screen overhead. It was a Beatles song. She glanced at Kyle, tall and distinguishable despite his retreat to Harmony's side.

Beatles songs had always been their weekend specialties at the farm.

He hooked an arm over his fiancée's shoulders and raised his pint in encouragement.

Holding a grudge against him would be ten times easier if she didn't like seeing him so damn happy. Returning her attention to the lyrics, she let the first piano notes drop. "'Hey Jude,'" she sang. "'Don't make it bad.'" The crowd whistled along to the popular tune and she managed a smile as she went on with the song.

It was a popular choice. Soon, she wasn't singing alone. Soon, it was simple to intone the familiar words. More comfortable, she closed her eyes, going full McCartney. The sore knot inside her unraveled. She tried sieving it out, one chord at a time. Raising herself onto her toes, she belted through the bridge and the tavern patrons joined her in an enthusiastic round of "nah, nah, nah, nahs."

On the third round, she opened her eyes. Her "nah, nahs" died.

Gavin.

He was three rows back, packed shoulder to shoulder with William's customers. The mic in her fist dropped to her hip, the knot in her strung tight again. It was tempered, though, by a sunbright flash of hope.

Gavin, she thought. His name soon became as much of a mantra as the "nah nahs." *Gavin's back.*

The song wound down to a finish. The crowd applauded. Those seated came to their feet for a standing O. Their buoyancy had smoothed over her glitch.

He was smiling. Gavin was smiling at her, in the quiet way that sparked heat inside her.

One of the waiters appeared at her side. Mavis jerked in reaction. She let him take the mic and dipped into a small curtsy as he led another round of applause for her. Exiting stage left, Mavis scanned the milling faces. If she'd thought hers had been hot under William's gaze…

Now it was awareness that brought the flush to her neck and cheeks. He was here, he was near, and she needed to get to him. "Scuse me," she muttered as she elbowed through the thick clutch.

Warm fingers wrapped around her elbow. They tugged her around. Looking up, she found him. Or, he found her. *Oh God. Gavin!*

He was clean-shaven. Someone had given his fade haircut a trim. He looked great. He looked *fantastic*. Her heart knocked against her throat. The tavern seemed to rock like a canoe. She could *smell* him.

Words stuck in her throat. She couldn't bring them up so she concentrated instead on leveling her breathing as she looked at him and he looked back. The low lights brought the warmth of metallic umber to his eyes. They flickered. Longing, an unbridled sweep, lashed her as his eyes caressed her.

Someone bumped into her from behind and she stepped into him, his circle of heat. When he laid his hand on her shoulder, the other on the small of her back, she shuddered…she didn't think about moving. In fact, she closed her eyes again. After a few seconds, under the cover of the crowd, she turned her nose into his chest.

Hard. Real. *Gavin*. She wasn't sure how the emotions came at her. They were there, hair-triggered.

They built and she had no recourse but to press her face to his shirt and hang.

His palm swept up her spine. Stiff, she tried not to buckle when it draped warmly over the nape of her neck.

He spoke against her temple. "You with me?"

"Mmm." She gave a half nod. "I'm just—" she groaned at the obvious "—emotional."

His hold tightened. "Sorry. I'm sorry, Frexy."

"You're here," she said on a tumult of air.

"I am now."

"Why…?" She began to shake her head. She didn't understand…

It took him a minute to answer. "I…wanted to come home. So I did."

"Just like that?"

"It was simpler this time." His voice was a rumble and it fired in her veins as his lips grazed her ear. "You made it simpler."

She was going to kiss him—the chick who didn't do PDA—right here, in front of everyone. She was going to kiss him so everyone knew he was hers. Keeping her nose pressed to the wolf beneath his collar, she breathed. In and out. It wasn't enough—not enough.

Harmony poked her head in. "Hi! Remember me?"

Mavis's head sailed back.

"Hi," Gavin responded. "And sure do."

"You're back!" Harmony chirped.

"Just," he acknowledged.

Harmony glanced to Mavis, then back to him. Her eyes were bright. "Where'd you go?"

Mavis saw reluctance pass over him. Kyle cut off any excuse by becoming the fourth point of their square. "He's back. There's a surprise."

Mavis circled Gavin's wrist, passing her thumb gently over the pulse point and daring Kyle to say anything else.

"You forget something?" Kyle asked.

"No." Gaze falling over Mavis again like gentle rain, Gavin's expression went from tense to intense in the flash. "I didn't forget. As for where I've been…"

"Don't leave us hanging," Kyle said.

"I was in Monroeville," Gavin revealed. "Visiting an old friend."

Harmony's eyes widened on her brother. "Tommy? You went to see Tommy?"

Gavin nodded affirmation.

Mavis's lips parted. Thomas Zaccoe was Benji's father. He lived in Monroeville in the same house he'd raised his son in—not but a walk from his grave site. When Gavin had trouble meeting anyone's eye, she caressed the inside of his arm.

"How was he?" Kyle asked. He didn't sound stern anymore.

Gavin nodded again. "Good. He's, uh…seeing someone. Some widow he met at the supermarket."

"That's sweet," Harmony said with a smile.

"I've been meaning to take Bea up to see him before the end of summer."

"He's got pictures of her everywhere," Gavin mentioned. "He needed a few things done around the house, so I wound up staying a few days."

"Did you see it?" Harmony asked quietly.

Gavin rubbed his lips together. "Uh, yeah. Yeah, I saw it."

They were speaking of the memorial the city had built in honor of its hometown hero. The statue stood at the entrance to the cemetery.

"It's beautiful," Harmony said. Her eyes grew damp. "Isn't it?"

"He wasn't one for show," Gavin said quietly. "But I think he might have liked it."

"Are you okay?" Mavis asked before she could think better of it in front of the others.

He grabbed on to her visually, like he was a squall and he wanted to hug her like a lighthouse. "Better," he acknowledged.

"Kyle!" William called from the bar. When he had Kyle's attention, he cupped his hands over his mouth to be heard over the music and crowd noise. "They want you to draw tonight's raffle!"

"Oooh." Harmony jumped to, drawing half a ticket out of her back pocket. "My number's seven-seven—"

"That's cheating," Kyle muttered as the two of them squeezed through the crowd to get to the raffle jar.

Mavis was alone with Gavin again. Thank God.

Gavin humphed as someone pushed into him from behind. She saw the dark look he tossed over his shoulder and grabbed his collar, turning him back to her. "Do you want to get out of here?"

He nodded decisively and smiled. "Hell yes."

She beamed when he fell into step with her. She pushed her way to the door. She moved quickly. The raffle would only last so long. Before anyone else could get in their way, she pulled him out into the tepid night.

No sooner had the doors whooshed closed behind them than she spun. Her arms twined around his neck.

He didn't fall back. Instead, he banded his arms low, boosting her up.

"Yes." She shivered, tipping her head to the side so that he could kiss her deep. *Inside.* Her brows arced together as he flicked his tongue over hers, dragged it out. "Mmm, *yes.*"

"Mavis." It escaped on a whisper, her name and everything behind it. His arms hardened. He said it again, bringing her hope to the joy of eclipse.

Her feet weren't anywhere near the ground. Her heart hammered against his breastbone. She felt the great muscle underneath his sternum responding at a gallop. With an unsteady breath, she pulled away slightly. "I—I missed you."

It took him a second to focus. The edge of need was thick, wrapped up tight in metal and ivy. When he realized what she'd said, his soul peered through the brush and ironwork and made her knees go stupidly weak. "I missed you, too." A bar twined between his eyes. "I missed you like crazy." Tipping his forehead to hers, he added, "I'm sorry. I didn't call. I made you think—"

"No." Mavis shook her head. "You're here. That's all that matters." She planted her mouth on his, inhaling in a quick rush. "Damn it," she cried. "You've made me sentimental."

"You make me a lot of things. Like happy. I realized that on the road. I thought I was ready before. You were right—I wasn't."

"And now?" she said, buzzing from head to toe. He nodded. "Now."

Never had a declaration sounded so finite. Or sexy. "Come home with me," she insisted. "I want you. With me. On the river. In my bed."

Those eyes darkened, glittering with promise. "Did I mention 'hell yeah' back there?"

"A girl doesn't get tired of hearing it," she suggested.

"Then 'hell yes' again." And he kissed her once more, in a bruising way that demanded. She felt immersed, just as she wanted.

THE RIVER. IT smelled like soot. Like home. Mavis had driven so fast, a tinge of burned rubber hit his nostrils, too, as he opened the passenger door to get out of her car. "I don't question why Errol drives you and Miss Zelda around anymore."

He saw her outline under the far-off streetlight, ghostly in black. The flowing bodice of the blouse he knew to be silk now that he'd had his hands on her draped low beneath her collarbone. The skin-hugging pants were leather—knowing her, some vegan alternative. Along with the high-scaling boots, she looked classy and edgy.

Every inch of him was taut. She wanted him in her round house, in her sheets. He didn't have a clue what Mavis's bedroom looked like, but he could see lowering her into the pillows. Losing the both of them there completely.

He could've shucked those leather pants right here under the carport but the air was misty. Yet another summer storm was on the horizon. "I need to get you inside," he said.

She began to take steps backward to the stairs. She blended into the shadows.

By the first step, he was beside her. Lifting her by the waist, he carried her up, up.

Her legs locked around his waist. He groaned. Grabbing her underneath, he followed the path of supple material and the round curve of her bottom, digging in. Her breath grew hot against his neck. Her lips kissed their way up to the cup of his ear. There, things got interesting.

He nearly stumbled on the last step. His hand got between her and the wall he nearly crashed into at the landing. He held her there as her attention centered on the spot she'd found that was turning his knees supple. "Whatcha doin' there?"

"Nerves." She sucked, bringing him to the bank of intense arousal. "They live in the cartilage." She laved. "Lots and lots of them. Waiting to be played with."

When the edge of her teeth joined the onslaught, he felt himself shiver. Once. Twice. The third time, he ground against her center and groaned.

She pulled back, licking her lips as she tipped her head against the siding of the house. "Erogenous zones. Men have them, same as women."

His breath was coming through his teeth, he realized. Hefting her beneath the thighs again, he transferred her to the door.

She endured being pressed against glass, his leg wedged between hers to keep her off the porch. As he unlocked the door with a grip that wasn't at all steady, she drew barely there lines across his chest until his skin grew sensitive beneath the cotton of his T-shirt and he wanted nothing more than to shed it or rend it in half to give her free autonomy. He felt clumsy as he boosted her high against his chest once more and stepped blindly into her dominion. "Where're the lights?"

"No lights," she whispered.

"None?" he asked.

"Do you trust me?"

"Frexy," he whispered against her lips. "You're

the only person I've ever wanted to come home to. What do you think?"

She sighed, scraping her nails over his scalp in slow motion. Her soft, shallow kiss caught him off guard. She was normally bolder. She slid her legs from around him and planted herself on the floor, using the neck of his shirt to bring his mouth down flush with hers.

He clasped her by the shoulders. He kissed her as she'd kissed him. Intimately. No rush. It took him back to her parents' house and the "accidental" lip-lock that had started everything.

She broke away. "Gavin?"

"Hmm?" he asked. He nosed against the hair that tickled the angle of her jaw. *Mangoes.* For days, he'd had a fierce hankering for mangoes.

"Give me your wallet."

The command struck him off guard. "Say what?"

She reached around to the pockets of his jeans. Cupping each, she dipped her fingertips into the one with the telltale bulge and dragged his billfold out herself. "What's the magic number?" she murmured as she peeled it open between them.

He tried to see her in the dark. He tried to carve her out of the outline in front of him. It didn't work as well as he would've liked. "Why lights off?" he wondered. Why not lights *on*, all the way on so if he studied her closely, every inch, he could pinpoint all the secrets she hid under leather, silk and mystery.

"We're even," she said in explanation. "I can't see you any better than you can see me."

"Mavis," he said, not for the first time.

"Two." There was a smile in her voice, woven smugly alongside approval. "You still carry two condoms in your wallet."

He planned to use them. Unable to hold off any longer, he asked, "Which way?"

"To the bedroom?" she asked coyly. He felt her tug along the front of his belt.

"Which way?" he said again.

"Up the stairs, to the left if you follow the—"

She'd told him once she hated brute male strength. He wondered then why she gasped in delight as he tossed her over his shoulder and made quick strides. Groping, he found the railing to the stairs and followed its smooth curve up and left.

He wanted to tell her everything he wanted to do to her. Everything, in stark detail. He wanted to tell her what it all would mean. It got caught in his throat, though.

The room was nearly pitch-black, but he sensed the panoramic view that opened up on the landing. He saw four posts. A bed. River lights shone beyond, gauzy. The bed was curtained and the curtains were transparent. Near his shoulder, the light from the street peered through more glass. The bedroom was the only room at the top of the stairs. Gavin set Mavis slowly on her feet. "No curtains on the windows?"

"They're tinted." Her voice was barely there. For the first time, he heard nerves from her. Then he felt her fingers rucking up the bottom half of his shirt. "So the neighbors can't see."

He didn't give a rat's ass if the army was posted outside buying tickets to the show. She pushed the shirt up, gathering as she went. Bending slightly at the waist, he let her tug it over his head.

It took her a moment to unlatch and unloop his belt in the dark. "It's almost senseless. How much I want you."

He felt his jeans unsnap. Heard the zipper rasp. He closed his eyes and harkened back to the conversation they'd had weeks ago. "What scares you most?"

Mavis stilled. In the light from the street, he could barely make out the shape of her face. "Emptiness," she said. "I used to think feeling nothing was better and that keeping my head was more important than embarrassing myself with emotion. Since you…" She peeled the waistband of his jeans down over his buttocks by scooping both hands under, molding the shape of him from his spine to the bottom curve of his glutes. "…the thought of being hollow… It's not what I need, any more than the cocoon my grandmother thought would be best for me."

He skimmed his knuckle up her arm, took it

over the point of her shoulder. "You're not cold," he
observed. Winding his fingers tightly beneath the
slight spaghetti strap of her blouse, he savored the
feel of the sliding silk. "I've touched you. You've
never been cold to me." He twisted the strap. It
snapped.

"What scares you?" she returned. She was trembling. And yet she was back to speaking to him in
that Zen hummingbird voice that soothed him to
no end. He'd missed the lure of her voice.

"Using you," he said, giving her the same answer he had weeks before. He pressed an open
kiss to the shoulder he'd bared. Then he turned
his mouth into her throat.

"Gavin?"

"Hmm?"

She sighed. "Use me."

Shit. His arousal took a jump. With a grunt, he
picked her up again. The silk had to compete with
the satin of her skin against his chest. It all went
in tandem with the leather. The triad of texture
was erotic as hell.

He found the bed and dipped a knee into it, taking her down to sheets that were already rumpled
and…

Silk. Dear God. The material would make him
lose his mind before daylight. The simple thought
of taking her wrapped up in silk sheets made him
moan. He sat up. Reading him in darkness, she
handed him the packet she'd stolen from his bill-

fold. He made quick work of the clasp of her pants and peeled them off, one leg at a time. He pushed the waistband of his jeans farther down and carefully fed the rubber around his girth. Then he grabbed her by the calves and dragged her closer, kicking off his jeans as he came down on his hands. He teased her mouth with a kiss before working his way down. The lone strap holding the blouse gave a satisfying *snap* when he balled the material near the neckline and gave a hearty pull. She helped him work it over her hips, down to her toes.

He turned his knee out against hers, opening her up. He couldn't see. But he could touch. He could taste. He'd take advantage of that. But first—

His weight settled over hers, torsos aligning. Grabbing her hands in his, he tugged them straight to either side. He fit his hips against hers. Her pelvis jumped. A hot gasp lifted. "Warm," she panted, dipping her head back into the covers. Her hips rose against his in a circling wave. *"You're so warm."*

"I'm burned up, baby." He brushed his lips across hers. He brought her knees up and arched, lifting his head when he felt her bloom and dampen. He turned his palms into hers, twining finger by finger.

She dug her heels into the mattress and hiked her hips until the head of his arousal met the juncture between her thighs. Then she dug her ankles into the base of his spine, inviting him in one glorious inch. "Warm me up, too," she ordered. "I want to be warm like you."

His restraint snapped like the strap of her blouse. Any thought of finesse climbed into the back seat and he found himself buried, his face burrowed in the sheet near her head.

She quaked from head to toe. Her legs didn't leave him, but the fine bones of her hands trembled under his. "Ah," she said as he remained deep inside her.

"I'm sorry," he said. "Mavis. I'm sorry."

"No," she said, pressing her cheek to his. She swallowed. "No."

"I've hurt you."

She shook her head. "No. Just…*ahhh*." Her lips grazed his cheek. Still, she trembled.

"What do you want me to do?" he asked, stiff and still.

"I think…" She sighed. "I think you should kiss me."

Instantly, he fit his mouth to hers. He treated her, kissing the way she always seemed to want. Curling his palms beneath hers, he kissed her slow. He kissed her deep. He kissed her as if they had the rest of their lives for kissing.

The tension in her muscles melted until her fingers laced with his and her legs loosened so her feet could venture down his calves. They flattened, caressing. She kneaded her center against his in circles, rivulets of friction. He caught on to them, drawing shapes from the center of his hips. Releasing her hands, he cupped the back of her head, spreading his fingers wide in her hair, guiding it back to the bed. He kept kissing, not giving up the link she needed as the circles grew wider and faster.

Her toes pressed against the tops of his, like boots in stirrups. It was her hands now that dug into the small of his back, mashing his pelvis into hers. He felt her nails. He felt her grow harried and piqued.

"What do you need?" he breathed. "What do you need from me?"

"Harder," she said.

His curse was reverent. He pressed down into the bed. She lifted. He thrusted.

"Oh," she said on a rush.

He dropped his chin to his chest. "I can't… I'm not gentle."

"Stop it." She brought her hips up again to meet his and kept circling. "Stop whatever makes you think this isn't right. That you're too big, too rough. Stop whatever's telling you you're wrong for me. You're worthy. This is good. So good. Gavin, if you stop, one of us is going to scream, and I'm afraid it might be me."

"I can't stop."

"Good." She tipped her chin up as he went from circling to rocking.

Light flickered against the windows. Heat lightning at a fair distance. For a second, he saw her, the parts of her visible to him. Her fists were wrapped up in sheets. The smile on her face and the high-stepping friction at the point where they joined... it was enough. Mavis disappeared again into the cloak of night and he closed his eyes to keep her painted against his eyelids.

She was right. It felt good. Like coming back to life. He rocked faster.

She began to make noise, little mewls.

Hold it together, he thought as the skin around the waistline of his back drew in tight and his nervous system went up in flames. *Hold it together*.

She cried out, once. Her head slammed back into the sheets. She cried out again, her feet lifting her lower half against the brunt of his charge. Gavin groaned in appreciation as the climax ripped through her. With an animal sound, he lowered his head and kept charging.

Her arms locked around his middle, not giving up the link. She raised her torso to his so the slide would be complete, toes to chest. She kissed him. Then she kissed the wolf on his chest.

He couldn't stop, he realized again. He ground to a halt as the dark room reeled and the badass sensations he'd felt up to this point tore off their wee lamb skins and went on a Hulk-sized blitz. They blitzed until he was nothing but a shaking, heaving beast. Then he dissolved over her, rubber all over.

She clasped him around the shoulders when he began to shift his weight off of her. "Don't," she said. He could hear the hum of satisfaction in her throat. "Don't you dare, Gavin Savitt."

"Taking you with me," he whispered raggedly. He shook his head to clear it. "Taking you with me this time, Frexy." Then he flopped the both of them back to the bed, her on top where she could nestle.

MAVIS FELT GAVIN wake three times in the night. Once to entangle himself with her further. The next to turn away. She curled against his back, caressing until she felt him subside. Nightmares jolted him even as sleep held him in repose—repose that was not repose. He kicked her only once, lightly on the shin before muttering a sleep-rasped, "Frex?"

"Still here." She kissed the center of his spine as proof.

He tugged her hand from his waist. He pressed it against the wall of his chest, covering it with his. She counted the beats beneath her hand until they dwindled back into an easy cadence.

I'm not going anywhere. The certainty had been there throughout the experience. She'd ride out his storms until he no longer doubted that she could handle them. Then she'd ride out some more, however many he had to endure. Touching her cheek against the warm press of his back, she gathered his heat. She let it cover her like a blanket and drifted back to sleep, satisfied he had done the same.

When next she woke, it was near dawn. The room was dark, yet the night had lost its inkiness.

Gavin was gone.

She padded downstairs, wrapping the loose sheet around her. Halfway down, she heard the shower running. At the bottom, she found the door near the landing closed, the light a golden stripe underneath.

She entered. The shower door was pulled to. She saw his outline through the glass.

Mavis shed the sheet. She made sure to make noise so that when she opened the shower it wouldn't trigger reflexes she knew he wanted buried.

His head was under the spray when she stepped in. He peered back over his shoulder and the arm he had posted high against the wall. The one good eye did a steep dive over her naked torso. "Beautiful," he greeted.

Nobody had ever called her *beautiful*. Not since she was a girl and her parents didn't know any better. She moved to him, admiring his lines. The perfect shape of his behind. He had a birthmark on his right cheek. It was shaped like an apple. A smile snuggled into the lower half of her face, right at home. "You're still here."

"Still here," he echoed.

She touched him. He smelled like the soap her mother made from scratch and sold at Flora. "Thank you."

His feet circled until she was looking at more than his lines. More muscle. More flesh. Ink and sex.

Then he kissed her again and the ache she'd thought he'd treated swallowed her up. Smoothing her palms up his chest to the column of his neck, she linked them over his nape. His hands planed over her, around and back to rest low on her hips. They melded together as one.

She broke away. "Did you happen to grab the last—"

"Condom? No."

She cursed.

He chuckled.

"What?"

"I've never heard you cuss that badly before." His head angled down to hers again before his gaze seized on her collarbone. He stopped, eyes narrowing as he tried to make out the shapes that ranged from one side to the other. His fingers came up to trace, barely there. "Ah. *This* is what got you in trouble."

"Moon cycles," she explained. Helping him, she moved from the first shape to the last, left to right. "Waning…to waxing. But this isn't the tattoo that got me into trouble."

His stare fused to hers. "There's another?"

Guiding his hand around, she planted it against the back of her ribs on the left. "This one got me grounded for an entire season."

"What is it?" he asked, grazing the skin. "Butterfly?" He grinned. "Dream catcher?"

Mavis turned her eyes to the feral thing on his chest. "Did you know that ancient Romans claimed they were descended from wolves?" she asked, quietly. When surprise dawned and his gaze swept back to hers, her nerves flared. "And in Scotland… there was supposedly this goddess named the Cailleach. She ruled the dark half of the year and was often depicted riding a wolf."

Gavin had stilled.

"They called her the 'protector of wild things.'" When he said nothing at all, Mavis shifted her feet. Water driblets had glossed the side of her face. She swiped them off. "I always wondered…what riding a wolf would be like."

Slowly, he brushed shower mist over the surface of her hair. He brushed her cheek, tipping her face to the light. His thumbs rubbed the space beneath her eyes. Makeup, she realized. The water, heat and sleep had no doubt spilled her eye makeup down her cheeks. He rubbed gently, methodically until it was gone. Then he scanned her, seeing beyond the shadows. "I like lookin' at you in the light."

She dragged teeth over her lower lip. "I like when you open your mouth."

"Thirty-seven," he pronounced. "You have *thirty-seven* freckles. Just on your face."

She didn't have an answer. Not yet. He was looking at her. Nothing between them. No pretenses. No expiration date.

Nakedness came in so many forms.

"You spook me."

She rubbed the back of his shoulders when the whisper caught. "You spook me, too," she said back. Her heart walloped her breastbone because it almost sounded like they were saying something else.

Like *I love you.*

"You know me," he acknowledged.

She nodded. "I know you."

He went back to exploring the moon cycles. "I was rough."

"The best things are," she told him. "But that doesn't change how lovely…emboldening—how *great* they can be in the end. My body's singing, Gavin."

"I haven't always been nice. I pushed in the beginning. Pushed you."

"You didn't push me away," she pointed out.

"I wasn't strong enough," he admitted. "I don't think I need just anybody. I needed you then. I need you now."

It felt good to hear. "I've pushed you, too," she

acknowledged. "I pushed you when some might say it was unwise to."

"Yeah. 'Cuz here there be monsters."

She smiled at his pronounced drawl. "I'm glad you're here, pushing me."

He looked at her in the stark way that made her forget he was legally blind. "Keep pushing me," he told her. A rakish smile took over. Mavis saw the old Gavin, and her pulse was slipping and grabbing all over the place again. "Good things happen when you push."

"I will," she vowed.

Carefully, he turned her to face the opposite direction. She let him guide her around. His hands swept, roving, over her torso. She felt him at her back, his heat. His sex. "No protection. Remember?"

He nibbled a concise path along her jaw, grasping her breast in a hold firm enough to bring her to attention. "Admit it that I hurt you."

Mavis moved, unable to help herself, when his fingers veered toward the apex of her thighs. As they rubbed her folds together in a light pinch, she felt friction. She felt an instant of recharge. "I'm okay, Gavin."

"Okay isn't acceptable," he said at her ear. "Okay's *basic*." He rocked her from side to side simply, soothingly. A contrast against his rough-textured fingertips. "You should have something else. Something nonbasic."

"Sounds excellent." She rocketed onto her toes, stretching her back along his front as he flicked her chief erogenous zone with his thumb, then delved inside her.

"Hurt?" he asked.

She shook her head. She latched on, roping one arm up around his neck. She swayed into the lance arcing against her back.

He panted against her shoulder. He kissed it. "Thirty-one. You have thirty-one freckles on this shoulder." He kept kissing, connecting the dots.

"If you don't stop counting—" she rocked on her toes again as he plucked her like a well-strung harp "—you'll never be done."

"You think so good, Frexy." He took her mouth when she offered it. "Come."

She nodded quickly because it *was* coming. Her back arched as the wave curled.

"That's it," he said as she rode it out. He groaned as the orgasm gripped her. "That's it, Mavis."

It released, tossing her messily to shore. Her knees buckled. His arms banded against her middle, keeping her upright.

"I aim to do that again," he whispered against the cup of her ear.

Mavis caught her breath and turned around. "That sounds good. *Really* good. But before you do that…" She planted her hands against his chest, backing him up until he was flush with the shower wall. She eyed him up and down, homing in on the areas that needed work. "Let me reciprocate."

"THIS ISN'T WHAT I had in mind," he noted.

"You got yours in the shower," Mavis reminded him. "Think of this as a bonus round. Inhale, roll the shoulders forward, releasing the neck as you tuck your chin into your chest. Round your spine."

Gavin pushed the breath out, following Mavis in what she called "cat-cows." The view wasn't bad. He sneaked a glance at the mat to his right. Dawn was just creeping through the windows, fresh new-day dew clinging to the screens. She'd opened a few panes so that the sounds of the river, the birds, could accompany the flow of respirations. She wore yoga pants and a sports bra.

As he toweled off after the deep-tissue massage she'd offered in the shower, she'd come at him with a pair of rolled-up mats and his discarded Fruit of the Loom briefs. "Put these on," she'd said, "and meet me downstairs."

By the time he joined her in her living room, she'd pushed the couches back to the walls to make space for the mats. They'd started cross-legged on the floor, breathing. He hadn't thought much of the exercise. What good was he at relaxing?

Watching her, though, in her element, was a trip.

"If your knees hurt," she murmured, "you can fold a blanket under them."

"Knees are fine," he answered.

"Good. Exhale, come back up. Broaden those shoulders. Press the hips back. Arch the spine, looking up… And exhaling, round forward and down…"

Here's what that Zen voice had been made for, he thought. It helped, as much as the stretch.

"If you draw your belly button in toward your spine, you can bring it deeper." When he couldn't stifle a groan, she added, "It's almost like massaging the abdomen." With a glance at him, she instructed, "Don't force your chin in. Just release the neck. Nice, gentle stretch."

He was neither nice nor gentle, but he did as he was told. The hell if it didn't feel good.

"Cat-cowing is great first thing in the morning," she said. "It creates room in the back and torso. It strengthens the abdomen, opens the chest. It eases the mind and is great for stress. It's really just an awesome way to wake up, warming up the body."

"I can think of other ways to warm up the body," he quipped.

"We've already done those things."

"Most of them." He smirked at her as they both came out of the stretch. He couldn't tell if she was amused.

Mavis stood. "Stay down," she said when he made a move to do the same.

"Why?" he asked, suspicious as she came to stand beside his mat.

"I'm going to guide you through a Fallen Angel," she informed him.

His jaw loosened. "Huh?"

She gave a low chuckle, rubbing her hands up and down his bare shoulders. Then she eased them down the length of his back to rest on both of his hips. "Bring these up."

"How far?"

"How 'bout all the way?"

"What are you up to?" he asked as she guided him up until his legs were straight.

"Press your hands down into the floor," she told him. "Good. Press the feet into the floor. You can bend the knees if you're not as flexible in the calves. Concentrate on the hips. Really try to draw them up and back. How do you feel?"

"Ridiculous."

"Well, it looks great."

"Thanks a lot."

"From Downward Dog…come to your knees again. Spread them wide. The tops of your feet are down and flat. Good. Try touching your big toes together. Now come forward, not in tabletop—keep the legs to the mat and cradle your belly between your thighs. It's simple," she said when he gave her a winged look. She helped him flatten against his legs. "It's called Child's Pose. Touch your forehead to the mat."

"What are my arms supposed to be doing?"

"Whatever feels natural."

"None of this feels natural."

"Give it a few seconds. You can either stretch your arms out in front of you, or you can lay them against your thighs. Just let them rest."

"Mmm-hmm. And what do I do now?"

"You breathe."

"Breathe," he muttered.

"Yes. In yoga, everything comes back to the breathing. After a couple of respirations, you should really feel yourself relax into it."

"Hmm." He did breathe. And after a few moments, he might've felt himself relaxing, just as she'd suggested.

"Keep breathing."

Keep calm. Keep breathing. Two of the hardest things to manage. Though that line of thinking might've been somewhat easier to overcome lately.

If he hadn't come home... If Mavis hadn't cornered him under the bougainvillea... Would he be in the same place, this new realm that felt something akin to the calm after the storm?

He might never be free of PTSD. He hadn't chosen it any more than he had chosen to be blind. But he didn't want to be defined by it, nor did he want to be defined by his visual impediments. Mavis had shown him that, too—the day they took her canoe downriver. She'd chosen not to be defined by her epilepsy. In spite of its intrusions into her life, she thrived.

He would relapse, he was sure, perhaps as long

as he lived. The idea wasn't an easy one to process.
What *was* becoming more and more easy? Believing that he could thrive one day, as well.

Gavin realized he'd been lying in Child's Pose
for some time. He blinked, pushing up from the
heels of his hands. "Frex?" he called.

"Kitchen!"

He gained his feet, getting up from the mat.
Padding in the direction of her voice, he reached
back for his neck, rolling it on his shoulders. More
range of motion. He rounded one of the columns
that separated one room from the other in the open
floor plan. He saw the low table in his path and
managed to skirt it at the last second.

She was busy at the island slicing fruit. "Feel
better?"

"I felt good before," he noted. "But yeah."

She extended a hand. He plucked the red strawberry
from her. "These are from Briar. She sent
me a basket a few days ago."

"I've got some fig jam I need to give you,"
Gavin recalled, popping the strawberry into his
mouth. His taste buds savored the fresh bite of
nature's bounty. "Mmm." He beckoned for more.
She obliged. When he growled and reached again,
she quipped, "Just open your mouth. I can bean
them in."

"Or I could just…" He scooped into the bowl
on the counter and grabbed a handful.

"Hey!" she said. He'd eaten them before she

could retrieve them. "Okay, at this rate, we're never going to have oatmeal."

"No control," he claimed, mouth full. "Not when I'm this famished. And oatmeal?" Lowering his brow, he walked to her refrigerator. "Woman, when you have an eight-hour religious experience, you gotta cap it off with a hearty breakfast." He opened the door and hunched over to peer inside. "Where're the eggs?"

"By now, I hope they're baby chicks."

"A hard-lovin' man's got to have the protein. That's the point of a meat drawer."

"Is it?" she asked. She eyed him blandly as he showcased the bottom drawer by sliding it open then closed, then open again. "There's quinoa. Hummus. Peanut butter. All rich in protein."

He shut the fridge, dejected, and braced his hands on his hips. "You were raised on a farm."

"What's your point?" She walked away. "I bought some canned salmon a while back for Prometheus. I can make patties and give you some whole wheat rotini with black onions. Would that be better for you?"

"You're giving me dog food." He glanced around. "Where is the beast, by the way?"

"We were at the farm yesterday when Harmony talked me into going out," Mavis said from inside the pantry. "I left him there since Mom and Dad were spending the night in with Bea."

Gavin waited until she reappeared. He watched

as she bent to retrieve a saucepan from one of the cupboards. As she filled it with water from the sink, he closed the gap between them. "Did he, ah…miss me at all?"

In the light beaming clearly through the windows around them, he could see her as well as he had in the shower. Her lips curved. "He'll be happy to see you. I'll be happy when he stops loafing." She took the pot to the stove on the island. "It's pathetic."

He leaned back against the sink. "Did you loaf some?"

"You'd like that, wouldn't you?" she teased. A quick *fwume* accompanied the switch of the gas burner.

Gavin lifted two fingers, taking his time drawing the sweep of her hair back. Gingerly, he tucked it securely behind the small cup of her ear before sliding his knuckles against the underside of her jaw in a featherweight caress. "It might be better for you if you didn't. I couldn't blame you for cutting your losses and moving on."

"I thought your time away would've healed all that nonsense," she said with a frown.

He dropped his hand from her skin, regretful. "I don't come with a warranty or any guarantee. I'm covered up in warning labels. At some point or another, I'm going to burden you."

"Warning labels don't scare me. I said once that

the people who matter will never see you as a burden, didn't I?"

"Doesn't mean I'm not," he said, refusing to budge on that point.

Mavis kept frowning at him. Then she shifted her body to face him and kissed his mouth.

His blood tuned in instantly to the offering, even if the kiss felt like a rebuttal. When she pulled away, they were both breathless. "I want every part of you," she stated. "That entails *everything*, Gavin. Even the dark side of you."

"I don't want the dark side." His lips had that bee-stung feel. He licked them, trying to gather her taste further inward. "I'm hardly going to hang it on your shoulders."

Her palm fit over the neck of the wolf on his chest. "You know why you're here, Gavin? Because *I* need you. That includes your dark parts."

Gavin swallowed. Nobody had ever come out and said it like that. *I need you.* He wondered if anyone had ever thought it.

To be needed...the concept was potent. "How long does that have to boil?" he asked of the rotini.

"I don't know. Ten minutes?"

"Good." He picked her up by the waist. Turning her away from the island, he set her on the counter safely away from the cooking eye.

"We're out of condoms," she said as she spread her legs.

He stepped into the vee and roped his arms

around her waist, boosting her forward on the counter. He brought her torso flush against his. "I'll take care of it. I'll take care of you. Just hold on."

CHAPTER THIRTEEN

AN ECCENTRIC LADY'S birthday would not be complete without a three-tiered cake, a steaming pot of gumbo and a menagerie worthy of a circus.

"Frexy."

Mavis nearly smiled at the name trickling down the back of her neck, thanks to Gavin's close press against her from behind. She ladled sparkling pink punch into a cup. "Yes?"

"Am I hallucinating, or is that a camel?"

She didn't have to look in the direction he indicated. "His name's Melvin. Don't go near him. He loves women, hates men and is liable to take a bite out of you if you get too close." Pivoting, she handed him the cup. "Not that I blame him."

He was still squinting in the direction of the paddock. "For man-hating or for trying to get a nibble?"

Mavis lifted a coy shoulder, scanning him. He looked good enough to taste. Sipping her bubbly, Mavis noted his demeanor. The crowd was thick. The slight odor of sulfur wafted by. Someone had handed out sparklers, though it wasn't yet dusk.

She noticed that Gavin had kept a fair distance from the cookers.

There was color in him, though. Lately his cheeks hadn't looked nearly as hollow as they had before. He was clean-shaven, which took her back to her balcony that morning where she'd stood with her legs on either side of his, leaning over his lap with a razor.

It was their newly minted Sunday ritual. Before breakfast, sometimes even before bathing, they took tea out into the river stillness. He watched her perform her morning yoga sequence. Sometimes she lured him into a short round of meditation. It was difficult getting him to sit still long enough… or to close his eyes. Today, she'd peeked at him two minutes in. His eyes had been open, on her, where she'd seen brushfires and electrical storms. At a glance, she knew he'd forgotten his mantra.

Meditation had shifted swiftly into a lesson in tantra. Right there. Out in the open.

It was a shame that now, here at Errol's, all the morning's relaxation was vanishing by the minute. She cupped the underside of his wrist. "Hey."

He blinked. His gaze pinged to hers, direct.

She did smile, softly. The muscles around his jaw were tense. In a moment, the nerve at his temple would start doing jumping jacks. "Close your eyes," she whispered.

A flicker of uncertainty crossed him. In a second, it was gone. He shifted his feet slightly, exhaled slowly and lifted his chin as his eyes closed.

Mavis licked her lips. *Trust.* Her pulse tripped at the raw display. Taking a quiet breath of her own, she stepped into him, like she was about to hug him. She spanned her arms around his waist. Through his shirt, she found the dip of his spine. Pressing her fingertips to either side of it, she kneaded, slowly. Using circles, she made small movements along his spine. Horizontal. Then winding. She began to travel up his back, giving every vertebra the same treatment. Tipping her face to his, she tried to read it. "Stop me if I hit a bad spot."

He didn't stop her. As she began to progress back down his spine, she touched her nose to his collar. Then the glossy button near his sternum. She didn't rest until her hands reached the top of his sacrum. There, she firmed them.

"Mmm," he hummed favorably.

"Not too loud, Tarzan," she said with a smile. "We'll scandalize all the people Zelda wants to scandalize herself."

"What people?"

"That's more like it." Her hands flirted with his belt before venturing up the back of his shirt again in a tender sweep.

"You won't have to do this every time we go out," he vowed.

Because she was feeling especially bold, she ignored the milling party guests around them and skimmed his jaw, which was tense no longer, with a kiss. "Here's to bringing you back and staying upwind with you in the meantime."

He took both of her hands in his, cupping the back of her fingers against his palms and raising them. There was a Creole-style band parading from one end of the wide lot to the other, blaring brass and thumping bass. For a moment, she thought he'd slide them both into the jaunty two-step. "You'd probably rather be over there with the guest of honor or mingling with everybody else."

Mavis snorted. "The guest of honor is currently entertaining what appears to be a small herd of half-dressed Dothraki men. She has no need for me."

"How does Errol feel about the Dothrakis?"

"Fine, I expect," Mavis guessed. "Why would he have invited them otherwise?"

"And Melvin, the man-hating camel."

"Actually, Melvin lives here." Mavis nodded at Gavin's surprise. "Errol's wife's passion was animals. She brought home strays and rescues on a regular basis. Errol eventually instituted an animal sanctuary here on the homestead. It was their retirement project."

"And he kept it up after she…"

"Yet another reason he never sold the house," she explained. "It would've been difficult relocating all of them."

"I understand why Melvin would have a hard time finding a new home."

"Melvin's better at parties," Mavis said with a nod.

"Bachelorette parties?"

She laughed. "I'll walk with you back to the dog kennels. I bring Prometheus back here all the time for play dates. Errol rescued him and the rest of his litter from the pound when they were just a few months old. They've all found forever homes except Lola, his sister. Anyway, I think you'll enjoy Tony most. He's been here since the beginning, like Melvin."

"You're going to tell me Tony's a tiger, aren't you?"

"Nope." Mavis grinned. "He's a wolf."

"She's not going to fix you."

The man hadn't sneaked up on Gavin. Gavin had felt him coming toward the viewing pane of the wolf enclosure. Mavis was inside with several other dogs, rolling, running, chasing. He hadn't known she could look so childlike.

It took him a jarring second to match the rusty tenor to the man. Gavin turned his head and took a good look just to be certain. Sure enough, it was Errol. Driving hat. Fading stature. Sun-blotched face. Gavin glanced again through the glass and braced his feet apart, cleared his throat. "I know."

Errol measured him sideways. "She'll try. The ones who love us…they always try to fix the broken bits. It's through them we see a pathway to something better. Something balanced. In the end, it's time. It's understanding ourselves. Recognizing what needs to be changed and achieving it day by day, even if it is by increments."

Gavin nodded. "Yeah. I think I got that."

"It's not easy finding one, either," Errol said thoughtfully. "Who doesn't scare easily."

Gavin barked a laugh.

"It took a while for me to see it and respect it— that she loved me, even when I was unlovable."

Mavis was petting the wolf now, ruffling his scruff, talking to him. Gavin's heart turned into a snare with a brisk march. He swallowed. "How much of it was about you, though—the issues— and not her?"

"Too damn much. My wife sacrificed. Zelda does, too. She's sacrificing right now."

"You threw her the world's most eccentric birthday party. You even invited the Momoa triplets."

"But I'm not there. She puts on a good face. It's what she's best at. That doesn't stop me from wishing I was the sort of man she didn't need to put on a good face for."

Gavin's mouth tipped into a frown. "Do you ever stop thinking they'd be better off if you set them free?"

Errol loosened a breath, his already sagging shoulders sagging a mite further. "No. If you do it right, though, the question does get quieter inside your mind."

Outside of the SEALs, had Gavin ever really

done anything right? Had anything mattered as much as this?

"Now," Errol said, "ask me if it was worth it."

Gavin met Errol's clear blue stare. "Was it?"

"Yes," he said. He didn't blink. "Hell, yes. I wouldn't be what I am if not for them."

Gavin lowered his head. Slowly, he slid his hands into his pockets where they fisted.

After several moments, Errol said, quietly, "War might never leave us. It can make you—it can break you. But it's not who you are. It's up to you who that son of a bitch is."

A half smile grew across the rough plane of Gavin's face, stretching the scars. It felt tight, but good. "Thanks."

Errol made a noise in his throat. "If you don't call her out of there, she'll spend the night with the beast."

"Why does she do that?" Gavin asked out of curiosity. And genuine perplexity. His eyes lit on Mavis again and the wolf beside her. "Why does she love the baddies as much as she does?"

Errol adjusted his driving hat and turned to leave. "It's a fool man who tries to figure out why a woman is the way she is. Especially ones like we got."

Alone, Gavin let the vet's wisdom turn in his mind.

Mavis lifted her eyes to him. When she beckoned, he moved to join her.

His cell phone rang. He frowned at the caller ID: Tiffany.

"Shit," he muttered. Looking to Mavis again, he saw her pause. Her head tilted, asking what was wrong.

He hesitated, then nodded toward the exit.

She must have read him like a fax sheet because there was concern and perception all over her face.

Gavin turned away from the viewing glass. He waited until he was on the other side of the door and it had closed. "Yeah?" he answered.

"What is the meaning of this?"

He held the phone a few inches from his ear. His mother was seething, and he knew why. She pounded through the speaker, and he heard nothing of the glacial tones he had grown used to hearing. She raged, cursing.

He walked away from the building behind him to put distance between the barking that could be heard from inside. He cut a path away from the party, walking across a long green field toward the distant fence line that marked the eastern boundary of Errol's expansive piece of property. No one would think to look for him here.

"This is because of them! You did this because of them—and that place! It's warped your mind, just like it did when you were younger!"

"Let me stop you right there," Gavin interjected. His eardrums were tired of being railroaded. "This time I'm going to talk and you're going to listen.

When I'm done, I'm hanging up and you and I are done, for good, since the papers clearly haven't told you that already."

"The papers. They're nothing. I'll take them to court. I'll take *you* to court. You have no evidence—"

"I have plenty of evidence," Gavin said. "Plenty of witnesses, too. You see, Mom, that's what happens when you harass someone for so long. You get careless, you get emotional and you screw up. Just like you did with Dad and Briar all those years ago."

"You know nothing about that."

"I know everything," he told her. "All the dirty little details you left out of the retellings. I know about the break-in. I know how before you harassed Briar for her real estate, your father, Douglas, harassed her mother for it. You even confessed to the crime, Dad says. And you got lucky. You messed with good people and they let you get away with it. But I've been evaluating the situation and I've decided that I'm not near as good as them. I'm done looking over my shoulder. I'm tired of you using me to take shots at the people who care about me, the way you never did."

"One goddamn piece of paper isn't enough to keep a mother away from her son," Tiffany charged.

"It wouldn't be," Gavin said, ruminating over the cease-and-desist his father's friend, Byron

Strong, and a team of lawyers had helped him draft and send to his mother, "if it weren't for that last PI you sent for me."

Silence jammed into the connection. After all of Tiffany's noise, the quiet was more deafening than the chatter. "Do you even remember his name?"

"I signed his damn checks, didn't I?" she hissed.

"So you know he's part of a pattern?" Gavin asked. "Once I tracked him down with some friends who trace phone records in DC, I learned that young Corbin Walker is an apprentice at his family's private investigation office in Jacksonville, Florida. Not far from that place in St. Augustine you were bragging about last time we met."

"So what?"

"So not only did I get good and acquainted with Corbin. I got to know three of his brothers, his stepfather and two uncles. All of whom, after learning how you sent Corbin off the books to track me down, informed me that they had all worked off the books for you at some point or another and were finally able to come clean about the things you've done through the years to me and a slew of other folks you've conned."

Again, silence on the other end. Gavin let it stretch for a few seconds more. Bittersweet seconds. "It seems you can buy illegalities with sex. But when you mess with one of their own, a young gun like Corbin especially, you can't buy loyalty."

"They'll only incriminate themselves by coming forward."

Gavin had reached the fence. He turned to lean against it, looking back on the party lights. "They've got friends. In law enforcement, as it turns out. They're willing to deal if the Walker boys testify."

"This is insanity."

"No," Gavin said, the scowl wearing into the bones of his face. "Tracking your stings through the years, *that* was insanity. All those people you've tricked or sued out of their hard-earned property and earnings… It doesn't help that you're Douglas Howard's daughter. You won't get away from his reputation. You won't get away from everything either of you have done. It hasn't all come to light, but it will. Like dominoes."

"Unless…?" Tiffany asked.

Looking for the bottom line. Always trolling for the bottom life. "I can't promise it won't come against you, especially if the Walkers decide to come forward without me. They can still do that, and I won't stop them. But for me, you're going to do two things."

"What are they?" she snapped when he paused. "Let's do this and be done with it."

Gavin almost couldn't believe it. She was willing to negotiate. His freedom was a few ultimatums away. "You leave my family alone. Dad, Briar, Bea, Harmony. The others, too. The Brackens, the Leightons, and every extended family and friend they call their own. Also, Benji."

"Benji's *dead*."

"His dad," Gavin said. "You said you had a source there. Not anymore."

"You do cover your bases."

He had to. She'd made him. "Finally…" Gavin started to pace in jutting strides. "I don't want to see or hear from you ever again. No more visits. No texts, calls or emails. You won't speak my name from this point forward. In fact, you never had a son. You're dead to me and I'm dead to you. Is that clear?"

"Profoundly." She was back to her glacial tones. "I won't be there for you when that place you're so desperate to be part of and those people you think you belong to teach you everything I've tried so hard to show you."

"There's something else I've learned," Gavin said. "That I get to choose where I go and where I stay, who I talk to and who I walk beside, who I am and what I want to be. I choose all of it. Oh, and I keep my promises. I promise you that if you don't follow through with everything we've talked about, I'll make it my mission to have you locked up for as long as it takes you to get the message."

"You strike a hard bargain," she replied. "A heartless one, too. I wish I could be proud. You may be cutting ties with me, but you'll always be my son."

"I'll live with it," he pledged. "It'll be easy because I won't have to live with you. Not anymore." He paused once more. Then, for emphasis, "Goodbye, Mom."

"ARE YOU SURE it's all right that we sleep here?"

Mavis folded the shirt she'd worn to the party on the chair in the corner of the guest bedroom of Errol's house. She unclasped the earrings from one ear and set them on the bed table next to the double bed where she and Gavin would be crashing for the night. "Why not?" She watched him tug off his jeans, pausing to dig the items out of the pockets. The long blade went to the surface of his nightstand, along with his phone and wallet. She saw him frown at the phone for a moment before moving on to his cash clip and change. Looking away, Mavis undid the clasps on the other ear. "I thought you said you liked the place."

"That was before you said we'd be sleeping here," he pointed out.

The earrings clinked in the trinket dish next to the lamp. Amused, she plopped onto the bed. It gave a satisfying *creeeak*. She bounced once, twice before lifting her ankle to her knee to unzip her boot. She was floating a bit—on punch, and on the evening's festivities. Errol knew how to give his Zelda a party, that was for sure. Also, her floating was one of the reasons they wouldn't be driving back to the river tonight. She couldn't risk it, even for Gavin's wariness. "It isn't that I told you this is one place we've confirmed paranormal activity, is it?"

"No," he claimed.

Mavis pressed her lips together, unzipping the other boot before toeing the both of them off. She stretched out on the bed, head on the pillow, toes pointed to the ornate footboard. Stretching, she purred. "Hmm. Well, that's a letdown."

"How?" he asked.

She tilted her head in study. He did look good in briefs. "If you were nervous about making contact, it means you've come to believe in ghosts after all."

The bed creaked again as he dropped to it. It dipped, making her tilt in his direction. He pressed his hands into the bed. "They still make beds this flimsy?"

"No," she said. "This one's at least fifty years old. Probably bought with the house. You dodged what I said there."

"I know I did." He lounged beside her, hesitating when he heard the protest from the springs. "Was it always like this?" he asked. "Always noisy?"

"I'm willing to bet nobody had discreet hanky-panky back in the day," Mavis drawled.

He glanced at her. A slow, wide grin spread across his mouth. "Mavis Bracken. I do believe you're tipsy."

"I told you I do indulge," she said, lifting a hand in a fanciful motion. The flash of her rings distracted her. Gold and silver clashing and shimmering. "Once every blue moon or so. Besides, my friend Zelda only turns…seventy-something-or-other every so often."

He gave a short chuckle. He reached up to trace the point of her chin. Then he seemed to indulge, too, skimming the back of his knuckles across her opposite cheek.

Mavis shivered warmly. "You're getting me all tingly…and we can't have hanky-panky. Unless we want the birthday girl and her main man to know all about it."

"Like they're not doing it?" he said.

Mavis's mouth formed into an *O*. "You think?"

"Well, yeah. Birthday sex." He raised a brow. "The older you get, the more necessary it is. You never know how many more birthdays you have until…"

"So," she said, turning further into him and nuzzling, "it's like a celebration—of life."

"Yeah," he said, smiling.

She tugged at his shirt. "Does it have to be *your* birthday?"

Gavin seemed to think about it. He pursed his lips. "Well, funeral sex is also a celebration of life. Usually, the people doing it aren't dead."

"No," she agreed sagely. "Because that's not right."

"*So* not right."

"Gavin?"

He turned his face toward hers on the pillow. Reaching over his head with the opposite arm, he dipped his fingertips into the hair on the crown of her head. They massaged lightly across her scalp. "Yeah, baby?"

She saw the shadows, even now after it was all over. The chaos of the party. Whatever it was that had reinforced those shadows after their visit to the wolf enclosure. After the phone call he'd yet to mention. *Who called you? What did they want? Are you hiding anything?*

She forced the last question aside, and all the others that hinted at suspicion. *Trust.* If this was going to work…she had to trust him. "Is everything all right?" She settled for a whisper.

His eyes cleared of repose. He blinked, caught. His breath rushed over her face before he turned to look at the ceiling. "Everything's fine." Shifting away from her, he switched off the lamp on his side.

Mavis sat up in tandem with him so they could discard the shams and decorative pillows and get under the quilt. She stayed quiet, sensing a moratorium on personal talk. Sighing, she closed her eyes, laying one hand over the other on the quilt's edge.

Gavin's voice ventured into the bedroom quiet. "Mavis?"

"Yes?"

"Is that your hand?"

She glanced down at her hands on her breast-bone. "Where?"

"On my thigh."

Turning her head to him, she saw him white against the cream-colored pillowcase. "No."

He didn't so much get out of bed as leap out. The bed shrieked at the sudden thrashing of limbs. A thump on the other side told her he'd landed hard on the wood. "What the hell?" he exclaimed. *"What the hell?"*

"Don't move, you meatball!" she cried, feeling along the now-empty covers.

He peered over the side of the bed, incredulous. *"What?"*

"Get back in," she said, motioning to him quickly. "Let's see if it happens again!"

His jaw hung loose. "I get felt up by a ghost and you want me to get back in the goddamn bed?"

"Well, what choice do you have?" she asked. "Are you going to sleep on the floor?"

"There's a couch somewhere," he said, climbing to his feet. He braced his hand against the wall. "I'll sleep outside with Melvin to avoid that again." He pointed to the bed in accusation.

"And leave me here all alone?"

"Oh, don't do that," he said, wincing.

"You can go," she decided, slinking back down into the covers. "But I'm not moving."

He shook his head. "How does this not bother you?"

She lifted a shoulder. "Just used to the idea, I suppose."

Shaking his head again, he stood mutely in indecision.

It took several minutes, but he got back in bed. Mavis stemmed a smile. "We can switch sides."

"I don't want her touching you, either," he said. "Scoot over."

She did, moving to the edge so he could lie in the middle. She turned on her side and he spooned fast against her back.

She could feel the tension in his arms across her middle. "If she paws at me again..."

"What makes you think it's a she?"

He stiffened further. "You said it was the wife. Errol's wife."

"That was just a guess. There's no way to confirm that."

"It touched me in a familiar way."

"Even so, that doesn't necessarily mean it's a female," she reasoned.

He spoke thinly now. "Thanks for that."

Mavis took pity on him. He was planked against her, hard as a board, and she could feel his heartbeat drilling against her spine. As silly as it was, he was here for her protection. She shifted her hand back to his hip.

He jerked and made a noise in his throat.

She swallowed a laugh. "It's me this time. Just

relax. Errol says as long as the presence has been here, it's never not been benign."

"Did it feel him up, too?"

"Pretend it's just you and me," she told him instead. She kept her voice down to a monotone. "Pretend we're back at the river house, in my bed... Breathe into me."

He did, once. Then again. Long respirations that gradually eased his tension.

Good, she thought. Her pride in him, her meditation student, her lover, ballooned. She rubbed his arm, dragging the tips of her fingers through the hair that grew there. His heart rate was slowing. His arms had loosened their grip. Still, she sensed that he wouldn't sleep even if she left the light on.

After a while of him breathing, her stroking, neither sleeping, she murmured, "Talk to me. If it helps."

"About what?" he asked, his lips close enough to trickle the words across the nerves of her ear.

"Anything," she said. "Whatever crosses your mind. Just talk to me."

She heard his swallow. He was silent again for so long she thought he wouldn't talk at all.

"I haven't been honest with you."

Mavis felt her lips part. She licked them, unable to stop the reverberations of dread inside her. Her stomach tightened. "Oh?" she replied.

"I told you I went to see Thomas Zaccoe but

nothing about any of the other places I went while I was gone."

"Want to tell me about those places now?"

"Yeah. But first…my mother would've come after you. She would've come after us. She saw we were together, at Zelda's. I've never had a healthy relationship. Nothing long term, anyway. Over the years she had me followed, more times than I know. Whenever I found myself sticking to one place or person for any length of time, I'd look up and see a man or a car tailing me."

"She stalked you?" she asked.

"She liked to hire out. Private investigators. Muscle. Anybody she could manipulate with the right amount of money or…"

"Has she had you followed recently?" she asked.

"I caught on to her man a couple weeks into my stay at the river. That day it was raining and you found me on your dock."

"You were bleeding," she remembered. "Did *that* person hurt you?"

"Not intentionally. He was jumpy, almost ran over Prometheus. I talked at him enough to get him to back off."

"Why?" she asked. "Why can't she just move on and let you do the same?"

"I think, growing up, she was a lot like me."

"She's *nothing* like you," she said, her hate for Tiffany palpable.

"Her old man was a lot like who she is now. He

moved her around, building his real estate port-folio. She never really had a home. Based on my knowledge of Douglas, I *know* she never had a happy home. My dad tried to make her happy, but I don't think she knew happiness when she saw it. Even after she had me..."

She'd stopped stroking him and was gripping him. She'd asked him to talk to her, so she let his voice fill the blanks.

"I didn't know what she did to Dad until years later, how much she'd hurt him just to establish a sense of control and self. Control was important to her. She used me to control him. She tried to control others."

"Did she at least try to be a mother with you?" she asked. "No questions? No bottom line?"

He thought about it. "She used to tell me it was us against the world, that nothing could hurt us as long as we were a team. But whenever I reached out for anyone else—it didn't matter who it was... friends, family—I'd see a change. She'd coddle me after, appeal to my better nature. As I got older, I saw the truth of her, though. I saw the bitterness and the drive. I was in high school when I told her I wanted to move in with Dad so that I could graduate with Kyle and my friends in Fairhope..."

"What happened?" she asked, wary of the si-lence now.

"She hit me. Then she tried coddling me, prom-ised she'd never do it again. By that point, she'd broken enough promises for me to know the truth. I was smart enough to walk away."

"She kept coming at you," she said, "in other ways."

"Every way she could," he said with a grim nod. "Until it wasn't just her anymore who didn't know what a happy home was. It was me, too."

Mavis felt the anger coil into her fingers. She had to take several breaths to empty it out. "Was it her who called you tonight?"

"Yes. That week, before I went to see Thomas, I had a cease-and-desist letter drafted. With some help from Dad and friends of his and mine, we found enough evidence to incriminate her."

"I can't imagine she was happy."

"Livid."

"Can she find a way around it?" Mavis asked. If she knew anything about Tiffany, it was how tricky the woman was.

"Not on my terms. Not unless she wants to lose everything."

"She's already lost everything. She threw all of it away with you." She'd been paying attention to more than just Gavin's words. "You've won."

A pause. "Yes."

He didn't sound like someone who had. Because Tiffany Howard would always be his mother, Mavis thought, no matter what she was. "You're wondering why you were never enough," she said, carefully. "You're thinking that if you were enough, she would have dialed back the bitterness and the anger, in some small way at least."

"Maybe."

"You must know it has nothing to do with who you are and everything to do with who she is? A parent who can use a child the way she used you isn't a parent at all. The fault, the sickness, lies with her alone. It has nothing to do with you." Stroking him again, she tweaked her neck until she could see the hardness of his face. "I know who you are. Remember?"

He nodded, once.

"You're you," she told him. "That's enough."

"For you?"

"For anyone."

He turned so that his nose grazed her cheek. "And you?"

"Yes," she whispered, wanting to hold him fast in the dark. "Me."

"Even if I'm a SEAL with more mommy issues than Carrie?"

"I think poor Carrie's got you beat." Pivoting on the bed until her front was pressed to his, she placed her hands on either side of his face. "She's gone now," she said. At his nod, she pressed her lips to the scars on his cheek. "You're still here." She kissed his other cheek.

His touch rose to her chin, tilting her mouth to his. They kissed in slow, luring increments—until they were both good and lost.

His exhale was ragged as he pulled back enough to press his brow to hers. "Mmm. Since we're both here…"

She smiled. "Uh-huh?"

"…and we're pretending that it's you and me in this room—nobody else?"

"Nobody."

"What do you say we get on with it?"

"With the birthday sex?" she queried, smug. "Hanky-panky? The celebration of life?"

"All that," he confirmed.

"Condom?"

He jerked his chin toward the wallet he'd left on the nightstand.

She ranged across him, nabbing the wallet. His hands on her waist pulled her back to him. She straddled his waist, beaming as her navel buffed against his and she found that his excitement was as precipitous and high-reaching as her own. She unfolded the wallet, spied the handy packet hidden in the fold… "Good man," she crooned.

He took the wallet, tossed it aside before bringing her down to him. "Come 'ere," he said.

"Last thing." She tugged the quilt up until it was all the way over their heads. Under the intimate enclosure, she took his kiss and his hands and they both folded into each other until the rest of the world was forgotten.

CHAPTER FOURTEEN

MAVIS HAD LEFT Prometheus with her parents again. In the morning after they said goodbye to Zelda and Errol (and Errol's ghost), Mavis and Gavin stopped at the farm to pick up her dog.

"He likes you sleeping at my place," Mavis said.

Gavin had spent the drive trying not to watch her. She made it difficult. Her face was bare, her freckles bright, and he didn't think he'd seen the smile fall from her mouth since they woke.

He feathered his fingers through her hair. There was sterling silver at her ear. He traced the shape of the metal. "I wouldn't blame him if he wanted you all to himself."

She glanced at him briefly. "Ditto." Her lips turned in on themselves as the road drew her attention again. "He's involved in this just as much as we are."

Gavin caught her drift. "I don't plan on things changing for the time being."

"I could let that slide," she mused. "Or I could ask what you mean by it exactly."

"What?"

"'For the time being,'" she answered. She shrugged. "What does that mean?"

The smile wasn't lost, but it didn't have to be for Gavin to know that she was set on this point. "What do you want it to mean?"

"I don't expect you to commit to us in the long term."

"No?"

She shook her head. "The long term's new to you, just like civilian life. I want you to find out who you are. Then decide if you want us to be part of that."

"You'd wait for me to figure it all out?"

She nodded, reflective.

His hand was braced on the back of her seat. It flexed to touch her. He stopped it. It took some effort but he stopped looking at her. If he looked at her any longer, he wondered if he'd be able to keep himself together.

She parked in her parents' drive. Neither of them said anything as they got out. He met her around the hood of the car. Before she could start for the house, he took her hand. She stopped and he drew her to him.

He'd nearly drowned as a SEAL candidate during Hell Week. Kissing Mavis was like that. Only in reverse.

Prometheus interrupted, greeting them with an excited yip. They broke apart just in time for the dog to finish his run. He dived at Gavin, then at her. As Mavis took her turn, Gavin's attention veered to the man near the side of the house where Prometheus had come from.

Kyle stood with his hands on his hips, frowning at the both of them in condemnation. Gavin straightened, planting himself in front of her.

James came around the house, too, saw the stare-down in progress. He proceeded across the drive. "Mavis."

"Dad," she said. "I hoped you'd be here. Zelda sent home a ton of shrimp."

James looked from her to Gavin. "You're just now getting back from the party?"

At least the older guy looked more curious than hostile. And because Gavin held James in respect, he nodded. "Yes, sir."

Mavis had retrieved the pot of shrimp from her back seat. "Here," she said. "I figured Mom could break it up and take it to Flora, split it among Olivia and Briar, too. There's enough to feed an army."

"That's fine, sweetheart," James said kindly. "Why don't you take it into the house? Then you and Prometheus can head on home."

"What do you mean?" Mavis looked to Gavin. "You fixed my canoe. I thought the two of us could take it downriver and try to find the eagle our neighbors say they saw earlier in the week."

"Later," James told her. "Right now, I think your man has business to attend to."

"He does?" Mavis asked, growing defensive when she saw Kyle, too, hovering in the distance.

Gavin squeezed her hand. "It's all right."

"You don't have to stay here with them," Mavis told him.

Gavin read James's expression. Yes, he did. "I'll get a ride home."

Mavis frowned at the three of them. "Here," she said, hefting the pot into her father's arms. "Take this." She stepped in front of Gavin, exchanging a silent look with him before she let go of his hand and returned to the driver's door.

Gavin held the air in his lungs as Mavis drove off. James waited until she'd disappeared down the wooded lane before clapping Gavin on the shoulder and turning him to walk in Kyle's direction. "Get in the truck, boys. I'll take this shrimp inside."

"Why?" Kyle wanted to know.

James answered, "Trust me, son. It's time we took a drive."

JAMES PICKED THE AIRFIELD, Gavin knew, because it was closed on Sunday and it was isolated. He let Kyle drive, Gavin sensed, because he didn't want the quarrelsome navy boys sitting elbow-to-elbow in the cab of the single-cab pickup with the Bracken-Savitt Aerial label on the side. The crop dusters were tucked inside their hangars and nothing broke the heat of the tarmac until the pickup's shadow swept across it and came to rest near the end of the first runway.

Kyle got out first. Gavin stepped out next, letting James disembark, too. The three of them came to stand at the back of the truck.

James lowered the bed and made a come-hither motion. "Let's have 'em."

Kyle waited a beat, then asked, "What?"

"Your weapons," James answered. "Any firepower and sharp objects you have on your person; I want it here first." He knocked on the tailgate.

Gavin hesitated. He saw Kyle do the same. The latter sighed, then reached warily around to the small of his back. He lifted his trusty Colt into the air.

James made the motion again. "Gimme."

Kyle unracked the pistol before relinquishing it. When James looked to Gavin, he handed him the long blade he kept at his hip.

"Very good." James placed the weapons in the bed and closed the tailgate with a bang that echoed into empty air. "All right. Here's the dilemma. You two used to be thick as brothers. For some reason or other, this changed through the years. It's a shame because our families are close-knit and they're about to be closer with the wedding next month. But now we've got another hang-up on our hands."

When James stopped, Gavin took the initiative. "That is?"

Kyle answered. "It's Mavis."

James nodded. "Mavis."

"Your problem isn't your sister," Gavin told him, resigned. "It's me. I'm the problem."

"You don't understand," James said, shaking his head. "The short of it is that she's in love with you."

Kyle cursed.

Gavin glanced from one man to the other. "How do you figure that?"

James lowered his eyes, solemn. "She's her mother's daughter. I've spent the last thirty years staring at the same spark in Adrian. There's no mistakin' it." He gauged Gavin's reaction. "She hasn't told you."

He was sweating, his mouth was suddenly parched, and the heat had nothing to do with either. He shook his head.

James nodded. "I won't ask how you feel in return. Hell, I won't even ask what your intentions are. I saw enough to know you're here for her, temporarily or not. What I will say is that whatever's going on between you and Mavis has little chance of survival if the two of you—" he pointed between them "—keep feuding. You may not think so. She may not, either. But nobody can get away from the fact that we're all in each other's pockets. And I don't think any of us are going anywhere for the time being. Mavis looks happy. I'd like her to stay that way. So…" He gestured them toward one another. "Let's do this."

"Do what exactly?" Kyle demanded.

"Well, that's up to you," James decided. "You want to talk it out, talk. You want to fight it out, fight. I'll be the ref. Just get it done." He checked his watch. "There's shrimp at the house and I want to be back before lunch."

"You'll stand there and let us punch it out?" Kyle asked, surprised.

"If you must," James said with a shrug. "You want rules, here they are. No killing each other. That definitely wouldn't make Mavis happy. No firing, no stabbing… That's why I have these." He patted the tailgate. "No eye-gouging. And no broken bones."

Gavin waited for Kyle to move. The man just frowned at him. "Are we doing this or…?"

"Depends," Kyle said. "Did you sleep with her?"

Gavin raised a brow. "Little bit, yeah."

The tension shuttered between them. The air took on the consistency of gunpowder. Kyle's death stare was enough to light it. "How long?" he wanted to know.

Gavin almost smiled. "You know that night with all of us at the tavern?"

"Since then," Kyle said, not questioning. Challenging.

"Since then," Gavin confirmed.

Kyle lips firmed together. "Why?"

"What?"

"Why her?" he wanted to know. "Why did it have to be Mavis?"

Gavin measured him closely. "If you think it's to punish you in some way, you're wrong."

"No?"

"It's got nothing to do with you," Gavin told him. "Or Harmony. Or anybody else. It's real. It's ours. And there's not a damn thing you can do about it."

"Until you take a hike, you mean?" Kyle ventured. "Until you leave her, and then me and Dad and the rest of us have to mop up the mess you made? You did it to your parents. You've done it to Harmony and Bea. You've made it clear time and again that you're not tied here. No matter how many times I try to drag you back, you get one whiff of responsibility and you leave."

"Responsibility." Gavin ran his tongue over his teeth. "That's what you think I'm afraid of."

"It's the same with women," Kyle said, unabashed. "Things get serious, you hit the trail. They're lucky if you call them beforehand to let them know you're leavin'."

Gavin set his teeth. "You're a better monkey on a gun than you are at running your mouth."

"Now it's Mavis," Kyle argued. "*Mavis*. Before a few weeks ago, there wasn't much you wanted to do in that department other than trade barbs."

"Things change," Gavin said. "Roll with the punches."

"That's hard, not knowing when you might swing wide and hit her."

Bastard. "What the fuck is that supposed to mean?"

"The dog gnaws at the leash when he isn't freed fast enough to suit him."

"Keep talking," Gavin muttered. "I'm curious as to whether I could take you still or not."

"You want a rematch, you tell me, boo. I'll let you take first shot."

"I call her Frexy."

"What?" Kyle spat.

"Frexy," Gavin said, slower. "It's a mash-up. Between Freckles and Sexy."

Kyle barked a laugh that had nothing to do with mirth and everything to do with intention.

"Her ass is as plush as her mouth," Gavin detailed. "I make a fine study of it, every chance I get."

Kyle had stopped laughing.

Gavin pushed some more because, somehow, it wasn't enough. "I'm thinking of having a mold done. It's that good. And the noises she makes... Christ. Like an alley cat in he—"

Kyle came at him. Gavin raised his hands in fighter's stance. "Come on. You know you want it."

Kyle leaned into it, landing a fist in the face.

Gavin saw stars. He reeled. *Ow.* He managed

to keep his feet. Shaking his head clear, he reacquainted himself with the version of pain he'd always responded to best. Dancing back on his heels, he rolled his head on his shoulders. He was feeling springy, light on his toes. "Been saving that?"

"Like you wouldn't believe." Kyle came at him again.

Gavin opened up his senses. He felt more in tune with them. Maybe it was the chance at action. Like old times. He bent backward, letting the blow whistle in front of his nose. As the momentum took Kyle forward, Gavin circled around on his hips, planted his feet and tackled.

The tarmac didn't absorb either of them as Gavin took Kyle down. With a deft kick to the legs, Kyle flipped Gavin over his head. The somersault disoriented him for a hair's second. Long enough for Kyle to launch himself at him, switching things up. Gavin found himself pinned under Kyle's heavy torso, the shadow of an arm arcing over his head. He braced for the second jab.

"Don't go for the nose," James called from a distance. "You break it, it's your ass, son."

The fist hit Gavin in the jaw. "*Ah!* Son of a bitch!" He gritted his teeth, tasted blood. His voice grated from his chest. He brought his knee up, going for a low blow.

Kyle crumbled. "Ah. Harmony's going to kill you," he said.

A sinkhole opened up inside Gavin, wide and

treacherous. The pit ached and he realized how much he missed what had been. He missed when friendship had been as natural between them as breathing. Before the world took too much. "You always were a sucker," Gavin informed him, throwing him off. He spat blood on the tarmac.

"You're still an asshole." Kyle heaved himself slowly to his feet. For a second, he wasn't steady. That was something, at least.

James asked, "Y'all done already?"

Kyle shook his head, braced his hands on his hips. "You still haven't told me. What it is about her? Why're you willing to change for her of all people?"

It was simple, Gavin realized. He spread his arms. "I choose her. Just like I choose this place. Because I'm free to do so."

"What was stopping you before?" Kyle was almost at a bellow. His frustration at its peak. "When it was your parents. When it was your sister. What the hell was stopping you then?"

Gavin breathed hard into the lull. He shook his head, the answer obstructing him.

The frustration cleared slowly. Little by little, Kyle's gaze cleared. "Tiffany?"

Gavin swallowed. "The only thing I can remember choosing for myself freely was being a SEAL. I didn't answer to her then, or her influence. I answered to the higher-ups. The head shed. And I was good at it. It's the first thing I felt good at.

Maybe because it was the first thing I did for my-self, aside from being your friend."

"Why didn't you tell me that she got to you here?" Kyle asked. "Why didn't you tell me it was her keeping you at a distance?"

"Because that wasn't all of it. She told me I didn't belong. I believed her."

"What's changed?" Kyle asked.

"I know better now," Gavin said. "Mavis and Dad, even Briar have all shown me what I should've known better all along. This is home. This is where I want to be. So that's where I'm at."

"That's where you plan on staying?" Kyle asked.

"I want to stay," Gavin told him. "But your fa-ther's right. I can't love her and have this battle with you. You're a part of her, and damn it, you're family. You're a part of my family. I can't ignore that anymore. I don't even want to."

Kyle didn't seem to know what to say. James had fallen silent, trying to fade into the background. Gavin breathed through his teeth. He was starting to hurt. His knuckles. The back of his ribs where he'd hit the ground. All this was nothing compared to the hollows that years of misunderstandings had carved out on the inside of him.

Kyle shifted from one foot to the other, going briefly up to his toes then back down. Gavin imagined his balls would be sore for a while yet. "You still owe Harmony an apology. And Bea.

I'd like you to say everything you just said to the two of them."

Gavin nodded quickly. "Every word. She's long overdue an explanation."

"You really want to stay?"

Both Kyle and James seemed to want the answer to that one. Gavin looked off past the airfield to the outline of trees in the distance. The farm wasn't that far. They could walk it, over the wildflower fields, the secret hills and glades, past the secluded pond to the rambling house that had been as much a beacon to him as Hanna's. To refuse it all again and again had been torment.

He wouldn't hold himself back anymore.

"I want to stay," he said finally. It rang clear and he felt liberated to say it.

James nodded. "That'll about do it." He looked to Kyle. "Son?"

Kyle continued to stare at Gavin, emotions bleeding to the surface, everything else...history. "Let's go home," he said. A smile touched his hard jaw.

Gavin agreed, then cracked, "I hear there's shrimp."

THE LADIES' LUNCHEON in the dining room of Hanna's Inn was packed with onlookers and skeptics alike. It was where Zelda and Mavis had met the Tea & Biscuits Society for their monthly business meeting. The Paranormas didn't do many speaking engagements, but when they did, Zelda brought her Alfa Romeo and plenty of pizzazz.

She was an excellent storyteller. Mavis was perfectly fine holding up the analytical side of the equation. Even she had to admit, it was fun spectating when Zelda was at the lectern. Today she had chosen to recount her overnighter at the Myrtles Plantation, one of the most haunted residences in the country.

"That's when the Baccarat crystals started shaking above my head," Zelda recalled, holding her arms up, "and my flashlight battery drained. As I looked up at the window in front of me, I saw a reflection. It was the face of a young girl. There was a scent, the stench of burning. Like what you smell when a battery goes bad. It disappeared as Mavis found me. And there on the pane was the perfect imprint of a child's hand."

One cynical laugh split the quiet din of the room. A few of the ladies jumped in their seats, then looked around in resentment to the woman sitting closest to the kitchen door. She was well-dressed and coiffed with a heavily powdered face. "You expect us to believe that?"

"Of course," Zelda said without a hitch.

"It's malarkey," the lady said. A few of the society ladies laughed in a nervous quiver, as if happy she had spoken if only to break the grip of Zelda's ghost story.

Mavis spoke up. "The Myrtles Plantation has

been inspected by *National Geographic*. Their photographer snapped the infamous photograph of Chloe, the slave girl. There's both film and digital tools that have captured photographic anomalies. People who've chosen to spend the night there have heard cars arriving that aren't there and footsteps and voices, as if ghosts are arriving to a party. Not only does the plantation's history support Chloe's story, it tells of lively dinners that took place during what is classified as the Stirling era."

"Well, I certainly won't be paying it a visit," another lady in a large red hat said. She threw off a shudder.

"Because it's a scam," the cynic told her. "A ploy."

"If you think so," Mavis said with a shrug, ready to let it go.

Zelda had other plans. "How long have you lived in the South?"

The woman shrugged. "All my life."

"You've never seen, heard or felt anything you questioned? You never heard a lucid friend or relative tell a story like mine?"

"Honey," the lady drawled, "I don't think anyone's heard a story like yours." She looked to a quiet woman sitting in the corner. "I swear, Ivy. I blame you for putting us through this charade. Have we heard all the sensible speakers in the near South? Are we to the point where you have to call on entertainers?"

"I do love to entertain," Zelda intruded smoothly. "Though that's not what Mavis and I do."

"We take our work seriously," Mavis added.

The lady snorted but subsided into silence.

Mavis could all but hear Zelda's *I win* vibes. She glanced at the clock above the mantel. "We have time for one more question."

For a minute, no one spoke. Then the woman, Ivy, who had hired them for the hour, raised her hand. "What do you think it all means? Do you believe it speaks to the matter of our death or what happens after?"

Mavis found Zelda ceding the floor to her. "We both have our own ideas and understanding of what happens when we die, just as I'm sure each of you do," Mavis explained. "But no matter how long we do this, it doesn't change our belief that we're not meant to know everything."

"But you call yourself investigators," the cynic pointed out. "Isn't that the point—to know everything?"

"Some people make it their life's work to understand what happens after life," Mavis explained. "Our work is listening, challenging or dismissing paranormal activity. When we do come across something we can't debunk, we try to bring our client some understanding of what it might mean and who may be present."

"Mavis recently uncovered the identity of another of our Louisiana ghosts," Zelda boasted.

"She was able to connect the present owners of a house with a distant relative, the descendant of a Civil War–era kitchen girl named America. They're conducting DNA tests to confirm that the owner and the kitchen girl are distant relations. It may help clear up an important part of the descendant's heritage and bring America's spirit a little justice."

"Fascinating," Ivy said. She led the society's applause. Briar breezed into the dining room to open the drapes she had closed for effect. Then she and a maid began clearing the dessert plates as the ladies rose to mingle or file out.

"Thank you so much," Ivy said as she approached Mavis and Zelda at the head of the room. "I believe this is the most interesting meeting we've had in years."

"It was our pleasure," Zelda said. "Let us know and we'll come back. I have more stories and Mavis has more statistics."

"You make a convincing team," Ivy said. "I'm sorry about Edie. She's a hard case."

"Edie." Zelda's lips folded in disappointment. "I was hoping she was more of a Hildegard. Or a Hatshepsut."

"I don't give a hoot what she thinks. Our next ladies' retreat will involve a drive to St. Francisville and the Myrtles Plantation. I have a feeling attendance will be at an all-time high. I was wondering, too, if you had any titles you could recommend for our book club."

Before Zelda could oblige, a decidedly unladylike voice broke into the room from the hall beyond.

"I don't care what you think about the presentation. Save the negativity for your departure."

Edie responded, "Well, I never! This is a ladies' luncheon of the Tea & Biscuit Society. What's a man like you doing here, anyway?"

"I'm glad you mention it. Mavis!"

Mavis realized her jaw had loosened on its hinges and was currently hanging wide. Zelda smiled. "It seems you have a visitor."

"Mercy!" Ivy declared, clapping a hand to her breast as Gavin filled the dining room doorway.

He looked like a man on a mission, one not to be trifled with. When he caught sight of her, he called out. "Mavis, over here!"

Mavis closed her mouth. She cleared her throat and lifted a finger to Zelda and Ivy. "If you'll excuse me."

"I'm tempted not to," Zelda said, mischievous. "Don't you just love male hysterics?"

"Oh, divinely," Ivy agreed, bobbing a nod.

Gavin filled the room. He bumped into a chair, righted it, then edged closer to Mavis. His urgency was at such a high, she placed her hand to the center of his chest. "Are you all right?"

"I'm great." He glanced sideways at Zelda and

Ivy. "I waited outside with Prometheus. Didn't want to interrupt your speech."

"Well, why not?" Zelda chimed in. "It doesn't get much more impressive than you, handsome."

He forced a laugh. "Miss Zelda." He bowed his head to Ivy. "Ma'am. I'd love to chat." His gaze seized on Mavis. "But I have something to say."

"I want to stay," Ivy said. "Do you think he'll let us stay?"

Zelda patted Ivy on the arm. "Honey, take a seat. I'll ring Briar. Maybe she can bring us another round of sponge cake."

As the ladies removed themselves from the immediate vicinity, Mavis scanned Gavin further, trying to gain some clue as to the reason for his insistence. "Are you sure you're all right? Your heart's beating like a drum."

He shrugged it off.

Mavis reevaluated. "Does this have anything to do with where you went this morning with Dad and Kyle?"

"Some," he said with a nod.

When he didn't go into detail, she let her hand fall. "You don't want to tell me."

"Your brother and I straightened things out between us," Gavin told her. "We'll leave it at that."

"You did?" she asked, stunned.

He skimmed the hair from her face with his first finger, parting it wider down one side, then the other. "It was necessary. Not that I wouldn't have preferred us going on to the river and staying in bed for a while. From now on, the only thing that will be taking me from your bed will be nuclear."

A bark rolled through the long narrow window close by. They looked around to see Prometheus's nose pressed against the glass. His tail wagged, eager to be included.

"And your dog," Gavin added.

Mavis rolled her eyes at the canine. "I think he's more yours than anybody's."

"I love you," he said, before she'd barely finished speaking. He said it, rushing, on a ragged exhale, as if it'd been trapped inside him.

Mavis's pulse misfired. She nearly fumbled for the mantel. He held her up with his eyes, so intent. The intensity was sincere. Now she wasn't breathing.

Something shattered nearby. They both startled. Mavis looked around to see that Briar had dropped two plates. She crouched on the floor, holding one hand with the other. "Go on," she said, smiling tautly. "Go on, please. Pretend I'm not here."

"Your hand's cut," Zelda said, rising to help her.

"It was the plate," Briar said, shaking her head. "Silly of me. I didn't want to interrupt, but it slipped and…"

Gavin moved quickly. "Let me see."

"It's nothing," Briar said. "Gavin, please. Say what you have to say to Mavis."

He took her hand anyway, the injured one she

cradled. The blood was running down her wrist. He cursed. "Is Dad here?"

Briar nodded shortly. "Yes, but—"

"Can somebody get him in here?" Gavin asked, snatching a white linen napkin off the table. "You're going to need stitches. And even if you have the supplies, I don't trust my eyes to sew it."

"I trust them," Briar said quietly.

Gavin's gaze arrested on her soft face. "Next time I drop a bombshell, I'll make sure you're not carrying breakables."

Briar laughed a tinkling laugh as he rewrapped the pristine linen around her hand.

He shook his head, holding the napkin tight to her wound. "I'm the one who breaks things." A strike of pain crossed her countenance and he swore. "Sorry. You need the pressure."

Her eyes were shining. "Your father did it here. Remember? He brought flowers and words. But the best part was that he brought you. It felt like the beginning of forever."

Gavin nodded, head low, mouth twisted into a sentimental grin. "You made me cinnamon rolls." After a moment, he looked back at Mavis. "I'm glad I got to say it here of all places. It feels right."

Mavis saw Gavin and his stepmother crouched together on the elegant, blood-dribbled rug. She broke. "I love you, too," she said, just as rushed and ardent as his admission had been.

His attention strayed to her again. Briar beamed.

Mavis was aware once more of Zelda and Ivy. The attention scrambled her. She focused on Gavin. How could she not? His relief was palpable. His joy was a living thing. It electrified her. "I love you," she said again, sure.

His mouth warped into a wide smile. "All right," he said with another nod. "All right. Give me a minute." He helped Briar to her feet. "Can you walk?"

"Yes," Briar said.

"We'll get her where she needs to go," Zelda said, replacing Gavin's hand with hers over the napkin. "Ivy, go to the garden. There you'll find a man with a shovel or a rake. You'll know him. He looks like that one." She measured Gavin's breadth with a sweep of her arm.

"We'll meet you in the parking lot," Ivy agreed, stepping into action.

"You'll be all right," Gavin said, relinquishing Briar into Zelda's care. "Just keep pressure on that wound."

"Thank you, Gavin," Briar said. She looked to Mavis. "Take all the time you need. Lock the door if you have to. We'll shoo everyone out."

Gavin watched from the doorway until they made it to the entry. Mavis took a few seconds to catch her breath. It had been an odd few minutes. Her lungs settled back into a normal pace.

She spotted the blood that had transferred to his

hand. Quickly, she picked up another napkin from the table. She went to him, taking him by the wrist.

He turned to her as she wiped the blood away in delicate sweeps. She kept stroking after the red had vanished. He had to take the napkin away from her. Even after he had, her heart lashed her breastbone and she struggled to look at him.

He raised his clean hands to her face, framing it. He lifted it so he could see her. His eyes scanned, searched. "It's okay. I told Kyle I'd wait on proposing. It seems he's not the only one who needs time to think it over."

She swallowed. "It's not that. I've just been afraid—not that everyone else wouldn't accept us in the long term. I wouldn't have cared if any of them refused. I was scared that you wouldn't want that—that after everything, she still poisoned you against living your life in one place. With me.

"I didn't believe you'd come back," she went on, purging the truth. "I didn't trust you to like I should've. When you showed up at the tavern, I didn't believe it when I should have. I'm sorry."

"Don't be," he dismissed. "I should've been upfront with you the whole time. The whole time I was away, all I could think about was getting back to you."

His eyes were clear, clearer than she had ever seen them, and they'd fused themselves to her. She found a smile and let it hang on her mouth so he could see how glad it made her.

He smiled, too. "While I was away, I stopped in at an old teammate's house. I'd asked him to hold on to a few things for me for a while because I didn't think I'd need them."

When he gestured to the item he'd left on the edge of a flower stand just beyond the door, she craned her neck. "What's that?"

He picked up the box, handed it to her. "Open it."

She did. So stunned was she by the contents that she nearly dropped the box altogether. "These are your medals."

He nodded. He wasn't smiling anymore, but was very solemn. "There hasn't been much about me that's permanent. There hasn't been much I've carried from place to place. That's what comes of being a drifter, I guess. But I have these and now I want you to have them."

She shook her head, trying to hide the sting behind her eyes by lowering her gaze.

His lips touched the crown of her head, lingered. "You brought me back to life."

"No," she argued. "*You* did that. Without your strength and your fortitude… I couldn't have pulled you out of that burning building if I tried."

"You would've gone up in flames, too," he murmured. He stroked her hair, tucking her head beneath his chin. "Ah, baby. You won't have to pull me out of the fire anymore. I'm going to make sure you never have to. I came home for me. I stayed for Dad. Then you wouldn't leave me alone in the bougainvillea. Before long, it was you I was staying for."

Mavis trembled. She placed her hands on the strength of his arms, melding into the line of his heat.

"I know what it is I want to be again because of you," he went on. "I know we'll be all right."

She nodded. "More than all right."

"Yeah," he said on a laugh. "Things will be more than all right. Do you know how long it's been since that was my truth?"

"It's true now," she replied, soaking in every inch of his resolve. She felt infinite under the glide of his bicolored gaze. "I've known you my whole life. When you came back…some part of me *knew*. It was overwhelming, like suddenly understanding all the unanswered questions in life. Why we're here. What we live for. I've never had the answers. But I want more than to know them—I want to live them. You make me feel alive. I never knew how much I wanted to feel that way until…" She licked her lips, eyeing his. "Until I kissed you."

"So it was *you* who came on to *me*?"

She closed her eyes and smiled, remembering. "Maybe."

"Maybe you should do it again," he suggested.

Focusing on him and all the sure things he'd come to mean to her, she closed the small gap between them until her boot-clad feet were nestled between his. Trailing her fingertips up his arms, she brought them up to his shoulder, scaling the fine hairs on the back of his neck. She clasped them over the back of his head and bowed him to her.

She kissed him until he was as breathless as her. He kissed her back until his heat had become her own.

"Damn," he said, coming up for air. "I don't have a ring."

"Don't need one," she said with a quick shake of her head. She took his mouth again, branding it for her own. "I don't need one," she said again.

"You'll have mine," he said.

Mavis wasn't sure her feet met the floor. "Only if you'll have mine, too."

"Okay." His cheek pressed against hers. She felt his smile as sure as she felt her own and she knew what it was like to be flooded with light. "Can we go back to the river? Can we make our own life there—the three of us?"

Lovingly, she turned her lips to the tender place beneath his ear and murmured, "I believe we've already started."

* * * * *